KILL SHOT

A KYLE PAYNE THRILLER

JT SAWYER

INKUBATOR
BOOKS

Published by Inkubator Books
www.inkubatorbooks.com

ISBN (eBook): 978-1-83756-584-9
ISBN (Paperback): 978-1-83756-585-6
ISBN (Hardback): 978-1-83756-586-3

PROLOGUE

DARRINGTON, WASHINGTON

THE LAST SIXTY SECONDS OF HIS LIFE FLASHED BEFORE HIM. As the Gulfstream G700 jet rapidly descended another thousand feet, he felt his stomach lurch into his throat. He gripped the armrests, glancing across the aisle at the flight attendant and other passenger, whose faces looked frostbitten.

It had been a smooth, uneventful flight until now. For the past three hours, the man had enjoyed seeing the terrain below transition from Great Basin Desert in the eastern half of the state to the forested peaks of the Cascade Range as they neared Seattle. The view was a far cry from the urban jungle of DC that occupied much of his frenetic life.

And now it seemed that life itself hung in the balance, the jet having become a metal torpedo whose control appeared to be beyond even the grip of the two pilots.

Pull up, damnit. Make it happen. You're former top-gun pilots, for God's sake.

Another abrupt descent was followed by the nose of the jet angling down further. He tried to remember his training, calming his breathing and focusing on the image of his wife and daughter. Instead, his concentration splintered apart as the young female flight attendant two seats up began screaming.

He swallowed hard, his heart slapping against his ribs as he dared another glance out the window. The mountains were no longer like a distant painting. He could make out the individual treetops and a dirt road snaking through the forest near a small town.

"Prepare for impact," yelled the senior pilot in a primal voice.

The man felt his cheeks quivering as the velocity increased.

Another scream erupted beside him from the female senatorial aide. Her shrieks and the flight attendant's blended together now into a high-pitched noise that nearly blotted out the groaning engines.

He glanced across the aisle at the young woman, who was murmuring a prayer as tears streamed down her face. The man reached out, resting his hand on top of her wrist, the memory of taking his eight-year-old daughter on her first rollercoaster ride flooding over him.

His daughter's face became his talisman as he whispered his own prayer of sorts, hammered out from numerous combat deployments over the years.

You'll get through this. You always do. You've been through a helo crash behind enemy lines. This is nothing. Deal with it, and you'll get the hell back home.

Then he thought about the sensitive nature of this trip and whom he was going to meet in Seattle. *Shit, this jet malfunctioning can't be a coincidence.*

He heard metal vibrating, then shearing off near the right wing. The G700 jolted forward, then dove uncontrolled this time.

The pilot's voice erupted over the speakers again. "Brace for impact. Brace for…"

CHAPTER 1
TWENTY-FOUR HOURS LATER

KYLE PAYNE GRIPPED THE BLADE, FEELING THE BALANCED WEIGHT and examining the fine edge. He set it down on the display table and grabbed another. While most of the other knife vendors at the Seattle outdoor expo catered to buyers of high-end hunting blades, Payne was looking for something simple with a particular edge that could augment the folder clipped on his pants pocket.

The next one he picked up seemed to fit his requirements: comfortable in the hand, just under four inches to avoid state legalities, carbon-steel material with a birchwood handle, and a quality sheath.

"Like the Scandi grinds, eh?" said the older man with the long beard behind the table.

"Yes, sir. Nothing beats a good Swedish Mora knife."

"You lookin' to use it for field-dressing game or just an all-around camp blade?"

"Carving around the campfire, mostly, and filleting the occasional fish."

"Well, that'll do both and then some, but I imagine you already know that if you know anything about Moras."

"You mean 'puukko,' right?" said Payne with a grin, referring to the traditional Scandinavian name for the tool.

The old man raised an eyebrow. "You're one of the few people who've come to my booth this weekend who knows that term. You a collector in addition to a carver?"

Payne shook his head. "I got my first puukko when I was nine; my dad bought it from an old Swedish guy who lived in town, which was mostly made up of Scandinavians. That blade was with me for nearly twenty years 'til I lost it on a canoe trip."

"Where'd you grow up that you had a bunch of Swedes in your neighborhood?"

"Upper Peninsula of Michigan. Home to the only Swedish College in the country. Lots of Scandinavian history there since so many Finns, Norwegians and Swedes came over in the late 1900s to work in the copper mines and the logging industry."

Payne pulled out his wallet, removing two fifty-dollar bills and handing them to the man. He could have talked with the old-timer all afternoon, but he needed to grab dinner and find a motel for the night. He grabbed a catalog and brochures and stuffed them in his daypack.

The vendor extended his leathery hand, both men shaking. "Remember, a knifeless man is a lifeless man."

"Indeed." Payne held up the sheathed blade, knowing the wisdom of that saying from personal experience. "I hope the expo treats you well."

Payne wove his way through the crowd, passing by rows of tables that he'd already inspected. Entering a new aisle near the corner of the auditorium, he noticed a man and woman in tan suits and white shirts making a beeline in his direction. Instinctively, he made a left turn, passing by more vendors and making another left turn into another aisle. The two suits had altered their route and were still heading towards him.

He continued walking, feigning interest in a first-aid kit seller's table while using his peripheral vision to see if the two individuals were going to bypass him as they approached. He pulled his ball cap lower and turned away.

"Excuse me, are you Kyle Payne?" said the blonde woman in the tan suit. Her partner stood back a few feet, scanning the crowd.

Payne kept a neutral expression as the woman slid back her jacket slightly to reveal a shiny bronze FBI badge and the hint of a pistol. *What the hell is this about? I haven't done anything illegal—lately, and not in this state.*

"Are you Kyle Payne?" she asked again in a more forceful tone.

"Depends."

"I'm Agent Carrie Walker, and this is my partner, John Fiche. We're with the Seattle FBI office." The other vendors were swiveling their heads between her and Payne. She gestured beyond Payne's shoulder. "Maybe we can talk over in the corner where it's a little quieter."

He sighed, motioning for her to lead the way.

Her partner didn't move, waiting for Payne to fall in line behind the woman, and the trio walked past the remaining vendors and over to an empty spot beside a hot dog cart.

Payne noticed a comms piece in her right ear. He glanced around the overhead girders, seeing several security cameras and wondering if these two agents had a third partner working the video feeds. That would explain how they were able to locate him inside this building.

Except, how did they know I'd be in this exact location?

The woman stopped, taking the corner position so she had the advantage of seeing the crowd, which forced Payne to have his back to the flow of people moving past. Her partner stood a few feet off to Payne's right, his hands hanging loosely by his sides. Both of them looked to be in their late thirties and had an air of confidence that, he surmised, wasn't born of time spent behind desks.

"You wanna tell me what this is about?" asked Payne.

She held up her phone screen, which showed the image of a man Payne hadn't seen in a couple of years. "Were you friends with Senator James Harrison?"

"You used the past tense. Did something happen to the senator?" Payne inquired.

She glanced around, lowering her voice. "His plane went down yesterday morning in the mountains northeast of here. No survivors."

Payne rubbed the back of his neck. "Damn, sorry to hear that."

"You were friends or work associates?" she asked.

"More of the latter, though that was quite a while ago."

"What line of work?"

"What does this have to do with me, exactly? I only knew the man briefly."

She scrolled on her phone, turning it around again and revealing a screenshot of the call log from a cellphone. "Your number and the other one listed were found on the senator's phone. Both were attempted a half-dozen times in the day leading up to the crash."

Payne scrutinized the image, his ribs constricting at not only the sight of his own phone number but the number of his friend Alisa Fairbanks in Virginia. She had been the analyst for his CIA team for years, but he wasn't about to reveal the connection.

"Any reason you didn't answer the calls from the senator?" she inquired.

"Yeah, because I only turn on my phone once a week or so."

"Seriously?" said Fiche. "Who has the luxury of living like that?"

"Someone on an extended vacation," said Payne, while mulling why Harrison was trying to reach him and how Alisa was involved.

The last time he'd interacted with the senator was two years ago when Payne had still been with the CIA. For several weeks Payne had been on the man's personal security detail for the duration of his visit to Algeria. During Harrison's time as the head of the Senate Armed Services Committee, his probing into a missing weapons shipment with US ties had led him on a fact-finding mission to North Africa, but the trail had gone cold. It was connected with the Operation Paragon debacle that briefly made news headlines once it was discovered that the State Department was moving weapons to rebel groups along the Algerian-Niger border.

I wonder if he uncovered something new and paid the ultimate price. And he must have recruited Alisa again to help him.

Payne looked around at the nearest exits, wanting nothing more than to head for his motorcycle and drive north on his planned trip to Vancouver and then spend the summer in Alaska. But first, he needed to contact Alisa and make sure she was safe. From the call log, it looked like she hadn't been responding to Harrison's attempts either.

"Look, this is a real tragedy for the senator. I'm sure his family and co-workers are devastated."

"Yes, it was quite a loss," she said. "And we've been tasked by our boss in DC to get to the bottom of what he was doing there and what may have led to the crash."

Payne clenched his jaw. *Good luck with the former investigation, since the senator was always looking into a half-dozen murky operations.*

Walker tapped on her earpiece while turning away and whispering something in response. She finished her conversation, giving her partner a sideways glance. "Some new information just came in. Let's finish this talk back at our office. It's only a few miles from here."

"What information, exactly?" he inquired.

"This is not something we can talk openly about in public, trust me," said Walker.

Payne angled his head towards a nearby hallway. "I saw a small classroom down there." He noticed Fiche looking on edge, his right hand hovering closer to his jacket.

"Lead the way," said Fiche as he nodded for Payne to move.

Fiche moved alongside Payne as they walked, their shoulders nearly touching. Payne wondered if they thought he was going to bolt.

After weaving through the crowd, they made their way down a cement corridor where the restrooms and an empty classroom were located. Payne entered the door on the right, Fiche following him inside. Payne set his pack down on a table.

Fiche shut the classroom door behind them, and in that instant, Payne caught a glimpse of two things that set off his alarms—the dappling of blood on the sleeve of the man's jacket and the fact that he was not only carrying an FN 5.7 pistol, an unusual weapon for law-enforcement in the US, but also a suppressor on the side of the holster.

No way they're feds. Payne suddenly felt the weight of the Swedish puukko in his back pocket.

From the window into the hallway, he saw Walker take up a sentry position outside the entrance.

He glanced at the wall to his right, where a narrow frosted window near the ceiling was located. The opening was barely large enough to squeeze through, but it would require time— time he didn't have.

In that microsecond, a lot of things flashed across Payne's

reptile brain. If he was wrong about his instincts, he'd be arrested for assaulting a federal agent—but at least he'd be alive.

It all happened in slow motion. Fiche turned and deftly flipped the right side of his jacket away as he reached for his concealed pistol. Payne exploded into action. He drove forward with a right hook that caught the man in the cheek, sending him into the door.

The fake agent's eyes widened in shock as he staggered backward, shaking his head. Taking advantage of the momentary disorientation, Payne followed with a round-house kick to the guy's left calf.

The man buckled but recovered faster than expected, lashing out with a vicious backhand that connected with Payne's temple. Payne crashed into a desk, sending chairs scattering across the classroom floor. Regaining his footing, he blocked an incoming straight punch and countered with a lightning-fast elbow to Fiche's jaw. The impact reverberated through the room with a sickening crack as the guy's head snapped sideways, blood spraying from his split lip.

The fake agent made a wild leap forward, tackling Payne and sending him to the ground. It was clear the fighter was well-versed in stand-up and wrestling skills. But so was Payne.

They rolled across the floor in a tangle of limbs, each fighting for a dominant position. Fiche's knee rocketed upward, narrowly missing Payne's groin but connecting with his thigh hard enough to numb the muscle. Payne countered by stabbing his fingers into the man's left eye, then slipped out from under Fiche's weight, getting to his feet and sending another kick into his attacker's lower back.

The guy reached for the edge of his jacket again, but Payne wasn't about to let him get to his weapon. He removed his ball cap and flung it at the man's face, then pulled out his new puukko, rushing forward. The man darted back, slamming against the door and narrowly averting Payne's incoming blade thrust.

He sent a vicious punch into Payne's left arm, knocking him off balance. The classroom door began opening as the woman pushed her way in, but Payne kicked it, catching her fingers in the crack. She howled and pulled back, and Payne quickly slid the lock in place and spun around to advance on his attacker.

The man yanked out his CZ pistol, but Payne slashed the weapon hand, slicing through the forearm, the handgun clattering to the tiles. Payne arced the blade down, slicing across the right quadriceps, then shuffled back out of range.

The man winced, trying to reach for his pistol, but Payne kicked it into the corner. Fiche groaned, retrieving a collapsible baton from his jacket. He swung it with his good hand, waving a series of figure-eights as he fought to stay upright from the leg wound.

Payne heard the woman slamming against the door; then the noise suddenly stopped.

"The security guards are looking this way," she said. "I need to move. Meet me at the exfil site."

Fiche sent a nervous glance at the exit. "Better not leave me, you bitch."

The man made a maniacal swing, trying to drive Payne back into the folding chairs. Payne ducked at the incoming head strike and shot his blade's tip into the man's abdomen. Fiche scurried back, pressing his palm into the bloody leak in his gut while he leaned against the door.

"Who sent you to find me?" said Payne.

"Piss off." A slight accent slipped out this time.

Payne heard a commotion in the hall as several people identifying themselves as security pounded on the door. He'd only have another minute to make his escape through the window. There was no way he was going to stick around for questioning and another attempt by whomever Walker was with.

Fiche slid down to the floor, dropping the baton as blood pooled beneath his pants.

"Last chance...who are you working for?"

The man shook his head, the grip on his abdominal wound weakening as his head slumped forward.

Payne moved closer, removing the guy's earpiece and patting down his jacket before locating a small booklet about Seattle with several loose photos inside. He shoved the items in his pocket and returned the blade to its sheath. Then he grabbed his pack and the CZ pistol, tucking it into his belt under his shirt.

Hearing the door lock being worked, Payne trotted to the back of the room and stood on a desk, lifting the narrow window and shoving his daypack out, then shimmying through the opening.

He dropped behind some shrubs next to a row of dumpsters. He squatted, hearing shouting from the security guards in the classroom as they discovered the dead man. Payne examined the route ahead, figuring he was on the opposite side of the building from where he'd parked his Indian motorcycle.

Only Walker will probably have eyes on my ride. He rose, limping along the back side of the dumpsters. He put on his sunglasses and made his way past some utility trailers, blending into the flow of attendees exiting the north side. Payne inserted the dead guy's comms piece into his ear, hearing a woman speaking in French. Though it had been a few years since he'd spoken the language, she was clearly indicating she and her partner had been compromised.

His mind was still reeling from the bizarre turn of events, but he needed to get some distance from this place and figure out his next move. Hopefully, he'd come back for his motorcycle tonight or tomorrow.

Payne removed his iPhone and placed it under the back wheel of a parked truck.

As he made his way to the shuttle buses at the northeast end, he wondered what tinderbox had just been ignited and its ripple effect upon his life.

CHAPTER 2

"Damn, it looks like you're dead," said FBI Agent Carrie Walker as she and her partner, John Fiche, stood near the bloody corpse in the classroom at the sportsmen's expo.

"Except I'm better looking," said Fiche, glancing over the man's fake credentials and the pistol suppressor.

"Yeah, sure." Walker examined the interior of the room, replaying what she thought had unfolded only fifteen minutes earlier.

She used her gloved hand to pull back the dead guy's jacket. "That badge looks pretty legit. And that's a pricey suppressor, but where's the pistol?"

"And the guy who entered the room with him?" Fiche handed her the tablet from the security guard.

She scrolled through the video images of two agents dressed in identical garb as her and Fiche as they walked with a man in a blue ball cap and a leather jacket to the classroom. The two guys entered while the woman remained in the hallway.

She enhanced the facial image of the man in the leather jacket, then glanced at the driver's license on her phone.

"This sure looks like the same guy we were coming here to talk with about the senator's plane crash. Kyle Payne."

"So, who beat us to it?" asked Fiche.

"Good question. These people strike me as pros, by their fake IDs and how they located our subject before we did. And if they know that Senator Harrison tried to contact Payne, then the senator's death in that plane crash just got a whole lot more mysterious."

A young woman with black shoulder-length hair came up beside Fiche. "We found Payne's motorcycle in the southeast lot. I examined the security footage, and he never went back to it." She pointed at the open window in the classroom. "After exiting there, he made his way into the crowd and headed towards the shuttle buses. I'm trying to locate where he was dropped off."

"We should post Payne's photos to TSA and border patrol in case he tries to catch a flight or hop over to Canada," said Fiche.

Walker shook her head. "Normally, I'd agree, but someone impersonated you and me down to the type of clothing we wear, and they knew exactly where to find Payne."

"We risk having him slip away, then," said Fiche.

Walker enhanced Payne's image again. "Not if we can anticipate his next move."

———

AFTER TAKING the bus from the convention center to a nearby high school that the expo was using for additional parking, Payne headed north on foot for three blocks, then walked east for a half mile. Seeing a Walmart, he proceeded inside, making a circuitous route through the store as he watched for pursuers.

Once he was sure he was clear, he headed to the electronics department and purchased two burner phones and a portable charger, then made his way towards men's clothing and grabbed a green ball cap and a black hoodie. At the checkout, he also purchased a water bottle and a packet of jerky. He exited the store, walking to the side of the building. He reluctantly passed on his leather jacket to a homeless man sitting under a tree near the curb.

It was a pricey jacket, but too bulky to shove in his pack, and he needed to alter his appearance given the cops would be searching for him, along with the fake federal agent.

Payne sat in the shade, removing one of the burner phones and activating the device.

The call went to a number in Virginia. Only it was sent straight to voicemail. "Hey, I'm just calling about that item for sale. Let me know if it's still available."

The message was for Alisa. She had been in his ear on countless operations and was one of the few people whom he considered family.

Those bogus agents either located me via my motorcycle's plates, my phone, or somehow through Alisa. How are you tied up in all of this? And where the hell are you now?

Payne watched a police cruiser exit the parking lot and head next door to the Home Depot, figuring they were just doing a standard patrol, but he didn't want to stick around to find out. He slid on the new hoodie and ball cap, then searched for taxis on his phone.

CHAPTER 3

An hour later, Payne arrived at a small county park in the northeast end of the city. He had taken two separate taxis and then walked the last mile to this location. He'd selected it because the park backed up to a few hundred acres of forest, which would provide escape routes and also a place to rest for a while.

He headed over to a picnic table under the shade of a large maple tree. He pulled out the confiscated booklet from the dead man. It was a pocket-sized edition of Seattle tourist attractions. Inside it were a half-dozen loose photos whose edges looked like they had been trimmed down to fit perfectly inside the book. It was an old-school surveillance technique that Payne himself had used over the years, allowing a seemingly unobtrusive tourist to cloak his motions of identifying subjects on the street while pretending to peruse the book.

All six of the photos were of a man and woman dressed in identical garb to the two FBI impostors at the expo. He examined their faces. They appeared to be in their late thirties. The woman had shoulder-length blonde hair pulled back in a tight ponytail and the kind of face that could have adorned fashion magazines. The man was a foot taller and built like a marathon runner with short-cropped blond hair cut in a military style.

Each photo was labeled on the back with the names Walker and Fiche, along with the cross streets.

Payne glanced at the background in the photos, which revealed skyscrapers and shops in the distance. *They were obviously being surveilled for a while, which means the impostors had time to set things up for their arrival at the expo.*

He glanced at the passing cumulus clouds overhead, replaying the brief verbal exchange. *If Harrison's jet was brought down, then this operation had to be in the works for a while since they already had phony agents in place.*

Payne thought about his options. Law enforcement agencies would be combing the city for someone matching Payne's description once the security camera footage from the expo was circulated. And without his motorcycle, he would be forced to get around on foot or via taxis, limiting his exodus from the city.

A large part of him wanted to disappear across state lines, except that would leave a lot of unanswered questions about Harrison's death and Alisa's whereabouts. *And if she's in trouble because of any of this, then she might need help.*

Alisa wasn't responding, but he still had a way of getting in touch with her via an old email account. He'd seen a small plaza with an internet café a few blocks away. That would be his next stop.

Payne studied the images of the FBI agents again, committing their faces to memory. He tucked the photos in his pack and headed off across the park, feeling the weight of the FN pistol in his waistline.

CHAPTER 4

AFTER ORDERING A BLACK COFFEE AND PAYING FOR THIRTY minutes of internet usage, Payne headed to a vacant corner table and set down his pack. He had paid in cash. While he carried a credit card, he rarely used it, keeping it on hand for emergencies or motorcycle repairs.

He sat facing the entrance, scanning the four other patrons, who looked like Europeans most likely connected with the international hostel a block away. Payne accessed the server, connecting to an old email account that he and Alisa had used in the past.

As he hoped, there was a message. It was from two hours ago.

If you're reading this, then I've had to go dark, and you're probably on the run. I was working with Harrison, and he had uncovered a new trail connected with your previous investigation in Algeria. He was heading to Pier 91 in Seattle to talk with the head of port security, Evan Whitmore, about a discrepancy in a recent shipment that passed through Jakarta after departing North Africa. I vetted Whit-

*more. He's solid. And Harrison trusted him. I gave the
senator your number, and he was going to reach out, but
something went horribly wrong. Sorry for getting you
tangled up in this.*

*Watch your back. This is a beast with a lot of tentacles in
high places. I'll be in touch as soon as I can and explain
more then.*

Payne leaned back, rereading the message. He pushed
away his coffee, no longer requiring caffeine in his system. *So
Harrison and Alisa unearthed something that has come back to bite
them…and me, apparently. It seems like riding off on my bike isn't
in the cards right now.*

He sent a brief reply to Alisa, explaining recent events and
his general whereabouts, then signed off.

As he saw it, there were two options: make contact with
the real Walker and Fiche and see what they knew about
Harrison's crash and the two impostors, or locate the port
security guy and figure out what he and the senator had
discovered.

The latter seemed like the smarter play since the feds
would want a face-to-face meetup, and Payne wasn't about to
sit in a holding room for hours, given how he'd poked a lot of
holes in the impostor at the expo.

Payne started a Google search for Evan Whitmore,
combing through property records and the online white
pages. There were two listed in Washington. One was in the
eastern part of the state, and the other had a residence a mile
away, near a marina.

He pulled up the map for the latter individual and studied
the pertinent landmarks and neighboring streets near Whitmore's house.

Time for a trip to the suburbs.

———

CARRIE WALKER HAD JUST SAT down at her desk on the second floor of the Seattle FBI headquarters building when her boss entered her room after a partial knock on the open door.

"Any ID on those two impostors posing as agents?" asked Derek Mentzer, whose immense frame nearly filled the doorway.

"Nothing showed up in the initial search, but Fiche is running it through other government databases as we speak."

"And that guy Payne?"

"Hopped on a shuttle bus after slipping out the classroom window at the expo." She sat upright. "That impostor disguised as Fiche looked like he'd been used for target practice by Payne. There were some precise knife strikes to the leg, arm and abdomen, and no defensive wounds."

Mentzer sighed. "And this is the guy Senator Harrison was trying to reach?" He glanced out the window. "I put in a call to several of my colleagues back in DC to see if they could pinpoint Payne's connection to Harrison, but nothing new came up beyond what you originally uncovered about him working as a risk-management consultant."

"I.e., for the State Department is more likely."

"DC is going to be all over my ass if we don't get some answers, so make this case your top priority and bring any other agencies or partners in to locate Payne. He's our only living lead right now."

"Don't you find it strange that the NTSB investigators are taking their sweet time to get back to us with a preliminary report on what happened to Harrison's plane? I know it's only been a day, but usually they want us on-site, and there've been no calls."

He shrugged. "Like I said, DC is going to be breathing down everyone's necks on this one, so they may feel a need to keep things airtight for now until they have something definitive, especially since Harrison was a former combat pilot and a two-term senator with quite a constituency. What I find strange is that there are people running around this city posing as federal agents."

"'Agent' since the woman's partner was bled out by Payne. From the surveillance footage at the expo, it looked like she suffered a broken hand after getting it slammed in the classroom door."

"It's a long shot, but put out a notice to the local ERs and walk-in clinics about that particular injury." He retrieved the buzzing phone from his pocket, scanning the text. "Gotta run. Looks like my video meeting with the DC office got moved up."

He left the office door open. Walker could hear the usual commotion of chatter combined with pecking laptops coming from the two-dozen cubicles in the main room, where other agents were busy working their cases.

She picked up the blue mug on her desk, staring at the cold black coffee with the oily sheen, deciding it would do. She pulled her chair in closer to her desk and flipped up her laptop, poring over the single page of notes she'd assembled on her own bizarre case, zooming in on one name.

Let's see what a deep dive into your background pulls up, Kyle Payne.

CHAPTER 5

PAYNE SPENT THE LAST TWENTY MINUTES HANGING AROUND THE small city park near Quaker Hill and watching the two-story corner house a block away. No dogs and no neighbors on their patios would make his job easier. At sundown, he went for a walk that eventually took him around the rear of the house. Hopping over the fence, he made his way through the yard, pausing by the steps to the back porch.

He heard music inside and someone mimicking the rock lyrics of a Guns N' Roses song, while the shadowy figure through the faded curtains lumbered around the kitchen. Payne stepped onto the porch and knocked on the door, then stepped back and kept his hands by his sides. The porch light came on, and he was sure he heard the sound of a shotgun being racked.

"You'd best get the hell off my property unless you want a chest full a buckshot."

"I'm not here to rob you, Mr. Whitmore. I'm a friend of Senator James Harrison. Name's Kyle Payne. I was told you were working with him on a sensitive matter related to port security and thought you could help me figure out what he was involved with that might have gotten him killed."

"I don't know anyone by that name. Now get the fuck out of here."

"I will as soon as you tell me what you two were going to meet about on Pier 91."

There was a long pause, and Payne watched the large figure shift his weight. "Who are you, exactly?"

"I worked on the senator's security detail a couple of years ago. He was investigating something in Seattle that I think was connected to a matter we were both looking into back then."

"You say you knew him—prove it. What did he always carry with him in his briefcase? And you'd better be specific, or I'm punching a hole through your goddamned chest."

"Padron cigars. He always preferred the Nicaraguan brands over anything else."

The shadowy figure beyond the curtains shifted again. The deadbolt clicked, and the door opened. Whitmore kept his Remington shotgun at a low ready while eyeballing the newcomer. "You think it mighta been a better idea ringin' my front doorbell instead?"

"Too many lines of sight around the other side, especially at that park."

"How'd you find me?" The man stepped onto the porch, causing Payne to back down the steps.

"A friend who was working with Harrison gave me your name. Said you and the senator were trying to figure out an anomaly with a shipment originating out of Algeria."

The man gave Payne a hard stare, then gazed around his yard. He stepped aside, waving the barrel of the shotgun towards the open doorway. "Let's talk inside."

Payne walked up the steps and followed the man into the kitchen, closing the door behind him. He inhaled the welcome aroma of chili simmering on the stove, realizing how famished he was.

Whitmore leaned the Remington in the corner and moved to the stove, turning off the burner under the cast-iron pot. "Damn shame about the senator's plane."

"Yeah, you're not kidding. Harrison was cut from a different cloth than the other politicians up on the Hill."

The man leaned his bulky frame against the counter and folded his arms. Payne noted the faded tattoos on the thick forearms, the most prominent being a mermaid with ample breasts and long red hair.

"I gotta admit, when I heard about the plane crash on the news, my first thought was that it was a helluva coincidence, given he was coming here to talk about something he said was related to national security."

"That's a thought we have in common, and in my experience, there are no coincidences in the occupation he was in."

The man canted his head towards the stove. "I was just about to sit down and have dinner. You hungry?"

Payne gave a hearty nod. "From the moment I walked in." He set his daypack down against the wall.

Whitmore turned and opened a cupboard, removing two bowls and handing one to Payne. They each got their fill and sat at the round table in the L-shaped kitchen as Whitmore recounted his work with the senator in between spoonfuls of steaming chili.

"How long ago did the senator contact you?" asked Payne.

The burly man leaned back, dragging a napkin across his lips. "Must be two months ago. Called me at work. Said he needed information on a manifest for a cargo ship passing through Jakarta, Indonesia, that had originated out of Algeria."

"Transporting what?"

"Cement and minerals mostly. Takes about thirty-two days to reach here from Jakarta via freighter. After that, it gets hauled off by eighteen-wheelers to the distributors."

"Why would something like that raise a red flag for Harrison?"

"Not sure. All he initially wanted from me was container tracking and customs logs for shipments heading to Seattle from Jakarta. After he first contacted me, he came out here, and I showed him around the port. He told me what he was looking for, but nothing raised any concerns until last week."

Payne finished his last spoonful of chili. "Go on."

"There were some weight disparities with two containers that arrived here, which is when I called the senator. After I sent him the manifests and files on the cargo, he said some woman tech wizard of his discovered that the inspection codes had been tampered with internally. Something about metadata this or that. I don't speak nerd so not sure what he was talking about, but he did say that someone was trying to create a clean digital trail to hide their smuggling network." He waved his hand out towards the window. "Next thing I know, he's on a flight out here, sayin' he needed to personally inspect the cargo on those two shipments."

"Did you have the shipments put on hold for him?"

"I told him they had already been unloaded, but he was as interested in the cargo containers as what was in 'em."

Payne rested his forearms on the table, fidgeting with the spoon in his bowl. "Seems like his next step should have been to contact Homeland Security."

"I did recommend that, but he said he needed to inspect the cargo boxes first before they started snooping around. He was very reluctant to have anyone from another agency check them out."

"What was inside?"

Whitmore flared his bushy eyebrow. "That's the thing, it

was just hundreds of bags of dried concrete mix and crates of rocks. I've worked this job for over two decades, and I've seen a lot stranger things before, so nothing set off any alarms for me. The interior walls were made of what seemed like fiberglass and were insulated, which isn't too common, but I had 'em x-rayed, and there wasn't anything of concern inside. Some of the refrigerated containers coming from Japan are like that since they have imported foods."

He gave Whitmore a hard stare. "Tell me more about the rocks."

The man spaced his hands a foot apart. "Nearly the size of footballs and had pink dust on 'em."

Payne thought back to his time with Harrison during their trip to Algeria, where they'd found an abandoned warehouse with a similar pink hue in empty crates.

The senator must have found some kind of credible evidence connected with Operation Paragon related to his search from two years ago. And if he wasn't willing to contact the feds, then maybe someone inside the FBI or Homeland Security was accessing the port authority databases and doctoring the manifests. That seems like a good motivation to stop further investigation...and down a jet.

"Anyone else involved in the investigation I should know about?" asked Payne.

"There was one person the senator mentioned. Said that a guy had been tracing the transport routes from here to Idaho."

"Got a name or any background on the individual?"

"All I know is it sounded like they were retired military. Harrison said the person specialized in data analysis and that he had spotted similar manifest alterations for semitrucks originating from here that didn't match up with data from the interstate checkpoints."

Whatever it is, someone is going through a lot of effort to conceal it and get it moving east.

Whitmore stood, taking both bowls to the sink.

Payne grabbed a pen off the table and jotted down his burner number and a code word. "I appreciate you taking the time to talk with me, and for that world-class chili." He handed the paper to Whitmore as the man sat down. "Call me if anything further turns up. But don't make any waves at work. Stick to your normal routine but document whatever seems unusual passing through the port." He nodded towards the shotgun in the corner. "And keep that handy, just in case."

He figured Whitmore was an unwitting but essential element in the smugglers' operation, since any disruptions with port security would create serious delays and red-flag shipments with customs.

Payne extended his hand, the two men shaking. "I'll be in touch if I learn anything new or find out what the hell is going on with the Idaho connection."

"Be careful. Those people brought down a US senator's plane."

CHAPTER 6

THE SUN HAD JUST SET, AND THE DOG WALKERS AND JOGGERS HAD returned home in the upscale Broadmoor neighborhood. The utility van sat on the quiet tree-lined street, parked along with dozens of other vehicles.

Today, the van bore the logo of a fictitious plumbing company; yesterday it had been a painting business with different license plates; the day before, it had had the vinyl skin for a dog groomer. While the driver had changed the exterior image frequently during the past week, he rarely changed the region he was surveilling.

Michael Dresden's handwritten notes regarding the neighborhood routines along with the photographs of his subject in the posh two-story mansion at the end of the street were about to come to fruition.

Dresden reflected on others he had stalked and eliminated in various parts of the world during the past three months, but this week's events would be the first time he was operating on American soil.

His home soil. The country that had trained him and

taught him to be a killer of his government's enemies, and the country that ultimately betrayed him.

One of the individuals, Senator James Harrison, had already been removed from the chessboard, his flight going down in a fiery wreck in the mountains northeast of Seattle. After tonight, there would only be two more. Two individuals who would be brought to justice. At least according to Dresden's way of thinking. Except, their deaths wouldn't come quickly. He would see to that.

And tonight's execution would send an unmistakable message to the two remaining targets on his list. That they were not only in his crosshairs but that their carefully constructed empire was about to crumble to the ground soon.

He leaned between the front seats, removing an HK 9mm pistol from a shoulder bag and sliding it into a Kydex appendix holster. Next, he clipped an eight-inch fixed blade onto his belt.

The HK was only for backup. The blade would be his primary weapon tonight. This kill he wanted up close and personal. *Bad-breath distance,* as one of his old instructors used to say at the Farm, eons ago when Dresden had still been a starry-eyed CIA recruit, unblemished by the horrors of the world.

He exited the van and made his way along the urban trail that wound behind the neighborhood. Ten minutes later, he paused behind the privacy fence bordering the upscale home. He climbed a mature oak tree until he had a clear view of the spacious backyard and patio. Dresden ran through his plans for the hundredth time as a steady flow of adrenaline surged through his veins.

———

IT WAS NEARLY 9 p.m. when Matthew Ellison pulled his black Audi A6 into the garage of his two-story estate. It had been a productive and enjoyable night of visiting with colleagues from the art world at a recently opened gallery in downtown Seattle.

As one of the premier art importers in the US, he was always front and center at galas, red-carpet events, and his billionaire clients' social functions. During his thirty-seven years as an importer, he had acquired and fostered connections in far-flung regions of the globe that had allowed him to rub elbows with sheiks, ambassadors, and Hollywood celebrities. But it was his side business in black-market antiquities that provided the bulk of his net worth, and tonight's function was as much about maintaining the façade as a legitimate art appraiser as it was about greasing the wheels with a couple of visiting businessmen from Tokyo and London.

Ellison exited his vehicle, the smell of cigar smoke following him as he walked to the side entrance in his garage. He typed in the numeric code on the keypad beside the door, disarming the house alarm before stepping inside.

He glanced up in irritation as the motion-sensor lights in the hallway failed to activate. He walked in the darkness, his right hand trailing along the wall until he arrived at the spacious kitchen. It was a place he rarely spent time in except when passing from the garage. His staff prepared his meals, usually serving him in the solarium on the west end of the estate or on the second-floor balcony that overlooked his three-acre flower garden.

A sliver of moonlight pierced the curtains in the dining room, providing enough light for him to make his way to the fridge. Ellison swung open the door, reaching for a bottle of Heineken.

The smell of leather crept over his nose as a gloved hand slid along his face.

Someone yanked him back, spun his body to the left and slammed his face onto the granite countertop.

Ellison began to slide to the ground, but the attacker held him in place, pinned against the edge of the counter. He felt something slice into his lower back as if a red-hot nail had just pierced his kidney. The man stepped back as Ellison slumped to the floor, the glint of a bloody blade evident in the attacker's hand.

The art importer groaned, trying to kick his Italian shoes along the bloody tiles and scurry back, but only managing to slide in a half-circle before feeling the energy drain from his limbs.

The attacker put away his blade and removed his ski mask, standing over Ellison.

"Who...who are you?" said Ellison.

"You won't know me. You were never directly a part of what happened to me, but those who learn about your death will sure as hell know it was me." He leaned in closer. "I want them to know it took a while before you died from that kidney wound. That you suffered because of them. And there was nothing you and all your money, influence, and security protocols could have done to prevent it. I want them to know they can be found—that they can be reached."

The man squirmed, his lips tightening in a grimace. "Please, you don't need to do this. I can..."

His personal reaper squatted beside him. "You'll what... offer me the world or riches beyond my wildest dreams. I was once a man rich in friends, and a woman with dignity beyond what you could have ever known. Your friends erased all of that in a microsecond."

Ellison tried to talk, but only managed a whimper, his eyes rolling back.

———

DRESDEN WATCHED Ellison take his last breath. He removed his leather gloves and replaced them with nitrile gloves from his jacket, dipping his index finger in the pool of blood beside Ellison's waist.

He stood, moving to the fridge and spelling out a single word that he knew would send a tsunami of panic through the halls of DC.

CHAPTER 7

AFTER LEAVING WHITMORE'S, PAYNE TOOK A CIRCUITOUS PATH through the neighborhood, his mind churning as he tried to make connections with the nebulous information Whitmore had divulged. He arrived back on the main street and walked for another mile past several blighted strip malls. With the interstate less than a half mile to the east, there were numerous budget motels along with a lone Waffle House.

Payne headed to the Starlight Motel, a sprawling establishment with a central hub for the office and four spokes of rooms that extended out. The old brick and mortar structure looked like something built in the sixties, and Payne hoped that the interiors weren't from the same era.

He realized being picky wasn't an option for a sixty-nine-dollar room that boasted color TV like it was a recent upgrade.

Payne stepped inside the lobby, his nostrils assaulted by cigarette smoke. An older man with flossy white hair on the sides and a shiny patch in the middle was staring at his phone and laughing. The man's furrowed face resembled a piece of driftwood, and his yellow teeth were evident with each chuckle at the video on his device.

"Got any availability?" inquired Payne.

"By the hour or the day?" The man didn't look up.

"Just one night. And I'll take one with a color TV."

The man sneered, setting his phone down. "Never heard that one before."

Payne shot his thumb towards the parking lot. "You ever think about getting a new billboard to reflect the times?"

He shook his head, then used his index finger to pick something out of his teeth. "The sign guy down the road wants to charge me three hundred bucks to swap that neon piece of shit out with a new saying. Hell with that."

The host extended his open palm, waiting for payment. It was clear he just wanted this transaction to be over with so he could get back to his entertainment.

Payne pulled out eighty dollars and handed it over. After getting his change and a key, he exited and sucked in a lungful of fresh air. He walked down the length of what had been described by the owner as the third spoke, stopping at door #39. He inserted the key, turning the knob, which felt like it was going to come off in his hand.

It's going to be one of those nights I barricade all the furniture against the door. He'd slept in more than a few run-down places over the years, but most of them were in less developed regions of the world.

At least the inside didn't reek of smoke or urine or beer, though the lingering odor of Lysol was probably responsible for the cover-up. He flicked on the lights, glancing around the austere setting. Table, chair, bed, TV, a towel on the rack near the bathroom. Life was good. Or at least tolerable for sixty-nine dollars.

———

AFTER HE SHOWERED and killed a cockroach near the toilet, Payne sat at the table and examined the photos again from the dead guy's booklet. He jotted down the cross streets labeled on the images and used them to locate a city block in downtown Seattle. A few minutes of studying Google Maps on his burner phone and he discovered that the little diner where Walker had gone several times was only three blocks from the FBI building.

He looked at the time stamp, seeing both numbers were around 0630.

Payne set his phone alarm for 0430, knowing it would be a ninety-minute walk to the downtown region, which would leave him with a thirty-minute window to scout the area adjacent to the diner.

Let's hope you're a creature of habit, Agent Walker.

———

AN OLDER-MODEL VAN with tinted windows turned into the truckers' parking lot across from the Starlight Motel. Paul Giletti was at the helm, and he turned off the engine and took a long swig from the energy drink cradled between his legs.

He glanced at the woman in the passenger's seat as she buddy-wrapped three of the broken fingers on her right hand. Giletti lifted the armrest, withdrawing a bottle of ibuprofen and setting it in the cupholder. "Better pop a few more of those until I can get something stronger."

"I have had far worse injuries. I'll be fine," she said with a faint French accent that always slipped out when she was exhausted.

Giletti tapped the call button on his dash-mounted phone.

A second later, the voice of a younger man came over the line. "How long you want us to keep an eye on Payne's motorcycle at the expo center?"

"You can call it off. He just holed up in a fleabag motel on Jamison Street for the night."

"Copy that. How'd you locate him?" asked the man.

"Our contact with the feds didn't ping anything on facial recog at the train stations or airlines, so I figured we'd hang around the motels near the bus depot. He showed up here a few minutes ago, on foot."

"You gonna soften him up and see what he knows about the senator?"

Giletti shot the woman beside him an irritated glance. "That approach was already tried. Tried and failed, big time, and now the feds and cops are on high alert. Get over to my location and hang out in the parking lot across from us."

"Copy that."

Giletti watched the phone screen turn black, then opened his door and got out. "Going to take a piss break. Keep your eyes glued to room 39. You got it?"

"Yes, sir."

Giletti moved past the row of eighteen-wheelers, whose interiors were lit up with truckers watching TV inside their sleeper cabs. For a moment, he wondered what it would be like having a job that didn't involve kidnapping, torture and murder.

He walked to the side of the burger joint attached to the gas station and pulled out his phone again. Only this time, he was dreading having to update his boss.

Giletti and Dresden had served together in the CIA's North African station for nearly twelve years and had spent the past two years painstakingly planning this mission of retribution on US soil. In a few more days, everything would come to fruition, and they could, once more, disappear into the shadows and live out their lives in some quiet corner of the world.

He drew a deep breath, then called.

"Saw the news yesterday. That's a real tragedy about the senator. He was an American hero," said Dresden, dragging out the last sentence.

Giletti chuckled. "That's one less headache to worry about." He watched a stray dog darting around the trash bins. "The last shipment from the port should be at the Idaho site just after sunrise tomorrow."

"Good. I've already spoken with our crew there to begin work on the next phase."

"Roger that." He balled his fist, mulling over his next words. "There was one glitch, but I'm dealing with it. That guy Payne slipped out of our reach earlier today, but we'll snatch him tonight and drop his body in the harbor."

There was a long pause; then Dresden replied, "Just sit on his location for now. He's sticking around that area for a reason; otherwise he would have fled hours ago. He might be tied to other players we're not aware of. If that's the case, then burn them all. But, Paul, make sure you 'deal with it' this time. We're too close to finishing this thing."

"I know. Trust me, I know."

"If you finish there in time, plan to meet me in Spokane. I can use your help."

"You got it."

The phone went silent. Giletti tucked it away and pulled out a pack of Marlboros and lit one up. He took a long drag on it, watching the ghostlike wisps of smoke linger in the air for a second.

Three exhales later, he stabbed out the cigarette on the brick wall and tossed it in the sewer. He headed into the gas station, knowing he was going to require a few more energy drinks to get him through the coming night.

CHAPTER 8

I T WAS NEARLY 1:30 A.M. WHEN A LISA F AIRBANKS EXITED THE interstate, making a right turn and heading towards a string of motels outside of Dayton, Ohio. It had been a long drive, and her nerves were frazzled.

After watching in shock about Harrison's crash on the news yesterday, she had grabbed her go-bag, laptop, clean IDs, and a HK pistol and quickly departed her town house in Alexandria, Virginia. Along the way, she ditched her iPhone and started relying on her burner phones.

Within minutes of leaving, she noticed a dark SUV that stayed three cars back for ten miles. She abruptly exited the highway at the last second, taking a hard left turn and proceeding several blocks past some derelict strip malls, then made a series of right turns. She lost the tail after stopping inside a parking garage. The incident had cost her precious time, but it had confirmed her fears…she had been surveilled and was now being pursued.

Alisa tried to push down her fear, but then reminded herself about Harrison's last words. *These people don't want any loose ends.*

She had driven her white Toyota Camry to a long-term parking garage at Richmond International Airport and swapped it out for a rental car under a fake name and driver's license.

The CIA and friends like Payne had taught her well about life on the run. Never maintain patterns. Change vehicles frequently. Keep conversations curt but mannered. And always watch your back.

While she had only served as a case officer in the field for a year before blowing out a knee and being reassigned to intel, she still remembered the old skills. And right now, old habits and old skills seemed as critical as being paranoid, though she would never devalue the latter trait.

Her first stop was outside of Richmond, where she used the Wi-Fi in a roadside café, sending a message to both Payne and her boyfriend overseas. The difference in sentiment between the two messages was stark. One was fraught with worry, even terror, while the other spoke of a hopeful future. She wished the latter was the only one she could focus on right now.

After leaving, she'd taken a winding route back to the highway, then drove west, stopping at smaller countryside gas stations to refuel and avoid the plethora of security cameras at the larger truck stops.

She recalled Harrison's words on the phone two mornings ago. *If this thing in Seattle goes sideways and you don't hear from me by nightfall, then assume the worst and get out of town for a while. Maybe for good.*

What started as a favor for a friend had turned into something beyond her wildest imagination. And her years as a CIA targeter and intelligence analyst had taught her that they were always to question the official reports in the media. *Harrison tells me he has a significant lead in his investigation, and then his jet goes down on the way to meet Whitmore!*

She silently corrected herself. "Our" investigation. That was what it had become after Harrison had approached her at the behest of her old mentor, Robert Kilkenny. She was supposed to provide just a few record searches and collate the dates and the data connected to freighters originating out of Algeria. But her digging unearthed a creature with numerous tentacles. Then Kilkenny found discrepancies with trucking manifests departing the Seattle port and bound for Idaho. Just when Alisa felt like Harrison was about to wrap his head around things, it all went to hell in a fiery plane crash.

This is bullshit. It's not how my life is supposed to turn out, being on the run. I got out of the clandestine services to live a boring fucking life.

Alisa drove for a half mile, then found a budget motel beside a Denny's restaurant. She glanced in her rearview mirror again, scanning for familiar vehicles. At this late hour, the two-lane road into town was relatively quiet, but she knew better than to relax. They were out there, methodically working through her possible locations and contacts.

Alisa turned into the motel parking lot, reluctantly coming to a halt near the office. She wanted to continue heading west, to reach Payne and her old mentor before either of them were located by Dresden and his people.

She just hoped she had enough of a head start to make it to them in time and finish what Harrison had started.

CHAPTER 9

THE NEXT MORNING, WALKER HAD SAT AT HER USUAL TABLE IN the café. She had just taken a sip of her latte when the barista stepped out from behind the counter and made a beeline for her. The young woman in pigtails extended a cordless phone to Walker. "Some guy wants to talk to you. Said it was urgent." She handed over the phone and casually headed away as if it were an everyday occurrence.

Walker cautiously picked up the phone like it was a grenade. "Who is this?" She leaned back in her seat, holding the phone to her ear.

"Carrie Walker, you should think about changing your routine," said the man. "Especially with someone running around the city impersonating you, like the fake FBI agent at the expo center."

Walker scanned the other patrons, not seeing anyone on their phones, then extended her vision out to the front windows. "And you are?"

"I'm the guy who was approached by your doppelgangers yesterday afternoon. I'm looking at photos I found on the dead man right now and thought you might want to see how well they copied your appearance, right down to those fancy suits you wear, though I'm guessing standard FBI gear doesn't include FN five-seven pistols with suppressors."

"Kyle Payne, I presume? We've been looking for you. In fact, we were headed to the expo yesterday afternoon to talk with you about recent events with Senator Harrison's flight. Where are you?"

"That depends on whether you and your partner come alone or bring a tac team with you."

"You were the one being targeted, Payne. It's in your best interest to come down to the bureau; then we can talk more."

"And you and your buddy were the ones being impersonated, so I'm not the only one being pursued. Based on the photos I have, you were being surveilled for a while. Seems like we both have questions that need answering, and since I don't trust anyone right now, we'll meet on my terms. Go to Fishermen's Terminal on the northeast side in an hour. And come only with your partner, Fiche. Anyone else shows up, I'm gone, and you'll never hear from me again."

"Why should I take your word on any of this? For all I know, you were behind the senator's death, and those bogus agents at the expo were coming to clean up the mess."

"Because I would be a continent away and not on the phone with the real Agent Walker. Besides, this is bigger than you and I, and even the senator. If you want to hear what I have to say, then come in an hour. In the meantime, you should research the open-source material on Operation Paragon. I think what happened to the senator is connected with that undertaking."

After she provided Payne with her cellphone number, the device went silent. She stared at it as if it were a crystal ball. She didn't like being told what to do. More importantly, she didn't like the fact that someone was surveilling her and had posed as her and Fiche. *What the hell is going on?*

Walker debated whether to share any of this with her boss. She knew the man's response would be to get a chopper in the air over the rendezvous point and have agents staked out on the street corners and rooftops. And her only lead in Harrison's death, and the other impostor at the expo, would be in the wind.

She stood and tossed her coffee cup in the trash, quickly making her way to the front exit. She moved under the eaves for a moment, scanning the street in both directions, then up at the other storefronts, wondering how many times she had been observed leaving this diner.

———

PAYNE CHOSE A NEWLY CONSTRUCTED parking garage near Fishermen's Terminal for the meeting. The latter was a sprawling marina complex northwest of downtown. At 7:30 a.m., the majority of fishing crews were out on the water for the day, leaving the docks relatively empty. He'd spent the past thirty minutes walking the perimeter, making mental notes of the access points and surveillance cameras.

Ten minutes before the appointed meeting with the feds, Payne headed up to the third level of the parking garage a few blocks from the wharf and got into position beside a concrete pillar near the stairwell. From here, he could watch vehicles entering the structure on the street below and see any tac teams along the sidewalks or surrounding rooftops. More importantly, he had three escape routes: the entrance ramp, the stairwell, and a maintenance ladder down the side.

A few minutes later, a black Suburban with tinted windows slowly drove down the street, parking near the east side of the structure. Payne watched the two agents exit their vehicle, seeing they resembled the images he'd found on the dead guy. He watched them for a few moments, noting their body language and the cautious way they scanned their surroundings, which helped reassure him they weren't relying on a backup team.

He texted Walker.

> Parking garage, third level.

As the two agents headed for the building, he did another visual sweep of the surrounding rooftops and nearby vehicles. He'd chosen this particular meeting spot carefully since it was a blind spot for the security cameras, along with having enough noise from the nearby streets to make eavesdropping a challenge.

A minute later, he heard the clack of their shoes in the open stairwell on the other side of the pillar. He waited for them to emerge and walk into the open about twenty feet away before shouting to them, "That's close enough. No sudden moves." He scrutinized their faces in the overhead lighting while keeping one hand on the stolen CZ pistol under his hoodie.

Walker and Fiche complied, keeping their hands by their sides. "We're really FBI, Payne, unlike the two from the expo," Walker said. While her partner had a face like a weathered boxer, she was hard to look away from.

"You mean the ones who knew exactly where to find me and had some legit credentials." He stepped out from the shadows. "My gut tells me someone had access to FBI intel to know the details of Senator Harrison's crash along with my connection to him. But tell me I'm wrong."

Walker and Fiche gave each other uneasy glances. "That's why we came here, Payne," she said. "We're in the dark on some of this, just like you. What else did they tell you about the crash?"

"Just that Harrison tried to call me numerous times."

Payne noticed the man's right hand drift towards his jacket. "Keep your hands still, Agent Fiche. I've had enough fucking surprises lately."

"I've got something you'll want to see," Fiche said.

Payne gave a nod of approval; then the agent removed his cellphone. He worked the screen, then set it down on the lid of a large trash receptacle near the cement post and stepped back. "Those photos are from the crash site. Tell us what you see."

Payne moved forward, keeping his body angled and one hand on his concealed pistol. He grabbed the phone, keeping the agents in his peripheral vision.

He swiped through the images of the Gulfstream wreckage scattered along a forested slope. He stopped scrolling on the sixth picture, studying the grisly coroner's photo of the senator. The charred skeletal remains labeled as the senator's were shocking to see but not as surprising as what he noticed upon closer examination, the implications causing Payne's pulse to quicken.

CHAPTER 10

THE INTACT PELVIC STRUCTURE ON THE VICTIM WAS THE FIRST thing that caught Payne's attention. If it had been Harrison, then his remains would have had a titanium hip on the right side, like the one the senator had received after suffering a skiing accident three years ago.

Either the coroner fucked up, or the senator is alive. His eyes darted along the pavement for a moment. *Was this crash site staged, or did someone target the wrong plane?*

"Something the matter?" inquired Walker.

Payne forced himself to maintain a neutral expression. "So there were no survivors?"

She shook her head. "Besides the senator, there were two pilots, a flight attendant, and one of Harrison's aides. Initial reports from NTSB indicate the jet rapidly descended after reporting engine problems. They were planning to make an emergency landing at a regional airport near the town of Darrington, about seventy-six miles northeast of here, but comms went offline shortly after that, and they impacted the mountainside a few minutes later."

"The black box hasn't been examined yet," said Fiche. "But the NTSB investigators are finding the rocky terrain challenging, so it might take a while to get more answers."

"Since when does NTSB allow immediate access to a crash site and let the feds walk out with photos that could accidentally make it to the press?" said Payne.

"Above your pay grade." Walker shrugged and motioned towards the phone. "Keep scrolling to the last image."

He flipped through several more photos of the wreckage and the remaining victims, studying a close-up of a burned fragment of paper with some handwritten numbers. "Looks like GPS coordinates."

Walker flared an eyebrow. "That was found in a fireproof case under the senator's seat. The other items were missing, but that was tucked in a side pocket. I figured the same as you and looked it up. It's for a location in North Africa."

Algeria. Has to be. That's where Harrison's previous investigation led us two years ago.

Payne realized he was in the dark without Alisa right now, and his main focus was making sure she was safe. He required the FBI's resources to move forward if he was going to make any progress. All he had to go on was the information from the recent shipment at the port, which wasn't extremely helpful. But he knew he couldn't reveal what he'd learned about Harrison or from Whitmore. Not yet. Not if the feds were compromised.

"I looked up Operation Paragon," said Walker. "If you're referring to the botched arms deal in Africa, then that's ancient history, and I'm not sure how it's even connected to Harrison. But one thing of interest is my boss just told me this morning that a murder case he's investigating in north Seattle had the word 'Paragon' spelled out in blood on the vic's fridge."

"Who was the victim?"

"A rich art dealer. He was knifed one time in the back. Bled out slowly and probably suffered like hell. Whoever did it was some sick bastard," said Walker.

"And also someone with sophisticated skills to bypass the guy's high-end security system," said Fiche. "Again, like my partner just asked, how is Harrison connected to Operation Paragon?"

"Harrison wouldn't have been in any of the headlines two years ago that you looked up, but he was deeply involved in determining what really happened in Algeria back then since it was such a black eye for American interests overseas. I know because I was on his security detail."

"Anything you care to share about what he discovered there?" asked Fiche.

He figured they had already done their homework on his background, but that wouldn't have taken them past his cover story with the CIA, so he decided to keep things simple to alleviate some of their suspicion.

"I knew the senator when I worked with the State Department. I briefly handled his security overseas on an investigation into a particular group of arms dealers that he was spearheading. He was looking into a weapons-trafficking network that he thought was connected with Operation Paragon, but the trail went cold in Algeria. We traced an illegal arms shipment to a shell company there, but then our leads disappeared. Literally. Three informants, including the moneyman, were found murdered in one week. After that, my role ended."

"Safety abroad for a traveling politician is usually a job for diplomatic security. Is that who you were with?" inquired Walker.

"Something like that. My security role was a cover. I was

only there to help Harrison and his team track down the weapons shipments."

She and Fiche exchanged glances again before Walker spoke. "State Department can mean a lot of things. But, in my experience, that usually means CIA, especially since you probably possess some experience or expertise in that particular region of the world."

He knew there was a question in there. "I'm going to throw your own words back at you and say it's probably above your pay grade."

Walker waved a hand out towards the skyline. "And now you're sightseeing, cruising around the West Coast on that Indian motorcycle of yours? That bike was put into FBI impoundment, by the way, so don't plan on it as your getaway ride."

He handed the phone back to Fiche. "To answer your question, I'm on permanent vacation. I left government work last summer and decided to see my own country instead of everyone else's."

"Well, maybe Africa isn't so cold after all," said Walker. "Those coordinates must be relevant."

"Or they were a ruse to throw investigators off from the real location," said Payne. "It's not likely anyone formerly affiliated with Operation Paragon would return to a site that had already been flagged."

"You mean somebody waltzed into a well-patrolled plane crash site and inserted false intel without being noticed," said Fiche.

Payne removed the dead man's booklet and tossed it to him. "You might want to analyze the photos of you and Agent Walker. They had been surveilling you both for at least forty-eight hours prior to the crash, so having someone sneak into an active crime scene to plant evidence is the least worrisome aspect about all of this."

He watched their uneasy gazes as both agents studied the pictures. Fiche whispered something about the location being near where they'd had dinner the other night, making Payne wonder if the two were more than just colleagues.

"One other thing you should know," said Payne. "After I acquired the comms set of the guy who tried to kill me, I heard his partner, the woman posing as you, Agent Walker, speaking in French. But it wasn't fancy Parisian—more like French Algerian. Whoever she is and whomever she's working for, these people are professionals with a long reach and plenty of resources. I'd watch your backs from now on."

She tucked the dead guy's booklet in her jacket. "And what about you, Payne? Who's going to watch your back? Or are you planning on disappearing after our meeting?"

"Depends." He looked into their faces, worried that the clock was ticking on Alisa's life, and he was more than intrigued to learn about the actual fate of the senator.

"There's something I need to look into regarding Harrison's movements. He was reaching out to me for a reason, and I think he may have bitten off more than he could chew. If that's the case, then I'd like to see what I can do—but I want to start at the NTSB command post by the crash site. There may be some additional clues there."

"No way you're getting in there without clearance," said Fiche.

"Does that mean you two will be my escorts?" Payne saw them mulling over the implications of having a civilian embedded in their investigation. "I think we can help each other. You need my background on this case, and I need your resources."

"That's why we were coming to you at the expo in the first place. We just got there a little behind our counterparts."

"When seconds count, the feds will be there in minutes." He listened to the squeal of tires on the street below, examining the entrance and stairwell again. "What are you going to do about the potential leak at your office? Whoever is involved probably already knows about this meeting."

"Just because someone knew our routines and dress code doesn't point the finger back to our bureau," said Fiche. "Like you said, this was a professional job, which could mean any number of outfits or freelancers."

"If an outfit connected with Operation Paragon is involved, then they'll have the paramilitary contractors to pull off something like that," said Payne.

She gave him a hard stare. "One step at a time. I'll look further into Paragon when we get back to the office later, but if you're coming with us to the crash site, then you need to follow my lead since you'll be walking into an active investigation."

"No problem. But just do yourselves and me a favor, and ditch your phones or leave them behind."

Walker gazed at her partner. "Not gonna happen. We have encrypted devices, so unless the NSA is also in on this, I think we'll be alright."

Fiche glanced at his watch. "You can ride with us, Payne. If we leave now, we can be at the crash site by lunch and have the place to ourselves, since there should only be a few staff on-site."

Payne relaxed his weapon hand. "No calling in this trip to HQ. Just the three of us."

Walker and Fiche gave reluctant nods at the request. "Seems like the crash site is the only concrete lead we have right now," she said.

"That and the connection to Algeria," said Fiche.

Payne didn't reveal what he'd learned from Whitmore, or the most significant lead—that Harrison was somehow alive.

Was he abducted, or is he hiding out?

Right now, he had more questions than answers. He was

hoping that would change once he examined the remains at the NTSB command post.

As he followed the two agents down the stairwell, he felt like he was descending to more than just the ground floor. Whatever fissure had just opened in his world following the senator's plane crash, he was sure it extended beyond the Western US.

CHAPTER 11

WESTERN IDAHO

THE ICY MORNING AIR BIT AT MICHAEL DRESDEN'S FACE AS HE exited the cabin and stepped onto the front porch with a steaming cup of black coffee. Idaho in early spring could be unforgiving and was a far cry from the desert heat he'd come to prefer during his many years with the CIA in Africa and the Middle East.

He sipped his drink, scanning his temporary domain. Eighty acres of rugged terrain, pine forests and rocky outcroppings. All of it backed up to a sheer cliff face that made the property virtually impenetrable except for the lone dirt road leading in from the two-lane highway six miles to the southwest. Scattered amongst the forest were numerous small cabins, outbuildings, a shooting range, a barn, and an immense Quonset hut that could house a grocery store.

The setting was perfect for a man who valued privacy, but it came with a small cost, and Dresden knew the wiry guy in the sheriff's jacket ambling towards him was coming to collect on that payment. Dresden leaned inside the cabin door, grabbing a small Pelican case off a side table.

"Nothing yet on the trucks," said Sheriff Miles Dwyer,

who was clutching a two-way radio in his gloved hand. "But the lookouts down by the main road will let you know when the rigs arrive."

Dresden handed the man the case. "This is the remainder for services rendered."

The sheriff grasped it, unclipping the latch and lifting the lid. A faint smile emerged on the guy's face before he closed the case. "This will go a long way towards providing some additional buildings and weapons out here."

"I imagine so." Dresden figured the hundred thousand dollars could equip Dwyer's neo-Nazis with a small arsenal and expand the man's extremist empire to recruit more whackos. Dwyer was the only one in his group of twenty militants who wasn't adorned with swastika tattoos on his neck or arms though Dresden was sure he had some visual proof on his body that he was a true believer. By all appearances, Dwyer was a respectable lawman, which wasn't hard to convey since he was the only law-enforcement officer in this remote region of Idaho.

The sheriff's childhood connection to Dresden's second-in-command, Paul Giletti, had greased the wheels for leasing this property for two months while Dresden gathered up the supplies he needed from Algeria.

Now, all Dresden had to do was gather a few more critical components and await the arrival of the incoming trucks from the Port of Seattle. Then his real work could begin. Fortunately, he was a patient man. Twelve years in black ops overseas had shaped his psyche and hardened his body. But it was the events of April 13, two years ago, that twisted and ultimately galvanized his will for the bloody carnage that he was about to unleash on US soil.

He could still see the faces of his direct-action team along the border of Syria and Turkey. Their mission destroying a fleet of stolen drones in the insurgent compound had been a success, and the helicopter extraction was finally at hand. Except no bird touched down at the designated spot, only a cruise missile that was sent to erase Dresden and his team— sent by his superior, who sat in the hallowed halls of DC while Dresden's world went up in flames.

Dresden, Giletti, and another man, Landon Keen, survived. The other five became a part of the desert floor in seconds, including his fiancée, Danielle. Now, every twist of his upper body or flex of a muscle caused the burn scars on his arms and neck to serve as a daily reminder of what he'd lost.

But the time for anguish and regret was almost over. And the hour was approaching when he would hold accountable the people associated with that horrific day.

The sheriff pulled up the sheepskin collar on his jacket. "Well, the drive back to town takes a bit, so I'd better get rolling. The guys already know to get you whatever you need, so just give 'em a holler. I told them to lay off the booze last night, so they should all be good to go."

"Will do." He extended his hand, shaking the sheriff's soft hand. "I appreciate your help and allowing my crew to operate out here."

"Anything for the cause, brother. Hopefully, whatever you're doing will help shift the balance of power to our side, even if it's only a fraction of an inch." The man held up a fist, then turned it into a two-fingered salute as he walked away.

"It'll be miles, not inches."

That seemed to make Dwyer smile. All the sheriff knew was that his childhood friend and his colleagues had some serious skills, cash and firepower, and they were going to teach the government that their days of overreaching into the lives of hardworking Americans were over. Or a similar anti-establishment message that bowed Dwyer's flexible morals. Dresden couldn't recall the exact wording, but it had all seemed to be smoothed over once a bag of cash was dropped into Dwyer's lap.

Dresden couldn't help but feel he was back amongst rival factions in Africa who were committed to a particular cause that was often funded by the US or Russia, who continually fought for control of the continent's precious mineral resources.

The sheriff moved down the muddy path towards the other vehicles in the makeshift lot below and drove off in his SUV.

A few minutes later, the radio in Dresden's hand crackled with a young man's voice, indicating the two trucks had arrived.

He glanced at his watch, seeing the semis were thirty minutes late. But he could overlook the delay. While punctuality was critical in his world, so was caution. Dresden would rather the men drive slowly and arrive intact than rush and draw attention from the state troopers along the highways.

His breath clouded in front of him as he shifted his gaze towards the Quonset hut to the right, where the shipment would be unloaded. It had taken months of careful planning getting the precious cargo from Algeria to Jakarta and then to Idaho.

He walked down to the building, entering through the side entrance and pressing the button for the large bay doors to open. Despite the weathered, rusty appearance of the building on the outside, the interior had concrete flooring, bright LED lighting, a fully equipped workshop, industrial shelving units, and a ventilation system. And the internal plumbing was tapped into a freshwater spring that emanated out of the riverbank below the cliff where the building was situated.

The noise roused the attention of a man seated at a large 3D printer in the far corner. He clicked off his work light and flipped up his protective visor, setting his gear down. He downed a bottle of water, then made his way to Dresden, wiping his greasy hands on his denim apron.

The man's horribly disfigured face would cause anyone but Dresden to avert their eyes. Landon Keen had been the third survivor in the Syrian missile strike two years prior, and the sulfur burns on his right cheek and ear caused his skin to resemble a melted candle. His eyebrows and most of his hair were gone, and he often had open ulcerations that had to be drained and covered in gauze.

Despite that, he still had the look of a rabid wolf in his eyes. The loss of his younger brother during that tragic night in Syria had fueled his rage, and he, Dresden and Giletti had been involved in every operational detail of this coming attack from its inception. With the arrival of this latest shipment, Keen's specialty as a munitions expert was about to come to fruition.

"About time. I've been freezing my ass off in this ice chest for the past hour, getting things ready," said Keen.

Dresden patted him on the shoulder. "Once this shipment gets unloaded, I'm off to Spokane to meet up with Giletti and his crew. We'll procure the remaining components we need and be back here by sunrise."

They watched the first truck roll up the driveway and pull into the Quonset hut. The stocky driver hopped out, nodding at Dresden, then walking around to the rear and removing the padlock on the lever holding down the sliding door.

"Any issues along the way?" asked Dresden.

"No, but we took the back roads the last ninety miles to avoid the weigh stations along the interstate," said the driver, his French-Algerian accent evident.

Dresden and Keen stared at the three dozen wooden crates inside. Dresden recalled the last time he'd seen the items was in a rat-infested warehouse along the Algerian coast.

The driver headed towards the forklift in the corner of the Quonset hut, while Dresden and Keen hopped inside the cargo container.

Keen grabbed a crowbar attached to a magnetic strip on the wall and used it to pry off the lid of the nearest crate. The odor of cedarwood shavings wafted over them, and Keen used the tool to slowly rake away the packing material and expose the carefully constructed faux rocks below.

He removed a football-sized piece and set it on top of another crate. Keen grasped one end of the rock and twisted until the coarse brown top unscrewed. He glanced down at the globular white substance inside, then angled it towards Dresden, both of them resembling treasure hunters.

"These geologic fabrications were worth every penny. The C-4 looks just like it did when I packed it up in Algeria."

The rock specimens Keen had created to house the explosives featured a shock-absorption system using viscoelastic polymers similar to those used in military ordnance transport. An area he was intimately familiar with from his younger days with the French Foreign Legion. The polymers could absorb vibrations, essentially preventing any shock waves from reaching the explosives during their long journey across the ocean.

The exterior shell was fabricated with actual mineral material that matched geological samples from the Algerian region, complete with natural-looking imperfections. This matrix was further reinforced with Kevlar threads for stability while maintaining the exact weight one would expect from actual specimens.

But the one thing that had ensured Dresden's smuggling efforts was the actual shipping containers themselves. The eighteen-inch gaps between the walls, floor, and ceiling were comprised of a multilayered aerogel insulation so the precious cargo could withstand the temperature extremes associated with international shipping. The aerogel material occasionally leached out into the air, leaving a pink residue when combined with the corrosive effects of a saltwater environment, but it wasn't something that had ever been a concern for customs inspectors.

Lastly, the carbon-fiber wall panels were engineered with a unique triaxial weave pattern that created a high strength-to-weight ratio while remaining lightweight enough for aeronautic applications.

When processed through Keen's industrial 3D cutting system, each eight-by-ten-foot panel would provide the exact airframe components needed for a small drone fleet that exceeded anything on the commercial market.

In the past, Dresden had used these specially designed cargo containers for transporting hundreds of stolen antiquities and artwork back to his former superior in the US—the same individual who channeled the art through black-market importer Matthew Ellison. And the same person who had rained down death from above two years ago in Syria. Life had finally come full circle, and the heartless politician behind the ending of all those lives was soon going to experience the consequences of their actions.

Dresden glanced at the vertical wood boxes lashed to the walls, which contained bundles of lightweight titanium rods. "How long will it take to extract everything and assemble it?"

Keen gazed at the other semi in the driveway. "Be done shaping the carbon-fiber panels into the design I need by tomorrow night; sooner if you and Giletti can lend a hand once you're back from Spokane. After that, I'll need another twenty-four hours to assemble the other items and install the explosive charges."

He patted Keen on the shoulder. "We're almost at the

finish line, my friend. And with Harrison out of the picture, there shouldn't be any more obstacles."

Dresden climbed down out of the semi and headed to his Dodge pickup near the cabin, looking forward to a change of scenery.

Soon, the final phase of their retribution would begin. The US government would brand it as terrorism. For Dresden and his men, it would be justice that was long overdue.

CHAPTER 12

WALKER DROVE THE SUBURBAN NORTH ON THE I-5 FOR NEARLY thirty miles before taking State Route 530 east for forty-six miles through the unincorporated communities of Cicero, Oso and Rowan, whose majestic wilderness backdrops were vistas that could be plastered on postcards.

Though the rear bench seat was comfortable, Payne felt a little uneasy sitting in the prisoner-containment section of the vehicle, with the lack of working windows and the mesh bars separating him from the front seat. There was an odd blend of aromas in the vehicle, which oscillated between a faint trace of what Payne figured was Fiche's aftershave mingled with the scent of strawberry shampoo emanating from Walker's direction. When he wasn't taking in the majestic mountains on either side, he found himself letting his eyes linger on Walker's tan neckline and blonde hair.

"Hard to believe we're only a ninety-minute drive from Seattle," said Payne as he craned his neck towards a snow-capped mountain to the south. "What do folks do out here for a living?"

"Hell if I know," said Fiche from the passenger seat, his voice laced with disdain. "Bunch of inbred motherfuckers, in my opinion."

"Don't sugarcoat things," replied Walker with a smirk. She glanced at Payne in the rearview mirror. "My partner was once with the dark side and worked for the US Marshals, serving warrants out here in the boonies, so he's a little jaded."

Fiche leaned back, pulling down his shirt collar to reveal an old scar on his neck. "Got this from a woman with a box cutter after we showed up at her cabin south of here. She didn't think that killing her husband in his sleep was a punishable offense and decided to re-enact the motions on me and my partner."

Walker fought back a chuckle. "Tell him the part about how she was sixty-two years old and it took both of you to subdue her."

"Shut up." Fiche shook his head, turning back towards the window. "That meth-head fought like a hyena."

"I think it was the Spartans who used to say that a woman's ferocity isn't measured by the weapons she wields, but the odds she's willing to face down," said Payne.

He noticed Fiche nodding in agreement, while Walker shot him an approving look in the mirror. "Are you sure that's a quote, or is it something gleaned from working with a lot of female operatives at the CIA?" she inquired.

"You watch too many movies, Agent Walker. I'm just a vagabond, roaming the country on my motorcycle. Or I was until yesterday. Speaking of my motorcycle, I'd like to get it back when we're done here."

"Very slippery, answering a question with a demand," said Walker. She gave her partner a sideways glance. "What do you think, is he a spook or not?"

Fiche briefly gazed back at Payne. "Given how he caused that guy at the expo to spring a few leaks, I'd say you're spot-on."

Walker adjusted the rearview mirror. "Above our pay grade, I know. But you're not denying it only makes for a stronger case."

"Let's just say I helped the senator, and people like him, follow threads that didn't like being pulled." He leaned in closer, alternating his gaze between them. "What about you two? You both look like you're far from your academy days. Surely, you must suspect something unusual going on when a couple of assassins in suits like yours try taking out a civilian in a public place."

"'Assassins'...that's a pretty strong word," said Fiche.

"The bruises on my body say otherwise."

It was nearly 10:45 a.m. when Walker turned off the two-lane blacktop onto a dirt road on the north side of Darrington, following the Suburban's console map to the rodeo grounds.

"Is this the main strip?" asked Walker as she slowed to a respectable thirty-five miles per hour.

"It's a couple of miles east of here," said Fiche. "With a little over twelve hundred people scattered around a few million acres of forest, there ain't much to this town." He clawed out air quotes at the last word.

A half mile later, Walker slowed and made a left turn. She paused before the main gate, where two armed security guards moved to either side of the vehicle.

She flashed her badge and explained they were there to examine the items recovered from the crash.

The bearded guard waved to the main building on the

other side of the rodeo arena, then motioned for his partner to open the gate.

"Local cops mean less of a chance of compromised federal agents," said Payne as they drove through the lot.

"Not everyone at the bureau is in on this, Payne," said Walker as they headed towards the two-story brick building. "Lots of good people I can personally vouch for."

"I realize that. But someone there is also on another payroll and doesn't care about collateral damage," said Payne.

"By the way you were standing earlier in the parking garage, I assume you're armed?" she asked.

He lifted the right side of his hoodie, revealing the FN 5.7 pistol tucked in his beltline. "Compliments of your phony twins."

"That guy also had a high-end suppressor that was a foreign make," said Fiche.

"It's his accomplice I wonder about…she's going to have a hard time squeezing a trigger or brushing her teeth for a while. Pretty sure I broke all her fingers when I slammed the door on her."

"I saw that on the camera footage from the hallway," said Walker. "You don't fuck around."

"My grandfather, who was in World War II, always used to say *he who lives by the sword lives one day longer.* I've found that to be a good mantra."

"Maybe we should leave him in the vehicle," said Fiche with a slight chuckle.

Walker parked near the front. Each of them exited and glanced around the empty grounds.

"You weren't kidding about having the place to ourselves," said Payne.

"The NTSB crew might be up in the foothills for the afternoon, so I'm not sure if we'll see anyone here for a while," said Fiche.

The place was laid out over sixty acres with a half-dozen buildings, horse stalls, bleachers, a barn and a spacious parking lot.

Payne noticed their tourist expressions. "From the photos you showed me earlier, I figured you two had already been out here."

She shook her head. "Those were sent over by the incident commander here after we requested it. From what he indicated, the human remains are in a refrigerated storage container they hauled into the barn yesterday. The rest of the personal effects are spread out on tables inside this building. We'll start here."

"How far away is the crash site?" asked Payne as they headed into the building.

Walker gestured to the mountains to the north. "About two miles. This town was damn lucky it was spared."

Payne wondered if luck had anything to do with it. Downing a government jet on a strip of homes and schools would draw even further attention to the senator's death. A part of him wondered if this location had been chosen for its proximity to the town since it would be easier for a mop-up crew to handle any evidence that might draw attention instead of the remote wilderness surrounding the area.

He gave one last glance at the perimeter of the property, reflexively scanning the exit points and high ground.

Fiche glanced back at the guards in the distance. "I feel like we should have notified Mentzer we were coming out here."

"And have him find out we were snooping around at a federal crime scene because we think there's a mole inside our bureau?"

"Well, when you put it like that."

Payne and the two agents donned nitrile gloves and examined the items on the three tables. Payne sifted through a slender silver watch, a man's leather boot, a melted laptop, a singed cotton jacket, and numerous fragments of clothing.

He moved on to the second table, which contained several burned carry-on luggage bags and a titanium briefcase. He flipped open the briefcase, which was empty.

"That's where those GPS coordinates were found," said Fiche as he walked by.

Payne was about to close the case when he noticed several strands of gold hair. He picked them up, holding them towards Walker's head. "Nope, not yours."

A frown formed on her face. "Really. I'm so glad for your insights."

He put the hairs back in the case, wondering why they hadn't been placed in an evidence bag. Payne moved on to the next table, examining the burned remnants of two documents sealed in clear bags, labelled as being from the cockpit. One looked like a fuel receipt and listed the amount of $176 along with a zip code. He pulled out his phone, entering the latter number into Google.

It only pulled up the small town of Marple, Idaho, near the Washington border. *There must be a small airstrip there where Harrison's jet refueled. But why in such a remote location?*

He zoomed in on the layout of the small town, which was listed as having a population of twelve hundred residents. There was a narrow strip of blacktop with a lone aerial tower a few miles northeast of Marple. The image was hazy, but Payne could make out several small planes parked near a Quonset hut and a refueling station. *Private airfield, so no guards on-site.*

He set down the evidence bag. *Was Harrison meeting with*

the military logistics guy that Whitmore mentioned? If so, then who was the dead guy labeled as the senator on the jet?

All signs kept pointing to Idaho. He needed to get back to his motorcycle in Seattle and be on his way to Marple if he was going to get any more answers.

"That's odd," said Fiche, standing near the front window. "The guards are nowhere in sight."

Payne walked over, moving up alongside him and staring out at the entrance gate.

The cracking of glass followed; then Fiche collapsed to the floor, the back of his head splintered apart by a lone gunshot.

Payne darted to the left as another gunshot splintered the window. He dropped to a squat and made his way along the side wall. He grabbed Walker's arm as she tried to rush past him towards her partner. "He was dead before he hit the ground."

"No, damnit." She tried to wrestle her arm free, but he tugged on it, pulling her along as a burst of rounds shattered the rest of the front windows. Glass shards flitted along the floor.

The front door swung open, and Payne saw two men in full tactical gear storm inside.

He and Walker took cover behind some steel fuel drums, clutching their pistols. She motioned to the back door, but he shook his head. "They'll have it covered already," he whispered. "We need to circle back to the front and take out those two guys before the others breach."

She gave him a wild-eyed look.

He pointed to the enclosed stairwell to their right. "You take the high ground while I stay here."

He patted her on the shoulder as he moved past her, moving along the rows of tractors as she bolted for the staircase. Payne took cover behind the massive rear tire of a John

Deere tractor, leveling his FN pistol at the gap near where Walker had just been.

A second later, he heard the crunch of broken glass as the shooters proceeded towards the fuel drums. He focused ahead, straining his ears for sounds by the rear exit. From experience, he was sure the assaulters were preparing to blow the door and rush inside any second.

Payne caught a glimpse of movement near the barrel. It was just a flash of black fabric. He aimed the front sight of his pistol at the first man's left knee, squeezing off a round that shattered the patella and sent the figure to the ground. He fired off another round into the guy's face, then bolted up, squeezing off two rounds at the second figure, who had started to backpedal away. One bullet struck the jaw while the other hit the neck. The shooter collapsed out of sight.

Payne was about to sprint towards the dead men to retrieve their rifles when the rear door exploded inward. Metal and wood splinters rained down on Payne, and he scurried under the tractor, sliding to the other side.

Leaning near the ground, he saw two sets of boots sweeping through the entrance. Payne gazed up to an open window on a second-floor room where Walker was positioned. She thrust her chin towards the front entrance, knowing he needed to bait the others into coming for him.

No way I'm going to get shot in the back. He glanced under the tractor again, this time lying on his left shoulder and pointing his pistol at the rear wall. He squeezed off a single round, piercing the fire extinguisher near the entrance, then rolled in the other direction and hopped up as the white haze filled the back of the building.

Payne sprinted down the main row of tables, then veered right towards the corner before making a sharp turn towards the front door. The room erupted in gunfire as Payne ducked beside a cart full of folding chairs.

He leaned out, seeing a ghostly figure emerge from the white mist from the shattered fire extinguisher. The front of his head blew apart from one of Walker's rounds, dropping him onto one of the evidence tables.

Payne caught a sliver of movement on the other side of the tractor. He fired four rounds into the pavement below it, one of the ricochets hitting their mark. A woman shrieked and fell to the ground. Payne squeezed off two rounds that struck her in the chest and neck, making her collapse onto her back and drop her rifle.

The clattering of boots to his right caused him to pivot and swing his pistol towards the oncoming target only to see Walker trotting in his direction. She was armed with a Sig Sauer rifle from one of the dead guys.

"We should assume there's one more person outside," said Payne. "Fiche was dropped by a shooter beyond the parking lot just before the others stormed in."

Her eyes were frozen on her dead partner. "Someone's going to pay for this."

"I agree, but right now we need to get clear of this area." He angled his head against the side of the shattered window, glancing at the Suburban in the distance. "Tires are flat, so I guess we're going out the back door on foot."

"Going where? There's nothing but miles of woods in that direction, from what I saw on the GPS."

He motioned for her to follow, running towards the rear entrance. Payne paused by the splayed body of the dead woman, noting three of her fingers buddy-taped together. He bent down, retrieving her Sig Sauer rifle and three spare magazines. "You recognize her?"

Walker shook her head, keeping her own rifle trained on the front door. "Should I?"

"She's your doppelganger from the expo." He gazed over the faces of the other shooters. All of them were in their mid-thirties with tan complexions and sandy blond hair. "Probably private contractors."

Payne moved to the splintered doorframe and peered at the dirt lot behind the building. "It's a hundred-yard dash to the woods."

"And after that?"

"I have a few ideas, and none of them involve the shooters on our tail coming out of this alive."

CHAPTER 13
SEATTLE

MARCUS ZHANG SAT AT HIS DESK IN THE CYBERCRIMES DIVISION at FBI headquarters, analyzing the GPS data from Agent Walker's vehicle along with her recent cellphone conversations from the past twelve hours. His computer skills and previous hacking abilities had allowed him unparalleled access to his fellow employees and their whereabouts.

The encrypted cellphone in his pants pocket vibrated, and he pulled it out, hearing Paul Giletti's beleaguered voice on the other end. "Things went to shit at the rodeo grounds, and Walker and Payne are on the run, heading north in the forest. I need an overview of the area and any houses in the region."

"Hang on." He closed his office door, then returned to his laptop. Zhang pulled up cellphone logs and overlaid it with satellite imagery. "Walker's signal is showing her about a half mile north-northwest of the rodeo grounds. It's pretty steep terrain, but there's a small structure on the plateau ahead of her, maybe a half mile farther."

"How many points of access?"

"One road, looks like a secondary route, so probably dirt or gravel." He zoomed in on the static location of the other signal. "Seems like Fiche is holed up in a building by their vehicle."

"Holed up is right. He took a round to the head, so he's no longer a concern."

Zhang's lower lip quivered. "What? You...you...you're joking, right?"

"What's the matter, Marcus...never get your hands dirty sitting at your keyboard all day?"

He watched Walker's signal again as it inched away from the rodeo grounds, then pulled up the location for Giletti, which showed him pursuing on foot. "You're not going to kill..."

"Get your head out of your ass. You didn't think we were just paying you to report on people's emails and travel patterns, did you?"

Zhang leaned back, his shoulders sagging. Since being recruited by Dresden, he had been the perfect mole, gaining access to all levels of the bureau's personnel, communications, and field protocols in his job as a senior analyst. Now, he was wondering if it was time to sever his ties and disappear using the contingency plans Dresden had set up for just such a day.

Giletti's voice flooded into his brain again. "While I'm hunting down Walker and Payne, I need you to work your magic on the surveillance footage at the NTSB command post here to erase my team's presence and create a new narrative. Can you do that?"

Zhang clutched the edge of his seat, the adrenaline surge rushing over him like he was back at the casino poker table he frequented each night. He focused on the thought of the next payment Dresden had promised, and on delivering some further, albeit violent, payback to his condescending colleagues at the bureau. "Yes, sir. I'll get right on it."

CHAPTER 14

PAYNE TROTTED UP THE NARROW GAME TRAIL WITH WALKER ON his heels. The pungent aroma of spruce trees reminded him of the miles of swamplands and forest around his hometown in northern Michigan, except the only predators in that region were the occasional wolf pack and not a hit squad.

After ten minutes of constant uphill jogging, he stopped on a level spot, both of them taking cover behind a massive fallen pine tree. In between catching his breath, he glanced over Walker for any injuries. "You alright?" he asked.

She cast her misty eyes down. "He shouldn't have gone down like that. Fiche was a good man."

Payne nodded, keeping his attention focused on the path they'd just taken. "I'm sorry for your loss, Agent Walker."

"Carrie. I think we're past the formalities. And I also think that there's a whole lot of shit you're not telling me about what's going on. I saw the look on your face when you were examining the initial photos of the crash victims on Fiche's phone earlier today. Care to fill me in?"

He thrust his chin up the trail. "We need to keep pushing on. My guess is that the kill team has orders to eliminate us at any cost. Once we're in a more secure location, I'll tell you what I know."

Before she could respond, Payne crept out from behind the fallen log and continued trotting along the trail as Walker followed. Given how choked the forest was on either side, there was no point in employing counter-tracking moves, mantraps, or venturing onto another route. Time and distance were essential, and he picked up his pace, knowing the pursuers could be sending another team to cut them off ahead.

Fifteen minutes later, the path intersected a narrow dirt road, which looked wide enough for a jeep to pass over. Payne glanced in either direction, seeing leaf litter and ankle-high grass tufts on the road, surmising it hadn't been used in a while.

"This way," Walker said, waving the barrel of her rifle to the right where the faint outline of a structure was visible through the trees.

They jogged beside each other, Payne constantly turning to check the path behind them. Rounding the bend in the road, they came upon a small clearing with a two-story cabin made of hewn logs and a barn to the rear. The windows on the structure were boarded up, and a canvas tarp was secured over the stone chimney.

He moved past the cabin, making a beeline for the barn. The double doors were secured with a chain, so he ran down to the side entrance.

"Got your CIA lock-pick set with you?" Walker quipped as they stared at the combination lock on the door latch.

"Something better, actually," he said, slinging his rifle and picking up a large rock. He slammed it down on the lock several times until the entire latch broke free. Payne tossed down the Stone Age hammer and swung open the door. An odor of rodent droppings and rotting vegetation pierced his nostrils.

"Once again, I don't hear any denial from you about being CIA."

"And once again, you're annoying as hell with your continual prodding."

He repositioned his rifle and followed Walker inside, both of them sweeping their weapons around the crowded interior. To the left were stacks of moldy hay bales, sealed barrels labeled as fertilizer, and a wall full of gardening tools.

To the right was a workbench along the far wall; in the middle was an old Ford pickup with a layer of dust on the windshield.

"Keep an eye on the front of the property while I check out this old rig." He headed to the truck, opening the driver's door and inspecting the interior. He flipped down the visors, hoping for a set of keys, but had no luck. Payne searched under the seats and the glovebox but to no avail. He popped the hood and went around the front, lifting it and inspecting the engine.

"You gonna give it a tune-up?" she asked while peering between the cracks in the weathered wood.

"Just searching for the damn keys, and also to make sure the mice haven't chewed up all the wires."

"Try the workbench," she whispered.

He gently lowered the hood and moved to the eight-foot-long workbench, which was lined at the back with dozens of coffee cans filled with nails, bolts, and galvanized nuts. He began dumping out the contents and rummaging through the items.

"Ever heard of a guy named Evan Whitmore?"

She shook her head.

"He's the head of port security in Seattle. I met with him yesterday evening. He was working with Senator Harrison, tracking down a shipment out of Algeria that arrived this week."

She pulled her head back from the cracks. "Same location as those grid numbers found in the wreckage. And you think that whoever was involved with Operation Paragon is moving illegal firearms into the US?"

"I don't think it's firearms. To be honest, I'm not sure since Whitmore inspected the containers and only found crates full of minerals." Payne sifted through clusters of nails. "Whitmore's been working at the port for decades, so he's no stranger to spotting contraband or illegal shipments. Even he was puzzled."

"But it was of concern enough to warrant a trip out here for Harrison. Too bad dead men don't talk."

He rubbed the back of his neck. "Well, actually, about that —Harrison wasn't on that downed jet. I don't know who the hell that guy was that Fiche showed me on his phone, but it wasn't the senator."

She narrowed her eyes. "What? You're shitting me, right? When were you going to tell me?"

"I just did, now that I know you're not in on any of this. I wasn't sure if I could trust you or your partner until things went down at the rodeo grounds." He dumped out a can of rusty screws.

"How can you be sure Harrison wasn't on that plane? NTSB seemed to think so from their initial report."

"The senator vaporized his right hip in a skiing accident in Vail, Colorado, three years ago and had to get a replacement. The photo of that victim had both hips intact." His eyes darted along the ground for a moment. "Now that I think about it, I wonder if that's why the NTSB investigation is dragging along. Harrison might be pulling some strings from the shadows to buy himself more time."

"Time for what?"

"Either to escape or to follow through on his investigation. Whatever hornet's nest he kicked was enough to have his jet brought down." He gave her a firm stare. "And to send a hit team after federal agents."

Payne spilled out a can of hex bolts, seeing a bronze key and a large silver key with a Ford logo. He walked to the double doors and used the smaller key to undo the padlock on the chains and slide them off. He retraced his steps back to the truck. He set his rifle against the side and leaned into the cab and inserted the silver key. "Good suggestion on where to search, Agent Walker. I mean Carrie." He turned it one click until the gauges on the dashboard activated. "Looks like there's enough fuel to get us out of the area."

Payne was about to start the engine when he saw Walker thrust up her fist. "Movement at ten o'clock. Four shooters closing in."

He slid out of the truck and grabbed his rifle. "Come with me," he whispered.

They skirted between the hay bales, arriving at the rear door. He motioned for her to head up the weathered staircase to the loft. "Same plan like in the warehouse. Only they're going to be more prepared, so expect a flash-bang before they enter through the side door. These bales will hopefully help dampen some of the effect."

She nodded, then ran up the steps and got into position behind a six-foot-high bundle of straw.

Payne moved to the last row of bales that overlooked the truck and side entrance. Like clockwork, he saw the side door swing outward and something being tossed inside. The metallic object clanked on the ground. Payne shuffled back, letting his rifle drop on its sling as he closed his eyes and covered his ears, leaning into the wall of bales. The shock wave was muffled, but he still felt his head rattle from the blast.

He immediately grabbed his rifle and raced back to the corner bale, fixing his rifle sights on the side entrance. Two people had already slipped in and disappeared around the hay bales on the opposite side, but the third figure in black tactical gear was exposed in the doorway. Payne squeezed off two rounds that hit the guy in the chin and nose, splintering apart the back of his head and dropping him across the threshold.

Payne backpedaled, weaving through the maze towards the center. In the tight confines, his rifle had become an encumbrance. He slung it over his back and reached for his FN pistol, but before he could retrieve it, he ran into the barrel of an assaulter sweeping in from his right. He grabbed the weapon and yanked it hard, then twisted it down, seeing the surprised face of a woman.

She winced, then sent a low kick that caught Payne in the left calf. His leg buckled, and he let go of the AR muzzle. The woman backed up, trying to raise her weapon, but struggled to maintain the grip. Payne rushed at her, shoulder-slamming her in the chest. She dropped her AR and sent a knee into Payne's chest that compressed his ribs, nearly causing him to vomit. He slid back and shot a right hook into her jaw, then scythed an elbow across her right cheek that sent her into the bales. He shuffled back, sliding out his pistol and firing two rounds into her head.

"Get down," yelled Walker.

Payne dropped to one knee, feeling something warm spray the back of his neck, and turned to see the third shooter collapsing as blood leaked from the bullet hole in his forehead.

"There's still one tango out there," he shouted.

"I've got him," Walker replied as she pointed her rifle out the upstairs window opening. "Shit, he just disappeared around the other side of the cabin."

"We need to get the hell out of here," said Payne. "He might be calling in reinforcements."

Walker's boots clattered along the creaky steps as she descended. He tossed her the Ford key as they trotted to the truck. Payne lowered his rifle into the bed, then ran to the double doors. "You drive while I handle things at our back side."

She slid her weapon onto the bench seat as Payne stood by the double doors. He waited until the engine sputtered to life, a black cloud of smoke belching out the tailpipe. Payne yanked the bolt back and shoved open the doors, then shuffled to the side as the Ford drove past. He ran for the side, hopping into the bed and grabbing his rifle.

He heard the metal beside his legs getting peppered by gunfire and saw a bearded shooter in an upstairs window at the back of the cabin. The man unleashed a brief volley as they drove past. Payne slid back against the rear of the bed, angling his rifle up as the truck sped by the front of the house. Once they swerved past the porch, Payne sent a flurry of rounds into the boarded-up windows on the second story.

The Ford fishtailed along the dirt road, eventually evening out as they moved out of sight of the old dwelling. Ten minutes later, Walker slowed at an intersection with another secondary road. Payne climbed out of the bed and moved to the passenger's seat with his rifle. She turned left and drove for a short distance until heading west back onto the two-lane highway.

Payne kept glancing at the road behind them, thinking about the bloody events of the past twenty-four hours. *That makes seven hitters down and one federal agent along with everyone on that plane. Whoever's behind this is sparing no effort to make sure their problems go away.*

He took a deep breath, inhaling the aroma of spruce trees, knowing things were probably going to get a lot uglier.

CHAPTER 15

AN HOUR LATER, WALKER GLANCED ONE LAST TIME IN HER
rearview mirror, feeling confident they weren't being
followed, and turned into a small gas station near Lake
Stevens just outside of Seattle.

She drove to the rear of the building and turned off the
engine. "I need to call my boss. I've already waited too long."

Payne swiveled towards her. "This is why I told you to
dump your phones when we first met."

She opened the door and stepped out, removing the
iPhone from her jacket. "It appears there are some hired guns
behind what's happening, Payne. You said so yourself—that
they could be French Algerians, so that doesn't mean there's a
leak in my agency."

He licked his lip. "I never thought I'd need to explain the
importance of operational security to an FBI agent, especially
given what just went down at the rodeo grounds."

She watched a blue camper van stop at the fuel pump and
an older man in coveralls exit. Walker returned her gaze to
Payne. "Look, I don't work outside of the law and dispense

with official protocols, all of which seems to be foreign to your way of thinking."

"I don't really trust anyone right now. He's going to want specifics on where you are, and this isn't the time to divulge our location. In fact, we should ditch this truck and acquire a new vehicle, then head east to Idaho. That's the next step. Escape and evasion are paramount right now."

"Criminals evade, and we've done nothing wrong." She hesitated before continuing, "My boss is a stand-up guy and not the type to be on anyone's payroll. Certainly not the kinda person who would put his own field agents in the crosshairs."

"But you're not entirely sure, are you? You'd be amazed at how a person's moral code suddenly becomes flexible when enough cash is dropped in their lap."

"Is that why you got out of your line of work, because your shiny armor was at risk of getting tarnished?"

Payne sighed, not wanting to engage in verbal jujitsu with the woman. He got out of the truck, leaning against the hood as he stared at her on the other side. "You do what you have to but leave any mention of Harrison being alive out of your report, at least for now, until I figure out my next move."

She blew a strand of blonde hair off her nose. "I'm sorry for what I said. I didn't mean to—"

He raised a hand. "I forgave you as soon as you said it. I know a little about losing a trusted friend and know you're probably wrestling with a lot right now. And for what it's worth, shiny armor is the first thing to get stripped away when you get involved in the line of work I was in."

Walker waved her phone at him. "I'll only be a minute." She walked to the corner of the parking lot beside the forest, sliding her phone off airplane mode and seeing a dozen voicemails pull up from Mentzer.

She didn't bother checking them and pressed his number instead.

He picked up on the second ring. "Carrie, thank God. I've been trying to reach you for the past hour. Where the hell are you?"

"Fiche and I drove out to the rodeo grounds so we could get Kyle Payne's take on some of the senator's wreckage and personal remains."

"Payne, the person of interest from the expo? Why didn't you bring him down here so he could be debriefed?"

"It's a long story, sir. I'll fill you in, but right now, I have to...have to tell you that Fiche was killed. He was..."

"Gunned down, I know. I'm so sorry, Carrie. Zhang just showed me the footage from the warehouse. I was getting ready to scramble a helo and tac team."

She felt the tension in her shoulders ratchet up. "What? Why would Zhang have security footage from the rodeo grounds? He's not even in data forensics. And we were only out there an hour ago or less, so how did he even have time to acquire and analyze the footage?"

"Pretty sure he was asked to assist with the NTSB guys in Darrington. That crew had security cams set up in and around the warehouse."

Mentzer is the assistant director of the bureau and he doesn't know who works for who? What's going on?

She chewed on her lip, fighting back the horrific image of Fiche lying dead. "You need to put out an alert for a lone mercenary who was just at the cabin a mile northeast of the rodeo grounds. Once you ID his dead teammates, you might be able to flag down who they're connected with. Payne thinks they're tied to the people posing as federal agents who attacked him at the expo."

"Carrie, all I saw was Payne taking out Fiche at close

range with his pistol, then pocketing some of the evidence from the investigation."

She felt her throat constrict. "What? No, that's not what happened at all."

"Where exactly were you when Fiche was killed?"

"In the back of the building, going over some of the flight logs."

"So you never actually saw Fiche get shot?"

The attack had happened so fast. She struggled to sift through the key details. "Fiche got hit; then Payne ran towards me as assaulters were moving in through the front door. I headed upstairs while he dropped the two attackers who were moving towards us."

"From what I observed, he grabbed some of the critical evidence from the back table just before you two bolted out the rear exit. There's nothing to indicate there was anyone else inside that building except you, Fiche and Payne."

"There were two shooters who entered the front door, then two more who breached the rear. After we took them out, we fled in the woods to this old cabin and barn, where four more assaulters came after us. We barely managed to escape."

"I've been over the footage a half-dozen times already. There are no other shooters."

She seethed out an exhale. "Sir, you need to examine that footage again because someone's fucked with it. Probably the security guards at the main gate of the rodeo grounds since they conveniently disappeared just before Fiche was shot."

Mentzer sighed. "Look, I want to believe you. I really do, but I just got off the phone with the security guards, and they said they were told to go home after you arrived, and there were no shell casings found in the building except the one from Payne's 9mm pistol."

Mention of the caliber echoed through her weary brain.

But Payne is carrying that FN 5.7, not a 9 mil. She shook her head. *Jesus, is Mentzer in on this cover-up too? Is he the mole at the bureau?*

"I don't know what the hell is going on, sir, but someone's trying to sell you a doctored version of what really happened. And the goddamned cuts on my face and arms from fighting the professional hit team who came after us sure as hell aren't a figment of my imagination."

A long pause followed before Mentzer replied, "Come in and we'll talk. Once I get your version of what happened, we can drive out to Darrington together, and you can walk me through what went down. You're one of my best agents, Carrie, and I want to believe you, but I'm getting pulled in two directions about what happened out there. Right now all the signs point to Payne, the very guy you're hitching your wagon to."

She thought about the gruesome damage to Fiche's skull. *No way that was done by a pistol round of any caliber. Payne was right all along…someone inside the bureau is behind this.*

Walker clutched the phone like she was gripping the edge of a cliff. "You know, I expected more. It's not like you to second-guess my every move when I've put my neck on the line countless times for you and my fellow agents over the years."

A pregnant pause followed until Mentzer replied in a calmer tone, "You need to come in. I'll look out for you the best I can, but, right now, I'm looking at Payne becoming the subject of a federal manhunt. You don't want to be tied to him."

"Inspect the ballistics report on Fiche before you pass any further judgment. You'll see they don't match the FN 5.7 handgun Payne is carrying. And have a handpicked forensics team comb through the building at the rodeo grounds. You have a shadow operating in your own department, boss, and they're going to try to bring down anyone who's connected with Harrison's death."

"This will work a lot better for both of us if you are here to help me sort through it."

"I can't. Not yet. We stumbled onto something at the rodeo grounds that I need to follow up on first. Give me forty-eight hours. If I don't find what I'm looking for, or I feel that Payne is compromising anything, then I'll return to Seattle." She sighed, glancing back towards the truck. "And for what it's worth, Payne saved my life today."

She hung up, pacing around the lot for a minute. Walker shuddered out a long breath as she lowered her head, feeling like the sky above had suddenly constricted. She returned to the truck, plucking out the SIM card from her phone, then stomping it under her boot heel and tossing the device in a trash barrel.

Walker rested both hands on the hood, staring into Payne's face. "Looks like going back to Seattle is not in the works right now." She looked into his eyes, his calmness reassuring. "Can't believe I'm about to ask this, but tell me more about your evasion plans."

CHAPTER 16

THREE HUNDRED MILES. PAYNE AND WALKER DID THE DRIVE TO the border of western Idaho in six hours. They made one stop at the halfway point to refuel and get some burgers from a drive-through, paying in cash for both transactions. After departing Seattle in the stolen Ford pickup, Payne had acquired another vehicle at a hotel. The blue Subaru Forester was an older model and probably wouldn't be reported stolen until the following morning.

For Payne, the drive felt like it lasted two days, with them rehashing the bizarre events of the past thirty-six hours, while Walker alternated between moods of anger and grief at the loss of her partner. In between, he tried to lighten the atmosphere by mentioning his upbringing in northern Michigan while she chatted about her youth in Seattle. Eventually, she slept for the last ninety minutes, giving Payne time to mull over his plan of action.

First, he needed to access his email and see if Alisa had messaged. Then he had to learn more about Marple and the airfield where Harrison's jet had supposedly stopped to refuel. From there, they might be able to examine the place's security footage and confirm that Harrison had disembarked there.

It was 9 p.m. when they pulled into a motel on the outskirts of Moscow, an hour north of Marple. They had both agreed that it wouldn't be wise to roll into the small town of Marple at night and opted to get some rest in Moscow and start fresh in the morning.

Payne had seen the signs on the highway just before exiting that Moscow was home to the University of Idaho, and the city boasted a population of nearly twenty-five thousand people. In addition to being the agricultural and commercial hub for the region, it appeared, at first glance, to be another one of those boom-or-bust college towns where socioeconomic life was stratified between working professionals and impover-ished students.

"Place still looks the same as when I was last here, five years ago." Walker glanced at the strip of motels and fast-food joints down the street as they exited the Forester.

He gazed at the distant plains to the west. "Poverty with a view. I've been in a few like this in my travels...Flagstaff, Eureka, Portland."

"Portland's just poverty with gray skies, compared to Flagstaff, at least."

He stretched his arms out, yawning. "You've spent time in Arizona?"

She smirked, taking a while to reply. "Yeah, went to the Grand Canyon with my now ex-husband. We did our honey-moon in Sedona and poked around northern Arizona for a week." Walker sighed. "It's never a good sign when the honeymoon is the best part of your marriage."

"Well, we all make left turns instead of right ones when we're younger."

Walker pressed her hands against the vehicle, leaning

forward and stretching her calves. "What about you? Ever settle down?"

He shook his head. "Thought about it a few times."

"Well, that's not vague." She walked around the car, leaning against the door. "Look, I appreciate what you did back in Darrington to help me take down that goon squad, not to mention contacting me in the first place, when slipping away would have been a lot easier. But it would be really helpful to know a little more about who you are, besides the nebulous comments you keep making about your travels and your past."

"Fair enough." Payne watched a young couple zip through the parking lot on their mountain bikes as they headed towards the dorms in the distance. "I was with CIA's Ground Branch for years before joining a small cadre of personnel-recovery specialists who were sent in to various hot zones to pull out high-value assets or diplomats."

She continued stretching, gazing at him. "That would explain how someone like the senator would dial you into his investigation, then and now."

"You were right earlier when you said that normally a traveling politician of his status would use diplomatic security when venturing overseas. Only, his senior bodyguard had recently retired, and he wanted someone from outside the pool of DS and, more importantly, a person who had some experience in North Africa. I had worked briefly as a case officer over there, so my name came up when Harrison was running his plan past my old mentor back at Langley."

Payne rubbed his sore shoulder. "I've had the misfortune of briefly interacting with some of the cake-eaters from the capital over the years, but Harrison was a different animal altogether. Maybe he's managed to hold on to his ethics in the DC snake pit because he was a decorated combat pilot. He was someone I'd definitely consider taking a bullet for if things came to that."

He thrust his chin at the motel office, wanting to end the conversation. "I'll go get a couple of rooms. I saw a pizza place next door when we pulled in. What do you like on yours?"

"Anything but pineapple or mushrooms. Those are disgusting."

"Good to know you're not picky."

Walker brushed a remnant of straw off her tan suit coat. "We drove by a secondhand store a few blocks from here. I'm going to grab some new threads so I don't smell like a barn and stand out so much."

Payne watched her walk away, his eyes lingering on her athletic figure, knowing her looks were still going to stand out whenever she was in his presence.

———

THIRTY MINUTES LATER, Payne was sitting on a bench outside the door to their room when he waved Walker over. She was carrying a plastic bag in one hand and a faded hockey duffel bag in the other. She tossed him the latter object, which smelled like an old sponge. "Thought we could use that for toting the newly acquired tools in the vehicle to and from our rooms."

"Good idea. And it's just one room. They were all booked up. I guess most places are since there's a birding festival going on."

She frowned. "Bird and nerd sound so similar, don't they? Oh, yeah, sorry. I forgot you were raised by wolves in northern Michigan and enjoy all that nature crap."

"Better than being raised in the home of Starbucks and grunge music."

She headed to the door and swung it inward. "Which bed you want?"

"I thought I'd leave it up to you."

"Such a gentleman."

He unzipped the duffel bag, shaking out some flecks of dirt. "I'll grab the pizza. It should be ready by now."

She set down her bag inside and turned towards him. For a second, he saw a look of desperation, or maybe fear, in her eyes. He knew that losing her friend and going on the run was beginning to sink in further. Probably for the first time in her career, she was bucking the very protocols she had always adhered to. And now, she was going to share a room with a stranger with a violent past.

"Payne, you sure about what comes next? Or any of this?"

He stepped closer. "I have some ideas. Let's discuss things when I get back with dinner. For what it's worth, this is the hard part: standing on the edge of the diving board, staring down, recalling the world you thought you knew and the murky waters ahead. But I promise it won't always be like that. We'll piece this together and find out who killed Fiche and all those poor souls on the plane."

She gave a half-hearted nod, then dumped out her new wardrobe on the bed.

Payne leaned in and closed the door, locking it with the key. After he walked across the parking lot, he stopped in the motel lobby and headed to the back room where the guest computer and snack bar were located. He grabbed a chocolate chip cookie from a tray and then sat down, checking his email account. He bit into the cookie, barely noticing the taste after seeing his inbox empty.

Damnit. You'd better be alright, Alisa.

He mulled over the possibilities. *She's either still in evasion mode and constantly on the move; holed up somewhere and remaining completely dark until the threat window changes; or...*

He drove away the latter thought. He couldn't let his mind go there.

Other than his father and a few close friends still working in clandestine ops, Alisa was as close to family as he had left in his world. She had saved his life countless times during operations with her intel abilities and decisive actions from afar. And he wasn't about to let her wade through this storm alone, whatever its scope.

Keep your head up, Alisa. I will find you. No matter what it takes.

———

TWENTY MINUTES LATER, the last piece of ham and pepperoni pizza was divided up between Payne and Walker.

She had showered and sat on the bed, wearing a black tank top and gray gym shorts she'd picked up at the thrift store. As he parked himself on a wooden chair across from the beds, he couldn't help but notice her incredibly tan and fit arms along with the way the lamplight played off her silky blonde hair.

"So why isn't there a Mrs. Payne—or was there once?" she asked, sliding back against the wall and stuffing some pillows under her back.

He dragged a napkin across his lips, then took a swig of his root beer. "There were some close calls, but being gone three hundred or more days a year didn't help."

"You make it sound like relationships were like a cold you didn't want to catch."

"Not relationships, just marriage." He winked at her. "The thing is, I'd just seen too many buddies of mine get hitched and then miss all the birthdays, anniversaries, funerals, you name it, and wonder why the woman they went home to was a stranger. It was hell on the kids as they got older, wondering why their mom was married but single, and their old man was never at their soccer games."

She pursed her lips. "Yeah, I've seen some of that with my colleagues at the bureau, but it's nothing on the scale of what you're describing. I'm happy to get back home after a few weeks of training in DC. I can't imagine being deployed eighty percent of the year." She rested her chin on her knee. "How long did you live like that?"

He glanced up at the ceiling. "Fourteen years or so, though the last few years involved more time in Virginia."

"Because you got benched with an office job for being such a wiseass?" she said with a faint grin.

Payne shook his head. "Got involved with personnel and asset recovery on a twelve-man team. There were four units, and we'd each rotate for a few months to a different part of the world so we could be on standby in case someone needed a hasty extraction from a hotspot."

"You said that with a hint of regret. You must miss it."

"Not so much the work as the man in charge. He was a great friend and mentor. He was killed by a bunch of drug-runners in Pineland, Arizona, last summer."

"Shit. Sorry. Did they ever catch who did it?"

He stared down into the half-empty bottle for a second. "It was handled. Those guys won't ever be a threat to anyone again, and their drug empire was pretty much burned to the ground."

Walker folded her arms. "Not sure I want to know any more. Or should know any more than that, Payne." She let out a heavy sigh. "If we're going to continue doing whatever it is we're doing, then I need you to know that you're, um, how do I say this…not overseas on an op or back in fucking Tombstone, Arizona. There are laws, and I plan to follow them to the letter."

"I expect you will, Agent Walker. I have no problem with

that, and I understand your reasoning. Just know that I won't lose any sleep in doing the opposite if that's what's called for, and it might very well be the case if we're dealing with another hit crew of French-Algerian mercs who have no qualms about who's in their crosshairs. The teams back at the rodeo grounds and the expo were professional killers, not bank robbers on the FBI's most wanted list."

"Since it looks like it's just the two of us embarking upon this investigation for now, I need to keep my sights focused forward and not be looking out for you, wondering if you're gonna turn vigilante."

He moved to his bed, yanking out a pillow from under the sheets and tossing it on the bed. He plunked down on his back, kicking off his boots. "I was just thinking the same thing. Am I gonna have to keep you from going full cop-mode if we run into more bad guys with guns?"

She flung her wet towel on his chest. "Go shower; everything about you stinks."

He sat up on one elbow. "I can honestly say that you smell quite pleasant, Agent Walker."

She gave him a puzzled look. "Stop your psy-ops bullshit and get cleaned up. The smell of rodeo dust and horse apples is going to make me lose my dinner."

He stood and walked to the bathroom, grabbing a fresh towel off the rack.

"Hey," she said, her eyes softening. "Sorry about your friend in Arizona."

Payne felt his shoulders relax as he looked at her. "Likewise, Carrie. It's not something you ever get over, but the pain will eventually ease up."

He headed into the bathroom and closed the door. He started the shower, looking forward to washing away the deluge of unpleasant memories.

CHAPTER 17

THE OLD WOMAN WITH THE SILVER HAIR REMAINED IN HER SEAT as the other passengers disembarked the plane at Missoula Airport in western Montana. Once the aisles were clear, she stood and removed her shoulder bag from the overhead compartment, then made her way to the exit.

After arriving in the terminal, she hugged the wall on the right so the frantic people trying to make their connections wouldn't trample her. Plus, she needed to use the restroom.

She glanced out the large terminal windows on the right, seeing the steady drizzle of rain that she'd just left behind on the East Coast.

Veering to the right, she headed into the bathroom and found a vacant stall at the far end. Locking the door, she hung her shoulder bag on the hook and unzipped it, removing a gray ball cap and glasses.

The woman removed the bobby pins holding her wig in place and slid it off, stuffing it into the bag. She pulled out the smaller clips holding her brunette locks in place and shook her hair back to its usual shoulder length.

Given the events of the past couple of days, Alisa Fairbanks felt naked once again, but another visual change was necessary in case she was still being tracked.

After all my years with the agency and time spent on evasion training in foreign lands, I never thought I'd be using those skills in my own damned country.

She tucked her false ID into a Velcroed concealment pocket at the bottom, swapping it out for a fake driver's license that she'd need to rent a car.

When she was ready, she took a deep breath, focusing on the next leg of this trip across the Idaho border. If she'd had a choice, she would have flown into Boise and driven up to the rendezvous point with her contact near Moscow, Idaho, but ever since leaving her Virginia townhome yesterday, she had to be certain she wasn't being followed by the same group that had taken down the senator's jet.

I was careful, but Dresden and his crew somehow pieced together that I was working for Harrison, so who knows how far their reach extends.

Before she could drive east of the city, she needed to check her encrypted email account and send an update to Payne and another to Harrison. She grabbed her bag and exited, retracing her steps back to the main corridor.

I hope you're alright, Kyle. Seems like the past has a way of catching up with people in our line of work, regardless of whether you're out of Langley's grip or not.

CHAPTER 18

SPOKANE, WASHINGTON

It was 11:15 p.m. when Giletti switched off the F-150's headlights and came to a halt on the dirt road that wound through the forest. He stepped out, opening the back door and removing a suppressed MK 12 rifle from under a blanket on the bench seat. The same rifle he'd used to take Agent Fiche out of circulation.

He heard a faint whistle coming from the darkness beyond the passenger's side. He responded with a similar sound while removing a pair of night-vision goggles from his pack on the seat. After adjusting them, he powered them on, scanning the dense trees to the right, where he saw four armed figures squatting near a tall chain-link fence bordered with razor wire. Beyond that was a six-hundred-acre facility comprised of three immense warehouses owned by the Willow Run Aviation Repair Company.

He quietly closed the truck door and made his way through the brush, squatting beside the lanky figure on the right. All of the men nodded to the newcomer, two of them refocusing their rifles on the distant security cameras on the first warehouse a hundred yards beyond the fence.

"Glad you're in one piece, brother, after what you described going down at the rodeo grounds," said Mike Dresden, who patted Giletti on the shoulder.

"We lost a lot of our crew, though."

There was a sorrowful look in Dresden's eyes. He hung his head low for a second. "Things sure sounded like they took a turn beyond what we expected with this leg of the operation, but we've still got enough people to see things through. We just need to avoid any further losses."

"It's going to be cutting it close."

"There are only two more steps beyond tonight to get everything aligned. We'll be in the home stretch seventy-two hours from now."

"I spoke with our two-man team in Virginia who were pursuing Alisa Fairbanks. She managed to elude them, so I told 'em to return to Idaho."

"That was a long shot but worth trying in case she was connected to anyone else in Harrison's inner circle. With the senator out of the picture, she probably won't rear her head again."

The stout figure on the other side of Dresden lowered his thermal spotting scope and leaned back, his face painted with black streaks. "The security guard outside the warehouses just made his second sweep and headed inside, so we're clear."

Dresden glanced at his shooters, giving the nonverbal command to snipe the cameras mounted on the warehouse.

Dresden reached over his shoulder, removing the lengthy pair of bolt cutters protruding from his pack. He stood and moved to the fence, snipping out a rectangular shape that was waist-high. "Giletti and I will head inside while the rest of you take up sentry positions around the perimeter of the buildings. Once we've neutralized the guards, we'll load up what we need in our vehicles and head back to the Marple location."

The men stacked up behind Dresden, stepping through the fence and splitting off into their respective positions. They trotted across the blacktop, moving past a dozen commercial planes parked in rows. Nearing the side entrance, Giletti and Dresden flipped up their now useless NVGs as the building's spotlights washed over their surroundings.

Dresden glanced back at his second-in-command. "Previous recons indicated three guards on the entire site, and they alternate between the three warehouses and exterior grounds every hour. Right now, they should all be in the main office in the right corner of this building."

Giletti kept his back pressed against the wall, covering the parking lot with his rifle while Dresden slid his suppressed AR-10 over his back and removed the two lock-picking tools from his vest. He kneeled and inserted the L-shaped lever implement with one hand while sliding the serrated tool in his other hand in the lock. The entire process to open the deadbolt took sixteen seconds…and twelve years of practical field application.

He tucked the tools back in his vest and stood, retrieving the rifle off his back and getting into position as Giletti swung open the door.

They moved silently along the concrete floor, weaving through aisles of shelves stacked with metal struts and spools of electrical wire until they arrived near the guards' office. From the raucous shouts and the drone of a basketball broadcast, it was clear the men had bets on the game.

Dresden darted to the left side of the door while Giletti moved behind him. Dresden removed a flash-bang from his vest and pulled the pin. He leaned closer, tossing the device inside. Both men turned away as the concussive blast erupted.

They rushed inside the room, Giletti dumping two rifle rounds into the chest of the man on the right as he tried to stagger to his feet. Dresden's AR-10 coughed out a series of double-taps that peppered the other guards in the chest, both men collapsing to the ground.

"Clear," whispered Giletti. He stepped over the dead man's body, examining the lone security camera they had left intact, which showed the front entrance to the property. "Shit, we've got a major problem. The main gate just closed. One of the guards must have let someone in just before we entered this building."

Dresden shuffled closer, watching the front gate close. A second later, they heard the sound of a vehicle coming to a halt outside the side entrance.

Dresden's ear mic crackled with the harried voice of one of his men. "There's a lone woman who just exited a Honda Accord near your six. She's carrying what looks like some takeout bags of food."

Dresden flicked off the office lights and bolted out of the room as Giletti followed.

"You want me to drop her?" asked the operator in Dresden's earpiece.

"No. I'll handle it once she's inside."

The side door opened. Dresden peered through the gaps between the boxes, seeing a woman in her late twenties carrying two large bags emitting steam into the cool air.

"Eddy, I've got the meatloaf you and the guys wanted..." Her voice trailed off as she paused near the entrance of the dark office. A gasp pierced the stillness as she dropped the bags on the ground.

"Don't scream or make a move," said Dresden, who had shadowed her movements, coming up behind her.

She stiffened but didn't make a sound.

Giletti moved up beside her, grabbing her hands and zip-tying them with restraints he'd removed from his pack.

The woman stared at the faint outlines of the motionless men in the office. "No, please, God. No. Are they—"

"Shut up," Giletti snapped, shoving her face against the wall.

"Easy," said Dresden, motioning to her waistline, where a slight bump was evident.

The two men gave each other uneasy looks. Dresden grabbed her arm and walked her to the left of the office, pausing beside a door listed as storage. He made sure to remain behind her so she couldn't glimpse his face. "What's your name?"

"Laura." She sniffled out the reply.

"Is this your first child?"

She shook her head. "I have two more girls. They're at my mom's house, waiting for me to come back."

He felt the weight of Giletti's eyes on him. His men had witnessed him executing others before without hesitation. But this was different. In another reality, it could have been his fiancée, Danielle. But her ashes were scattered in the winds of Syria, another lifetime away when Dresden's world had still been full of possibilities and alternate outcomes.

"Boss, we're burning up precious time," said Giletti, who moved up closer. "I can handle this."

Dresden opened the utility room door and walked her inside. He grabbed a rag from a stack on the right shelf and gently tied it around her mouth, then removed the iPhone from her back pocket. "Laura, if you want to see your girls again, you're going to sit still and be quiet for the next hour. If you don't…" He let the threat hang until she nodded frantically while tears streamed down her face.

He helped her to the ground, then backed up and closed the door. He removed a section of 550 cord from his vest and tied one end to the doorknob and the other to a shelving unit along the wall next to the room.

He tapped on his ear mic, indicating two of the sentries should head into the warehouse while one remained outside on overwatch. Then he waved at Giletti to follow him to the central part of the warehouse.

"That woman's a fucking liability, and you know it," said Giletti, who walked alongside him.

"She's an innocent."

"Technically, so were the security guards."

"We're not animals, Paul. Besides, she didn't get a look at us or what we're doing. And in an hour, we'll be long gone from here with what we need." He paused to glance back at Giletti. "What the hell is eating at you?"

Giletti pursed his lips. "That guy Payne got away. That's why we suffered so many losses in Darrington."

This time Dresden came to a halt. "You fucking said he would be taken care of by now. Hell, when you said your team was wiped out, I thought it was because of the feds, not one guy."

"He was with an FBI agent, Carrie Walker."

Dresden paced back and forth. "I looked into Payne after Zhang intercepted that message from the senator's phone. He was the guy who was with Harrison two years ago in Algeria, poking around our warehouse just after we moved out the last of the explosives and drone tech. He's former Ground Branch and a heavy hitter."

"By now, he's probably in federal custody or on the most wanted list, since I had Zhang work some of his magic to get Payne off our trail."

Dresden leaned in towards Giletti. "It's not like you to get sloppy. Have Zhang find out what happened to Payne. I'm not going to have him fucking things up at the last minute. Not when we're this close."

Giletti nodded. "I'll get with Zhang after we leave here."

Dresden turned without comment and strode across the stadium-sized warehouse until he arrived at bay 6, where his other two operators were waiting. One of his men, a bearded man with a shaved head, was sitting at a metal desk, accessing the warehouse inventory list on the computer. A minute later, he pointed to an aisle three rows to the right. "Looks like 29A has what we need."

Dresden trotted to the location, scanning the eight-foot-high shelves. He paused partway down and grabbed a cardboard box on the left. Slitting open the top with his blade, he peered inside, feeling the tension in his neck ease up. "These are the radio receivers. Grab twelve boxes and then let's locate the batteries."

The bearded man relayed the aisle, and Giletti bounded off across the warehouse with the other operator.

Dresden glanced back at the man at the computer. "Adjust the manifest so there are twelve fewer boxes of receivers and forty lithium batteries. I'm going to grab our truck and wheel it in here."

He trotted to the side door and then ran across the parking lot towards the opening in the fence. He glanced at his watch, knowing they would just make it back to Marple by sunrise.

Looks like Lady Luck will be on our side tonight. He couldn't say the same for the dead guards in the warehouse or the people who were going to be on the receiving end of his forthcoming fleet of weaponized drones.

CHAPTER 19

SEATTLE FBI DIRECTOR DEREK MENTZER LEANED BACK IN HIS desk chair, tilting his head side to side to ease the tension in his neck muscles. For the past hour, he'd been poring over the ballistics report and crime-scene photos from Darrington.

He opened his desk drawer, pulling out a bottle of Tums and popping two into his mouth, wondering if he'd go through the entire container before the morning was over. He knew his sour stomach was as much the result of the troubling ballistics findings as it was from the sit-down meeting he'd had earlier with Fiche's wife.

His widow now. Mentzer sighed. *Damnit, he should be alive. What the hell happened?*

He stood and paced around his office, eventually pausing before the large window overlooking the treed courtyard below. Mentzer searched the distant skyline, wondering what could have happened to Walker that caused her to go on the run with the prime suspect in Fiche's murder.

Mentzer's search on Payne hadn't turned up much, leaving him to fill in the blanks on the man's background.

Walker thought he was former State Department. He had to have deep ties to Senator Harrison.

Mentzer had known Walker for four years, and she'd always been a model agent, strictly adhering to protocols and holding her own in a male-dominated field. Which was why, against his better judgment, he had held off on sending out an APB on Payne.

He returned to his desk, pulling up the video images from the interior of the NTSB command post at the Darrington rodeo grounds. The blatant murder of Fiche by Payne, who callously drew his Glock and fired a single round into the agent's head.

He rewatched the interior video several times, focusing specifically on the moments leading up to Fiche collapsing from the gunshot. Something was off. A less experienced viewer would have missed it, but Mentzer had interned in the ballistics lab with the Seattle Police Department early in his law-enforcement career. He leaned in, replaying the footage again, this time focusing on the relation of Fiche's head to the angle of the front window as Payne aimed the weapon with one hand.

Just before Payne leveled the Glock at Fiche's skull, the agent's head briefly tilted back. It was only for a microsecond, but it was enough to set off Mentzer's radar. The other thing he noticed was that Payne's right shooting arm was slightly crooked at the elbow, which should have affected the recoil enough to cause the pistol muzzle to slightly flip up, but the weapon remained steady.

He replayed it three more times, his gut tightening with each viewing. Maybe Walker was onto something. Besides, even if Payne was brazen enough to kill a federal agent, why wouldn't he also take out Walker? And with his background, he would have known there were cameras at the investigation site.

Mentzer pressed the button on his desk phone for the forensics lab in the basement. A woman's voice came over the speaker. "Tammy, I'm reviewing the footage from the Darrington rodeo grounds and have some questions regarding Agent Fiche. Could you come up to my office for a few minutes to go over some things?"

"Um, I can, but I haven't even seen the footage yet, so not sure how much help I'll be," the head of forensics replied.

Mentzer narrowed his eyes. "What do you mean? Zhang said you passed the footage onto him to analyze and told him to send it up my way."

"That's not at all what happened. I was working late yesterday evening, and he stopped by to tell me he was going to clean up the video so the background noise from the highway didn't interfere with the audio inside the building. He acted like you knew."

Mentzer growled back a reply. "Where is Zhang now? Have you seen him?"

"Hang on." He heard the clatter of her footsteps as she must have stepped out into the hallway to peer into Zhang's office next door. A second later, she returned to the phone. "He's not in. In fact, I don't think he's been in all morning since his trash can is empty, and it's normally full of empty energy drinks by now."

"Alright, I'll be down there in a minute to go over the ballistics reports you sent me earlier. Something doesn't add up."

"Sir, I appreciate the faith you have in my abilities, but I am just now finishing up the report and was going to email it to you."

He pulled up the typed documents and scanned the findings again. "I'm looking at it right now. It was filed at 0530 this morning."

"When I was just crawling out of bed. I don't think so."

Mentzer chewed on his lip. "Stay put. I'll be down there shortly." He disconnected the call, ringing the security desk in the lobby. After conversing with the guard, it was clear that Zhang had left work at 8 p.m. last night and hadn't returned nor called in sick.

He grabbed his keys and ID badge off the desk and exited his office. With his pulse already racing, he didn't have the patience to wait for the elevator, so he took the stairs and trotted six floors down to sublevel one. He swiped his badge along the security keypad, then stepped into the hall.

Mentzer headed down the hallway, passing the forensics lab and then peering briefly into Zhang's office before striding to the room beside it. He opened the door and leaned in, staring into the surprised eyes of Zhang's young assistant, Amy Vickers.

She hastily set down her coffee mug, some of the steaming liquid spilling down the rim. "How can I help you, sir?" Vickers stood, her shoulders back.

"Seen Zhang at all?"

"Not since yesterday afternoon."

"Don't you usually work evenings?"

"Yes, but he let me go early. Said he didn't need any help."

One of my agents is killed, and Zhang decides to lighten his load?

He thrust his thumb at the cyber expert's office. "I need you to get inside his system and pull up everything he was working on regarding the death of Agent Fiche at the Darrington rodeo grounds."

"I can do it from here, actually." She sat down and went to work on her keyboard as Mentzer moved behind her right shoulder.

She arched her back, typing beyond anything Mentzer was capable of. "I go into his files regularly to add in my findings, so it will only take a second."

"Did he call you today?"

"No, but if he pulled an all-nighter, then he could still be sleeping. He's done that before, but he'll usually text me about coming in later."

Vickers accessed the FBI cybercrimes unit, then scrolled down to Zhang's name and clicked on it. She entered her numeric passcode, then whisked through a half-dozen headings before settling the pointer on the file labeled "Darrington."

"That's interesting." She pointed at the figures on the right side of the screen. "He's already logged in a lot of information for an investigation that's just gotten underway. Maybe he's working from home after all."

She clicked on the file. The screen went black, a 3D image of a silver snake spiraling into view before rearing its head as the body coiled up. The overhead lights in the office and hallway flickered.

Mentzer stood back like the snake image was going to lunge forward. The room went dark. A second later, the emergency lights in the hallway flickered to life.

He grabbed the phone off the desk, but the line was dead. Mentzer removed his iPhone, noticing there were no service bars. He exited the room, nearly running into Tammy and her three staff from the forensics lab.

"What the hell happened?" Tammy asked.

Mentzer waved his hand down the hall. "Gather the rest of the staff and have people check to see if the stairwells are accessible, then get everyone up to the lobby." He pulled out the small flashlight from his pocket that had habitually become a part of his everyday carry since being in law enforcement. He trotted down the passage, taking a right turn and continuing to the utility room at the end.

This section of the sublevel was part of the original design and still had standard locks and deadbolts. He removed his keys, recalling the dormant bronze key that opened the steel door.

A single emergency light was on inside, and he scanned the circuit breakers and computer mainframes. The room should have been aglow with the blue lights emanating from the computer towers, but everything was not only dark but lacking the usual hum from the cooling fans.

He heard footsteps approaching and swung around, shining his flashlight on Tammy's flushed face.

"We can't access the stairwells or elevators. We're stuck down here," she said.

He balled a fist, staring at the other faces of his staff who were trotting towards him. *Shit, Zhang has crippled our entire system.*

———

ZHANG PULLED off the exit for Lamont in eastern Washington, his GPS indicating it was only another thirty-seven miles to Moscow, Idaho.

He turned into a gas station, parked near the side of the building and stepped out of his red Porsche. He stretched his arms towards the cottony cumulus clouds and yawned. It was time to re-caffeinate and get a burger, but first he needed to check in with Giletti.

Zhang walked towards the edge of the parking lot, standing under a lone pine tree whose trunk was littered with wrappers and empty pop cans. He tapped on his ear mic, anxiously waiting for Giletti, who picked up on the fourth ring.

"I'm out of Seattle. About two hours west of our rendezvous point."

"Good. I need you to check on what happened with Payne and that female agent, specifically, if he's in federal custody."

"I'll see what I can do. My reception out here is pretty spotty, and I'll have better luck in the university town coming up."

"And the trail behind you after you left Seattle? You followed the evasion protocols I told you about?"

"Yes. My condo was scoured clean, and my digital tracks eliminated. And I left a little goodbye message for my colleagues."

"What do you mean?"

"They won't be finding anything of use on my hard drives in my office, and once they try to access the files, those clueless troglodytes are in for a shit-ton of surprises, since they'll be sealed in the building for a while."

"I told you to just cut and run. Not dole out payback for some bullshit grievances you have against your colleagues."

"It'll slow them down in their investigation with that dead agent, while giving me time to get off the grid."

"For a guy with a high IQ, you sure are a fucking idiot. You've just turned the bureau's entire attention to the Seattle office. They're going to be swarming with a critical response team and getting assistance from other agencies, who will form a task force to hunt you down and dig into what you were doing. And that means you put even more of a bullseye on our backs."

Zhang felt the blood drain from his face as he fought to swallow. He took a deep breath, recalling a YouTube video by a Navy SEAL who spoke about being confident in the face of adversity. "I was just trying to slow them down. Which I did, using malware that is light-years beyond anything other cybercrime units are even familiar with. It's the same shit I used to take down the senator's plane. They're going to be tied up for months, trying to figure out what happened, and there won't be any blowback to the next phase of your operation."

"We'll see. In the meantime, I'll send you another set of coordinates to meet at. Don't be late, and don't try any James Bond bullshit again."

The device in his ear went silent. Zhang felt his ribs ease slightly as he sucked in a breath of air like he'd been free-diving in the ocean.

He respected, and certainly feared, Giletti, but the man was a door-kicker. He was a rook, or maybe a bishop at best, on the chessboard. A shrewd and efficient killer who only understood the world through the prism of destruction and killing. Zhang could cripple an entire city, or even a country, without breaking a sweat by depressing the Enter button on his laptop.

Me and others like myself are the future of warfare and geopolitical control. Not apes like Giletti. Dresden's another story. He's the king, though, and I need to show him more of what I can do.

He thought about the latter figure, whom he'd only met once via online video when signing on with Dresden's outfit. The man seemed like a match to his own ambition and was the master of a physical domain of skills that were beyond Zhang's cerebral realm. Not that the bureau cared about Zhang's abilities, but he was sure an apex predator like Dresden would appreciate his skills and continue to employ him after this current operation ended.

Eventually even guys like Dresden would become obsolete. The world was reaching a point where the real masters would be those who wielded their malware soldiers and, eventually, coupled it with AI-driven generals.

And when that time came, Zhang planned to be at the top of the pyramid.

CHAPTER 20

CIA HEADQUARTERS, LANGLEY

Deputy Director Benjamin Stratton stepped off the elevator on the seventh floor, glancing up occasionally from the newsfeed on his phone as he walked past his staff at their workstations.

Rounding the bend that led to his office, he paused before his secretary's desk and waited for her to go over his meetings for the day.

The petite woman stood, her eyes darting nervously towards his closed door. "You have a visitor. She arrived twenty minutes ago."

He gazed at his secretary's computer screen, noting the calendar slot for 0700 was blank. "Fill me in again...who am I scheduled to see?"

"No one, actually, but Secretary of State Brittany Colson is here. She said it was urgent."

He flared an eyebrow. "I assume so if she crawled out from her cave."

Stratton walked to the office door and headed inside. Colson was standing with her arms folded near the large window to the left of his desk. She swiveled towards the movement, a plastic smile emerging as she walked towards him and extended her hand.

He reluctantly shook it, then motioned towards a chair as he walked around the other side of his desk and sat. "Quite a surprise, seeing you in these parts, Madam Secretary."

She gazed at the framed photos on the walls, waving her smooth pale hands at the medals near his bookcase. "Finally made it to the top, running the show here after all these years. Good for you, Ben. I remember during our senior year at Cornell when you said you wanted a seat at the 'clandestine round table,' as you called it, and here you are."

He smirked. "Cut the bullshit, Brittany. What do you want? Or better yet, what do you need and think, in your wildest dreams, I'll sign off on?"

She brushed a fleck of lint off her blue slacks. "Oh, you'll sign off on this. Trust me."

"Not likely, especially the trust part. You put on a good show for the media and when you're in front of the UN, but people like me...people who really know what you're like, know that even Satan wishes he could rescind his offer to you."

She chuckled. It was a genuine laugh, and when coupled with her striking blue eyes, almost made her seem likable.

He leaned back, interlacing his fingers behind his head and smiling. "There it is...that honey-sweet charm you were always good at. Hell, I almost fell for it years ago when I was younger and less worldly."

"It's the worldly part I'm here to talk about. You've seen enough in your career to realize that what I'm about to tell you is a powder keg of biblical proportions."

He seethed out an exhale, regretting the double espresso he'd just consumed since his heart rate was already spiking. "Go on. Spit it out."

She stood, walking back to the window and gazing out.

"I know when you were promoted to your current position this past winter, your predecessor read you in on current and recently completed covert operations abroad." The woman turned towards him. "But did you ever hear all the details regarding Operation Paragon? It was connected with a CIA-fronted arms dealer who went rogue in Syria two years ago."

He rubbed his smooth chin. "All I know about that op is that it began in Algeria and ended with a cruise missile raining down on the dealer's encampment in Syria, which put a stop to the weapons flowing in and out of North Africa. I assume that was to eliminate any potential connection to the agency there."

"That's the sanitized version. The dealer was actually one of your predecessor's senior case officers. Michael Dresden." She gave him a firm stare. "The man was a Ground Branch pipe-hitting, scary motherfucker."

Stratton stood and moved beside her, both of them gazing at the gray skyline. "Something tells me there are some loose ends still dangling in the wind after all this time."

"Dresden's alive. He resurfaced in the Western US, Washington State to be exact."

"How do you know?"

"An intelligence contact of mine who used to work here and is now at the NSA informed me a few days ago. Plus, a good friend who was a consultant of sorts in North Africa years ago was found brutally murdered in his home in Seattle." Her lower lip trembled. "His blood was used to spell out the word 'Paragon' on his fridge, for God's sake."

Stratton's eyes widened. "Wait...let's back up...you have the Algerian operation red-flagged after all this time, using the NSA's resources to surveil US cities. Why?"

Colson reached in the pocket of her blue suit jacket, removing a folded envelope and handing it to him. "This arrived at my home address. After it was vetted by the Secret Service, I examined it."

He lifted the flap and shook out the contents. A stamp-sized microchip landed in his palm.

"Not sure how up close and personal you've gotten with CIA drone technology lately, but that's a microprocessor for a weaponized drone capable of delivering enough ordnance to take out a city block. It's identical to the ones on the armada of drones that were shipped to Algeria during Operation Paragon. I got that package last Friday around the same time my NSA contact told me Dresden was spotted on a traffic cam near downtown Seattle not far from the home of where my friend was murdered the next day. Dresden's clearly sending me a message."

"Jesus, Brittany, I figured you meant RPGs and AKs, along with a small contingent of observation drones for intel gathering, were sent to Algeria. Are you telling me the agency was doling out a fleet of weaponized drones in North Africa?"

"Don't act so surprised, since the CIA has bases with such hardware dotting that entire continent."

"And those bases don't allow lethal hardware on that scale to fall into enemy hands." He clutched the microchip like it was a pearl as his mind raced over geopolitical events in Africa in recent years. Since his specialty had been Russian and Eastern European affairs, he tried to recall the rumor mill at the agency two years ago when the debacle of Operation Paragon made the news cycle. "Was Paragon connected with arming the rebel factions along the border of Algeria and Niger, or was that just a smoke screen for something else?"

He could see a faint glisten of sweat above her upper lip. It was an unusual tell for a woman who was as stone-faced as they came.

"POTUS needed the rebels in Niger on our side then since the Russians were beginning to establish a foothold in that region. But when I met with your old boss, he wouldn't sign off on it. Apparently, he had more balls than I gave him credit for, so we ran things through the State Department, farming out Dresden to act as the middleman who would funnel the drones to his contacts amongst the Niger rebels. He was the key to making this happen, since he knew the region and had a team embedded in North Africa."

"A regular shit show but not too unlike something I'd expect from State. I still don't get why you're standing in my office. You have someone threatening you, then go to the head of your Secret Service detail."

"In case you haven't been paying attention to recent events, Senator Harrison's jet went down in Washington State three days ago. Since he was on the Senate Armed Services Committee, I believe he may have launched his own investigation into Dresden if he suspected he was back in the picture."

"That's a stretch. How would Harrison even know about Dresden and his past?"

She averted her eyes. "Let's just say there was a workaround required to get the funds for the drones headed to Algeria two years ago, and Harrison was, unfortunately, instrumental in making that happen."

She angled her chin towards his closed palm. "Not all of the drones sent to Algeria ended up being used in Niger. At some point after delivery to the rebels, a half dozen went missing. It wasn't discovered until a few months later when a diplomatic helicopter of ours was nearly brought down by a drone near the Syrian-Turkish border. The explosive device didn't go off, probably due to the idiot controlling it. When ground investigators located the wrecked drone, they discovered a microchip with serial numbers related to the batch that had headed to Niger."

Colson shook her head. "If it ever got out that we had

provided weaponized drones, and not simply observation drones, to not only the Niger rebels but that some had made it into the hands of our enemies elsewhere, it was going to be an unmitigated disaster for the president."

He waved a hand. "Especially since he'd be coming up for re-election."

"Fuck you, Ben. You know how this works. Perception and politics are the same damn thing."

He grabbed her hand and dropped the microchip in it. "Sounds like quite a mess you have to clean up, Brit. And I assume since Dresden wasn't obliterated in that cruise-missile attack, he's got some payback in mind."

Stratton returned to his desk and sat, gripping the armrests like he was on a plane or a rollercoaster. "That's why you're really here, so that this clusterfuck from Algeria with a former agency case officer doesn't bite you in the ass, especially with the summit you're hosting just around the corner."

"Doesn't bite any of us in the ass, most of all, the man you and I answer to in the Oval Office."

Stratton rested his forearms on the desk, clasping his fist as he gave her a long stare. "Dresden scares the shit out of you, but not because of a political scandal, either. He sent that package to your house, and he wants you to know he's back in the game. Hell, you might be next on his list."

She emitted a wolfish smile. "Wow, nothing ever got past you. It doesn't take a genius to figure out that the man's deranged and clearly bent on revenge."

"It's the last part that interests me. The cruise missile that was directed down on him and his team...that took someone with considerable clout and access to issue that order. Someone above the State Department. Someone wanting to ensure there were no loose ends once the missing drones were eliminated. POTUS signed off on it and had you pull the strings, and now it's threatening to derail your career, and your life."

She walked to the chair, resting her hands on the backrest and drumming her fingers on the leather rim. It felt like the air in the room had suddenly pressurized. "I already spoke with President Buchanan about this. He agreed that Dresden and anyone associated with him needs to be handled. Discreetly."

Stratton replied, "Maybe you've forgotten the mandate here about running covert ops on our own shores."

"There is no line in the sand right now. Not with this. A scandal on this scale could vaporize all the work with our allies abroad and set things in motion for a presidential impeachment."

"Your predecessors all had teams *off the books* for such things, and don't give me any shit to the contrary. Get them on the ground in Washington State and make sure Dresden, and everyone associated with him, is permanently removed before the headlines are riddled with news of a domestic terrorist attack that had its origins back here with one of your former operatives."

The Secretary of State walked to the door, pausing before turning the handle. "Ben, just remember, the last time this agency suffered a black eye on the world stage, it had a devastating effect on our operational capabilities abroad for years to come."

She gestured at the commendations on the wall. "And if that call to patriotism isn't enough, then you should consider not wanting to be the shortest-lived director in the fucking history of the CIA."

———

Stratton remained seated, staring at the door for a full minute as a rare headache began squeezing on his skull. Finally, he stood and paced around his office. He removed his loathsome feelings for Colson from his mind and focused on the broader implications of implementing her demands, both on the agency and his own career.

The first thing he needed was to talk with Langley's head lawyer. He needed to know how they could create a work-around for sanctioning a black-ops kill squad on American soil. It wouldn't be a crew with any direct connection to the agency, and he already had one man in mind.

He thought back to what the Secretary of State said about having a contact at the NSA notifying her about Dresden re-emerging. *She's been keeping a backdoor channel open on Dresden and the Operation Paragon debacle for a long time.*

He mulled over the players and the politics of the region along with POTUS' undertakings during that time. That was just after the president got into office, but Colson had been involved in North African affairs long before he was sworn in. Hell, she'd spent part of her teenage years over there since her old man was the ambassador to Egypt, so she'd probably had plenty of connections when she became Secretary. She must have orchestrated Operation Paragon from the ground up, even reaching out to Dresden—or maybe she knew him ahead of time.

Stratton sat and pulled up classified files from Algerian operations during the past five years. On three occasions, there were mentions of a high-value political operative from Washington who had undertaken unannounced visits to the safe house in Algiers on the coast. While no names were listed, the individual was referred to by her gender.

Two things became evident as he read on: The transfer of illegal weapons to the Niger rebels had been planned a full year before the current POTUS took office. And the personal aide of Colson's had once served under Senator Harrison during his time on the Armed Services Committee.

So the usual inbred bullshit of life on Capitol Hill. Only this time, it's come back around, and the sharks are circling Colson. He mulled over the recent death of the senator. *That can't be a coincidence. The only question is: was Harrison's jet going down the work of Dresden or Colson?*

When he was done reviewing the files, he leaned back in his chair. He agreed that Dresden and any potential threat he was involved with had to be dealt with, and quickly. He also knew that the threat to his own safety and career had just exited the building, and she was a beast of a different nature that would require careful contingencies to prevent any blowback and allow him to weather out the coming storm of sending an agency-sanctioned hit team onto US soil.

He opened his front desk drawer and removed a tattered address book. The names were all listed under codes only he knew along with phone numbers containing alpha-numeric figures. He found the listing for his former chief of clandestine field operations and grabbed his landline phone, feeling like the floor beneath his shoes was splitting open.

———

AFTER LEAVING STRATTON'S OFFICE, Brittany Colson strode past the main elevators and proceeded down a narrow hallway on the right, where the head of her Secret Service detail was waiting beside the service elevator that went to the parking garage in the basement.

They stepped inside with the tall guard remaining at the front, while she stepped back a ways and pulled out her phone.

"He's on board. Or will be shortly, once he realizes there are no options," she said.

"Good. I figured if you strong-armed him, he would do the right thing," said President Neal Buchanan.

"And the other problem of ours has been dealt with thanks to Dresden."

"I'm actually going to visit with Harrison's wife in a few hours."

"Guess that whore won't have such a smug grin on her face now."

"God, I'm glad I didn't make you my press secretary, Brittany."

"No, you put me in charge of furthering your reach overseas, and as soon as Dresden gets taken care of, that legacy of yours and mine will no longer be in jeopardy."

CHAPTER 21

THE DRIVE TO MARPLE WAS PUNCTUATED WITH SCENIC MOUNTAIN valleys and seemingly endless high-elevation rivers whose banks were still lined with icicles. If it weren't for the fact Payne was trying to piece together the mystery of what had happened to the senator and dodging further encounters with a kill squad, he would have liked to do some hiking or fishing.

In between sips from her coffee cup, Walker was scrolling through information about the surrounding region on Payne's burner phone. Her hair was pulled back in a tight ponytail, and with the sweatpants and T-shirt she'd acquired from the secondhand store, she looked like she was ready for a morning jog.

"Says here that Marple has a population of 8,200 people, and the economic base is tourism from hunting, skiing and fishing along with sightseeing trips to the nearby ghost towns and old mines. Apparently, Idaho is the leading state for silver production in the country."

"Interesting. I would have thought it was the leading state for militias from what I've read."

She smirked. "That too, I'm sure. We've gotten our fair share of notices at the Seattle office about the concentration of extremist groups in the backwoods along the state border."

Walker pulled up the map of the town. "Looks like Marple covers about two miles of shops and motels and is surrounded on four sides by national forest."

"That must make a city girl like you uncomfortable. But don't worry, I'll make sure you don't stray too far from the sidewalks and cafés."

"Shut up, acorn-lover. I'm actually comfortable in both settings. I just prefer to avoid places with ticks, mosquitoes and snakes."

He gave her a questioning look. "Uh-huh, sure. I saw your shoes when we first met. They were polished. And your suit and pants looked like they had been pressed. You were in your natural habitat in Seattle, Agent Walker."

She looked out the window. "You can skip the 'agent' part. I'm not sure what the hell I am right now. Pretty sure 'fugitive' or 'assistant to a fugitive' would be a better fit."

"Your boss back in Seattle, that guy Mentzer you mentioned before, you made him sound like a straight shooter, but can you say the same for everyone else around him?"

Walker didn't hesitate. "Before he came to the bureau years ago, Mentzer was a homicide detective with Seattle PD. He's old-school and always has our backs, as do the rest of my colleagues." She lowered her eyes. "Or, at least, I thought so until yesterday."

The shootout at the rodeo grounds and the cabin seemed like it was months ago, but Payne was sure every agonizing detail about Fiche's death was constantly cycling through Walker's brain. The exhaustion written on her face was from more than just lack of sleep. It was the kind of weariness that came when you suffered soul-shredding loss. And no amount of rest was going to drain that wound. Time, and plenty of it, was the only suture.

"If Mentzer's the guy you describe, then he'll wade through the bullshit and figure things out. There's no way someone could have sanitized the entire scene at the rodeo grounds and the events surrounding those two bogus agents who came for me at the outdoor expo."

She stroked the bruise on her forearm. "I hope you're right. I joined the bureau to track down criminals, not go on the run like one of them."

He slowed, taking a sharp turn by a roadside waterfall. "You never played escape and evasion roles or urban games where you pretended to be the fugitive while your fellow agents pursued you?"

She shook her head. "Only during whiteboard exercises." Walker gazed at his face. "But I'm guessing yours involved more than classroom training."

"Our evasion course lasted a week and was preceded by another week of hands-on training in vehicle acquisition, countersurveillance, urban concealment, and dead drops. When it came time for the practical phase, we were blindfolded and handcuffed, then dropped off at midnight in some graffiti-riddled alley in Baltimore. We were told to blend in to the urban wilds of that city for two days and then could make our way to Philadelphia over the next five days by any means we chose and with only the five dollars that was provided."

"What prevented you from just grabbing a motel or shacking up with a friend?"

"There were three-man surveillance teams assigned to each of us. In fact, I was on such a team a few weeks later for another class so I could practice my shadowing skills. Plus, everyone knew it was a ticket out of the program if you cheated and avoided life on the streets."

She grinned. "So, that must have made a country hick like

you uncomfortable, straying so far from the woods and all the jerky shops."

"Haha. One thing I've learned over the years is that survival is survival, regardless of the setting. Your body doesn't care if you're in Yosemite or downtown Chicago when you're hungry, thirsty, or hypothermic. The only difference between the two is the nature of the predators, and I'll take the four-legged kind over those from my own species any day."

She nodded. "Amen."

————

THEY HAD both agreed that the diner on Main Street in Marple would be the best place to informally gather local information as well as just providing sustenance. Going to the sheriff's department had been quickly dismissed since Walker was considered MIA from the bureau and Payne might already be on a watch list.

Payne decided to recon the town first, and after driving to one end, he doubled back, heading on a route that ran parallel to Main Street. It quickly became obvious that Marple's tax dollars went to maintaining the central strip of businesses and not addressing the dilapidated parks and weed-choked sidewalks skirting the run-down homes on the eastern flank.

Once again, poverty with a view, like so many places out West.

Arriving back at the other end of Marple, Payne pulled the stolen car into the back of the diner's parking lot beside a row of other vehicles. Both of them donned their ball caps, keeping them low over their faces. Payne had taken an extra measure at limited disguise before leaving the motel and shaved his scruffy beard down to a goatee.

They stepped out of the Subaru, glancing around the parking area, which was a gravel lot that backed up to the forest. A quick glance at the newer-model trucks and SUVs, which were lacking in mud, told him that many of the other patrons were probably visitors from Moscow or Boise. The few older-model trucks to the left were caked with dry mud and had worn bumper hitches, which he figured were used by locals for pulling horse trailers or flatbeds with animal feed.

He caught Walker gazing over his face. "Not sure that goatee is an improvement. It makes you look like a scary ex-con."

"I was going for a hillbilly look, actually."

She shrugged. "Yeah, I can see that. But people will get that vibe anyway as soon as you start talking."

He chuckled. Despite having known Walker for only twenty-four hours, there was an easy banter between them, and he felt like they'd been on a road trip for a few weeks. "As long as I walk inside with you, nobody's eyes will be on my face."

"Quite a charmer. Those bullshit one-liners work often on women?"

He locked the vehicle. "Sometimes, but I think it's my rugged jawline and cool motorcycle that do the rest."

"And your obvious humility."

"That too."

They came around the corner of the café and paused before the entrance, taking in the breadth of downtown. There were only two stoplights and dozens of T-shirt and trinket stores mixed in with a handful of cafés and ice-cream shops.

It resembled a dozen towns he'd been in during the past few months of travel, except this one had an old-timey feel to it with its faded murals on the buildings and antiquated architectural styles reminiscent of many old mining towns dotting the Western US.

Entering the lobby, they stood behind an older couple who were waiting to be seated. Payne glanced over the large bulletin board on the wall to the right, which was filled with event flyers, business cards and photos of missing dogs.

He thrust his thumb at the ad for a cowpie-throwing contest that was coming up in two weekends. "Bet you've never been to one of those before."

Walker stared at the flyer, her lips going flat. "It troubles me that you probably have—and more than once."

"That's nothing compared to the cherry-pit-spitting competition in Oregon I saw a few months ago."

"They say travel expands one's education. In your case, I'm not so sure."

His eyes swept over the board, studying the cards for companies that weren't likely seen in Boise or Spokane: blacksmith, country vet, farrier, dog-sledding trips, hunting guides, well-digging, septic system installs, tractor repair, and ATV tours.

His gaze settled on a flyer on the far left. It showed a color photo of three stunning palomino horses with the caption indicating there was a ten-thousand-dollar reward for information on the poisoning of the creatures.

Walker tugged on his jacket sleeve. "We're up."

They followed the petite hostess. The café was laid out in a U-shape with a central bar with stools in the middle, while booths were lined up by the windows. The woman led them to the booth second from the rear emergency exit in the right corner.

Much to his chagrin, Walker sat facing the front door. It was an old habit, positioning yourself with your back to the wall so you could see who was approaching, along with being able to scan the other patrons. He saw her already performing the ritual, as most law-enforcement types do.

At least he had a clear line of sight to the parking-lot entrance. When he wasn't watching the slow waves of traffic on Main Street, he glanced around the inside. The central bar seemed mostly occupied by the older locals adorned in faded jeans and dirty boots, with hands that matched. He was within earshot of two of the eldest men, who were complaining about the rising cost of hay and how it would impact their ranches.

The hostess reappeared at their table, clutching an order pad. "We're short-staffed today, so I'll get in your orders, if you're ready, and then get 'em back to you as soon as I can."

"No problem," said Walker. "I'll have the blueberry pancakes and coffee."

"Same for me but add in three scrambled eggs, please," said Payne.

"You got it." She jotted down the orders and flitted away towards the kitchen as another couple entered the front door.

"I'm going to check the newsfeeds again for Seattle," said Walker, pulling out her burner phone.

Payne continued his people-watching, seeing a thirty-something woman with brunette hair get up from a booth on the opposite side of the diner. She gave a brief hug to a short lady with coiffed red hair in a floral-print dress who had evidently joined her for breakfast. After the redhead departed, the other woman donned her sheepskin-lined jean jacket and made a beeline towards the two older guys sitting on stools near Payne.

He only caught snippets of their conversation, but it sounded like she was a veterinarian relaying the medical results of a recent test. It was the part about poisoned cattle and horses that caught his attention. He slid his and Walker's glasses of water to the side. "We'd better stick with bottled water while we're here. Something's going on with pollution or chemicals leaching into the soil."

Walker glanced up from her phone, then over to the brunette chatting with the two ranchers. "Eavesdropper."

"Or maybe I can read the minds of women."

"Then why didn't you order for me?"

"I didn't want to step on your independence." He leaned forward. "What do you notice about those two ranchers and the woman talking at the bar?"

The thin man was crumpling a napkin like it was a ball of clay. The other guy had his gaze down, and his lower lip was trembling.

Walker put away her phone, casually glancing to her right. "They seem nervous as hell."

A second later, the trio hastily exited the diner and resumed their conversation in the parking lot. By their body language, it wasn't a friendly conversation, though there didn't appear to be any hostility directed at the female veterinarian.

The waitress arrived with their meals, setting down the plates and two cups of black coffee along with a small bowl filled with packaged creamers.

Payne slid closer, lowering his voice. "I saw that flyer in the lobby about the recent poisoning of horses…what's that all about?"

The woman's cheeks became taut. She fidgeted with her pen, clicking the top repeatedly. "A bunch of ranches up north have been losing animals…cattle, chickens, some horses. The sheriff thinks it's from pesticide runoff from the farms in the next county over, but who knows for sure."

"Any issue with the water supply in town here?" asked Walker.

"Not that I'm aware of, but you'll be hard-pressed to find any bottled water at the stores in town. People are a little worried and buying it all up." She forced a smile. "But the motel water is all good, so you won't have any issues while you're visiting. Y'all have a nice day." She tore the bill from her pad and placed it on the table, scurrying back to the lobby despite a lack of new arrivals.

THE DRIVE north along Highway 3 was uneventful. An ocean of spruce and pine trees occasionally interrupted by a scenic pullout on the right shoulder. Seven miles later, Payne slowed and turned onto a blacktop road on the left. It wound down a gradual slope for another mile, then ended at a double-wide chain-link gate.

Beyond was a two-hundred-acre runway bordered on either side by red lights; on the far side was a small admin building next to an open hangar with a helicopter covered with canvas; a row of similarly covered small planes sat dormant on the opposite side with one immaculate white jet with six windows, which was not cloaked.

The entire property was bordered with a twelve-foot-high fence, a third of which was choked with tumbleweeds at the base. From the old tufts of grass in the cracks of the road heading to the hangar, it looked like the place was seldom used.

Payne stopped his vehicle beside a steel post anchored in the ground with a security keypad and lowered his window. "I've seen places like this before. Kept afloat by a handful of wealthy locals who go on joyrides a few times a month, and for the occasional visitor from out of state. No full-time staff on-site, which is good." He paused, pointing to the nearest fence corner, a hundred yards away on Walker's side. "Those security cameras are pretty low tech, but I think we should come back when it's dark and poke around."

Walker craned her neck, staring at the other planes. "Why would Harrison stop here? Does he have a personal history with Marple?"

"I don't ever recall him talking about Idaho; then again, I didn't know the man that well. But that port authority guy, Whitmore, said Harrison mentioned working with somebody out here, so that has to be the connection."

Payne stared at the lone jet for a minute, then reached in the back seat and removed the small binoculars from his daypack. He scanned the vessel, noting the shiny paint job and new tires before settling his gaze on the logo of a black German shepherd. "K9Air.com."

She pulled out her iPhone and typed in the website, reading the description. "A first-class private charter service for dedicated owners who desire to travel with their pets cage-free."

"Interesting. That's a pretty sleek jet. What would something like that be doing here with these rusty tin cans?"

"K9 Air provides flights all over the world."

"My guess is there are no mutts allowed. Only designer dogs with gold-painted nails and bows in their fur."

"You're not a dog guy, Payne?"

"Pff, quite the opposite. I just prefer an actual dog, not a circus clown that costs five grand."

She swiveled towards him, holding up the phone. "Check out who the CEO is."

Payne looked at the image of the female veterinarian they'd seen in the diner. She was wearing a blue blouse, and her dark hair was curled and accentuated by hoop earrings. "Wonder how a small-town vet can afford a bird like that. Maybe we should pay her a visit and ask if she's seen anything unusual going on out here...or a particular US senator?"

He set the binoculars down and put the vehicle in reverse,

backing up and turning around. "We need to locate a hardware or sporting goods store first. There are a few things we're gonna need before we come back tonight."

"Those are probably one and the same store in Marple. What did you have in mind?"

"Just gotta get some ninja tools."

She smirked. "That doesn't sound illegal at all."

CHAPTER 22

I⊤ WAS JUST AFTER 3 P.M. WHEN PAYNE AND WALKER CHECKED into the Riverside Motel at the south end of Marple. This time, he paid in cash for two adjoining rooms.

Once inside his room, he dumped the items he'd bought at the hardware store onto the bed and removed the price tags and packaging. His shopping spree yielded a square canvas tarp, a two-pound hammer, a crowbar, glow sticks, a paint gun, a package of red paintballs, a Silva baseplate compass, and a spotting scope with night-vision capabilities.

"What's the hammer for, or do I not want to know?" asked Walker, who was doing a weapons check on the rifles she'd pulled out of the hockey duffel bag.

"It's a step up from the rock method of opening doors," said Payne.

She set down the Sig Sauer rifle. "Now, we just have to wait for nightfall."

"Actually, I thought we'd take a drive south and talk to a vet about her jet."

"After we stop at that burger joint down the block. I'm starving. And I'll drive this time so you can eat."

"I can do both."

"No, really, I can drive. I'd prefer not getting motion sickness for a change with you behind the wheel on these mountain roads."

Payne didn't mind. He'd be able to take in more of the stunning scenery, including the woman behind the wheel.

———

AFTER GRABBING carryout at Burger Lord, they ate in the vehicle at the rear of the parking lot while going over their recon plans of the airfield a final time.

It was almost 5 p.m. when Walker drove to Marple's lone veterinary clinic three miles southeast of town. It was a spacious property surrounded by dense stands of mature spruce trees and manicured shrubs that lined the driveway.

On the left, set back near the forest, was a two-story home whose modern look seemed out of place in the rustic setting. The vet clinic was a hundred yards to the right beside a dozen fenced kennels under a sloped roof. The dogs began barking in excitement as soon as the visitors parked.

Payne and Walker exited at the same time as a woman stepped out from the clinic. She gave them a puzzled look and walked towards them, leaving the door ajar. "We're about to close. Can I help you with something?"

"Just wanted to inquire about your services," said Payne.

A golden retriever darted out from the office and eagerly trotted to greet the new arrivals.

"Sorry, this is Maize. He's my personal assistant," said the woman.

Payne kneeled, leaving his hands by his sides and letting the dog inspect him at his own pace. Finally, the dog pushed his nose under Payne's wrist.

"He wants his back scratch now. And he doesn't ask for those from strangers often."

Walker extended a hand. "I'm Carrie Walker, and this is Kyle Payne."

"Darla Engels."

"We were hoping to talk with you about your air-taxi service. We saw your jet at the airfield north of town."

The vet's color seemed to drain out of her face. She abruptly withdrew her hand from Walker's. "Are you with the state...did Sheriff Dwyer call you?"

Walker smiled. "Oh, God, no. Sorry, I didn't mean to alarm you. We're just in from Washington, passing through. We were out sightseeing earlier and came across that little airport. When I looked up the logo on your jet, it pulled up your website and photo."

"We actually saw you at the diner this morning," said Payne. "And when we noticed the jet at the airfield, we wanted to drop by and find out more about your business."

"It's hard not to notice that jet. It's obnoxious as hell," said Darla. "And it's going to be sold off soon if I have any say in the matter." She sighed, her shoulders relaxing.

Payne stood. "We glanced over your website. It's a pretty unique business."

"Yeah, too unique, actually. Seemed like a great idea at the time when my business associate, aka my father, pitched the idea. I had the animal expertise, and he had the piloting skills and wealthy contacts. But us flying the occasional rich doctor from Boise or Jackson Hole doesn't pay the bills. I think we need to be based in LA for it to take off...no pun intended."

"A friend of ours arrived at that airfield in a Gulfstream jet a few days ago. Did you, by chance, hear anything about that?" said Payne.

"No." She angled her head towards the clinic. "Now, if

you'll excuse me, I have to wrap up my notes on a recent necropsy of a client's horse."

"From poisoning?" Payne asked.

Her eyes widened. "You sure know a lot about things in our small town for someone just passing through."

Payne smiled, trying to ease her concern. "I overheard you and those two cowboys at the diner talking about the poisonings. And I saw that flyer about it on the bulletin board in the lobby."

That seemed to deflate her worried look. "Weird shit going on around here lately. Lots of new faces, beyond just tourists, and now a bunch of livestock and horses keeling over from chemical contamination of some kind. I need to get a handle on what's causing it before Sheriff Dwyer steps in any further than he already has."

"He sounds heavy-handed," said Walker.

"You could say that. Guy thinks it's the 1950s and probably couldn't even tell you what the Miranda rights are." She turned and walked towards the clinic, whistling for Maize to follow. "Enjoy your visit to Marple."

Payne and Walker returned to their vehicle and drove back up the driveway.

Pausing at the entrance to the main road, he glanced down at his pants. He brushed off a swath of Maize's fur, then held up a blond strand. "I was wrong in Darrington. That hair found in the fireproof briefcase from the crash site wasn't from a person." He glanced in his rearview mirror at the clinic. "Harrison was here, with Darla."

———

DARLA WATCHED the two strangers depart through the thin white curtains of her office, then reached for the phone on her desk.

A familiar voice picked up.

"We might have a problem. There was a man and woman at the clinic, asking about our jet. And also about whether I knew anything about a friend of theirs who arrived on a similar aircraft recently."

"What'd you tell them?" he asked.

"I said no, of course. I gave them the business spiel about K9 Air, and that was about it."

"Okay, why don't you head over to my place? There are some new things that have developed." The man's normally unshakeable voice sounded tense.

"That bad?"

"It's not pretty. I'll explain the rest when you get here. Just drive the route I showed you, and you'll be alright."

———

THE TWO MEN sat on their Yamasaki dirt bikes on the forested ridge a quarter mile from the veterinary clinic. Seth Beckham, a stout man with a swastika tattoo on his neck, lowered his binoculars after watching the two outsiders depart the veterinary clinic in their Subaru Forester.

As the leader of the White Nation Brotherhood, Beckham was more than pleased to pick up some lucrative work tailing a couple of out-of-towners. Having grown up west of Marple, he knew every deer trail and dirt road in the region, which made his job surveilling others a literal walk in the woods. Or in his case, a bike ride along familiar paths.

He pulled out his cellphone and pressed one of three preprogrammed numbers on the burner. "They just talked with Darla. Now they're driving back towards Marple. Probably heading to the Riverside Motel they checked into earlier."

"Okay, I'll get some eyes on them in town," said Sheriff Miles Dwyer.

"One other thing, they went to the airfield earlier. The place is locked up, so they didn't go past the gate, but they were there a while, scanning the grounds."

"Hmm, wonder what the hell that was about." The sheriff was quiet for a moment before responding, "Unless they're somehow connected with Darla and her air-taxi business."

"Maybe they're not the people we're supposed to be looking for," said Beckham.

"I was told to watch out for a man and woman in their thirties who come across as law-enforcement types and ask a lot of questions. They fit the bill so far, given what else I heard from my contacts at the hardware store and the diner."

"You want me to keep an eye out here in case they come back?"

"No. Let's wait and see what I can learn once they're back in Marple, and after I talk to Giletti. But if they turn out to be the ones he told me about, then you're gonna be diggin' a few graves in the backcountry soon."

CHAPTER 23
WASHINGTON, DC

CIA DIRECTOR BENJAMIN STRATTON RAISED THE COLLAR ON HIS tan trench coat to keep the cool wind at bay as he walked through Folger Park and sat down at a picnic table tucked into the trees.

His three-man security detail was staked out in a triangle within thirty feet, but to any passerby they would look like any of the dozens of businessmen or politicians enjoying a walk in one of the largest parks in the Capitol Hill region.

A minute later, a sixty-something man in jeans and a black leather jacket walked up and sat across from him. His Yankees ball cap was pulled low, and despite the overcast sky, he was wearing dark shades. The man's knuckles were scarred over, and his leathery face made him appear twenty years older than Stratton, though they shared the same birth year.

"Just like old times, eh?" asked David Sheldon, who removed his sunglasses, his hazel eyes darting around at the three bodyguards.

"I wish it were that simple again. Sometimes I prefer the days when it was all about fieldcraft and acquiring assets.

Now, everything is done from a goddamned laptop and whatever we obtain from satellite feeds."

"Glad I retired."

Stratton smirked. "Bullshit. I know you still have your hands in the game, just in the private sector now. Can't blame you. Better pay and less red tape."

"And don't forget about the private jet and yacht."

Stratton reached into his coat and removed a manila envelope, handing it to Sheldon.

The man pulled out a handful of black-and-white photographs. "Jesus, you really are stuck in the Stone Age. You know they have these things called digital files now."

"Says the fucking guy who just learned to cut and paste on his computer a few years ago."

Sheldon examined the images of the individuals. The CIA director remained quiet, letting the man take in the visual details of the people and the locations. Some of the photos were recent, while others were at least a decade older given the grainy quality.

"You no doubt recognize Brittany Colson and James Harrison but tell me about the others, since you ran field ops in North Africa for years."

He saw Sheldon's cheeks grow taut as the man stared at Dresden and his crew of French Algerians. Having served as a case officer and later as the station chief in Tunisia and Casablanca for nearly twenty-five years, Sheldon had seen, and been instrumental in, a tidal wave of political upheaval in those turbulent regions.

"Dresden was a hell of an operator. Good instincts, gregarious, a man's man. A natural at recruiting assets, and his crew thought he could walk on fucking water."

"And the woman in the second photo standing next to him?"

"Danielle Boucher. Born in Algeria. Father was a minor

diplomat at the French embassy. Dresden recruited her when she was probably twenty-three. She was on his team for years. From what I recall, they were a thing."

Stratton pointed to a tall man in the third photograph. "That guy shows up in other footage."

"Paul Giletti. Dresden's sidekick, if you will. He and Dresden go way back; started at the Farm together and were later assigned to North African ops. Interacted with him a few times. He had an edge about him—not like Dresden, though. Giletti was the unofficial interrogator of Dresden's crew. The guy liked inflicting pain."

He slid the photos back in the envelope and handed it back to Stratton as a sour look formed on his face. "Why do I feel like this is all connected with that shit show of Colson's two years ago, Operation Paragon?"

Stratton leaned in. "I know what I know from case reports, which is minimal, so go on."

Sheldon recounted the events that Colson had discussed but with more expletives and less emotional detachment. It was clear that the Secretary of State had stepped into waters beyond her job description, and that Dresden had been at the epicenter of it all.

When the former station chief finished, Stratton slid closer. "Dresden and his crew were supposed to be KIA in Syria two years ago, after they were sent in to eliminate the missing drones from the Algerian shipment. Except Colson came to me recently, scared shitless, since Dresden is apparently alive and is looking for payback."

Sheldon pursed his lips. "Not sure what's more interesting —that he's still kickin' or that he waited two years to resurface."

"He sent her a message—mailed a fucking microchip from one of the weaponized drones to her home. And one of her old friends from North Africa was murdered in Seattle. Guy was a high-end art dealer with ties to politicians and celebs around the world."

"And now you're having to run damage control for Colson, is that what this is all about?" He didn't wait for Stratton to respond. "Those microchips are probably how Dresden's been funding his little op. What Colson failed to mention is that a bunch of those also went missing. He probably sold them off to support his efforts and recruit more mercenaries."

The director drummed a finger on the manila envelope. "You didn't mention anything about Harrison's photo. It's never really been clear to me how he was involved in all of this. I know Colson indicated needing him to sign off on things with the Senate Armed Services Committee, which he headed, but her version of the truth is often a far cry from reality."

"Not sure. The political machinations up on the Hill are your domain not mine, amigo. But I can tell you that his old man and Colson's had a connection from Harvard, or maybe it was Yale—wherever they went to school. When Brittany's father, Nigel Colson, was the ambassador to Egypt, he would entertain various guests from overseas, and some of my guys would assist with diplomatic security if there was a shortage at State. I know Nigel and Harrison's old man would always spend time visiting museums. They were two art freaks, I guess."

Stratton gazed up for a second at the setting sun behind the dense clouds. "That I didn't know. And the fact that the guy stabbed to death in Seattle was a major importer of art makes me wonder what else Colson's old man had his hands into."

Stratton leaned back, sighing. "One last thing." He removed his phone and pulled up a color photo of a man and woman in their thirties. "This is footage my targeter uncovered at a gas station in Washington State recently. Recognize either of them?"

Sheldon grabbed the device, his eyes narrowing. "Don't know the woman, but the guy is Kyle Payne. He's one of us. Or used to be. Worked under John Heller for years, doing search and destroy missions, personnel recovery and other black-bag shit that probably isn't in any official documents. He's involved in this, too?"

"Not sure yet. They were investigating Harrison's crash."

Sheldon canted his head. "Better hope Payne isn't working with Dresden. Two demons from hell on the same team is a recipe for the world to burn."

CHAPTER 24

THE TRUCK STOP'S NEON "OPEN 24 HOURS" SIGN AND FADED cowboy logo looked like it had seen better days, thought Alisa as she pulled her rental car into the side of the parking lot off of I-90 just east of Coeur d'Alene, Idaho.

The sun was barely visible through the dense trees at the back of the parking area where dozens of semis were idling. She watched the other patrons coming and going from the diner adjacent to the gas station. No one raised her hackles, and she had taken a circuitous route after leaving the airport in Missoula to make sure she wasn't being followed. During the three-hour drive west, she had tried to enjoy the snow-capped mountains and windswept valleys, but having a bullseye on her back erased any notions of being a sightseer.

Alisa adjusted her rearview mirror, scrutinizing a weathered GMC Yukon as it rolled in and parked a few lanes over from her. An older man stepped out, ambling to the truck-stop entrance, walking through the store and into the diner on the right. He had a neatly trimmed salt-and-pepper beard and was wearing a dusty plaid shirt, jeans and cowboy boots.

The man blended in with nearly every other guy she'd seen here. Except he walked with a limp on his left side.

She waited a few minutes, watching the man meander past the side counter before settling into a window booth that was vacant on either side. Alisa exited her vehicle and headed inside, following a similar route through the store and into the diner.

She slid into the seat across from the man, noting the other patrons at nearby booths, the emergency exits, and the numerous security cameras.

"You look good, given all that's going on," he said.

She smiled. The first smile in what felt like weeks. But Robert Kilkenny was always the person to elicit such a response from her.

Alisa canted her head towards the parking lot. "I see you're still driving that old tank." It was the same SUV he'd had when she was a junior analyst at the agency. The vehicle he'd take on weekend fishing trips where he'd dispense wisdom about tradecraft more than casting techniques.

"That 'old tank' is on its second transmission and shows no signs of slowing up, unlike me." He chuckled.

Even though he was nearing the horizon of seventy, his eyes still held that look of sharp intelligence and situational awareness that came from a life in intelligence gathering.

He leaned forward, patting her hand and giving it a squeeze. "You should get something to eat here. My rental house is a ways off, and my cooking's about what you remember."

She watched a tall man in a hoodie walk past and turn into the bathroom. She'd seen him having a smoke in the shadows by the dumpster when she first arrived and figured him for a trucker, but he moved with an athleticism that didn't come from sitting in a big rig for most of the day.

Alisa returned her gaze to her old mentor. "I would've hoped to meet you under different circumstances."

He shrugged. "That's how these things go. Trouble comes knocking, and you either face it head-on or bury your head in the sand. And you aren't no ostrich."

A heavyset waitress appeared, setting down two empty mugs and a pot of coffee. "Already know what you want?"

Kilkenny leaned back, squinting at the large menu on the wall. "Cheeseburger with mushrooms and fries."

"And for you, hon?" she asked, glancing at Alisa.

"Um, same, but without the mushrooms."

"Sure thing." The woman turned and headed to the kitchen at the same time as the man in the hoodie exited the bathroom.

Alisa watched him weave through the store, pausing in the snack aisle, then disappearing around the corner towards the laundromat.

"Were you able to uncover anything further about the senator's crash?" She poured coffee into both of the mugs, then slid hers closer, cradling the hot sides.

He shook his head. "I tried to gain access, but the NTSB crew in Darrington haven't compiled their findings."

She flared an eyebrow. "Sounds about right."

"My question is: was Dresden or Colson behind the crash?" He stirred cream and sugar into his coffee.

Alisa leaned in closer, lowering her voice. "Seriously? You think the acting Secretary of State was involved?"

"Not directly, of course. You know how it works. Proxies within proxies all run through cash transactions. She may be corrupt as hell, but she's not stupid. Once Colson discovered Harrison was looking into what happened in Algeria two years ago, and the resulting fallout with the near-miss drone strike on that helo of ours in Syria, she had to move fast and squash his efforts."

"You really think she'd be that desperate?"

"Two years ago when she orchestrated the Algeria deal with POTUS' permission, she used her position to bypass congressional oversight and had the guys at State create a shadow program to arm the moderate rebels in Niger."

She tapped the side of her mug and stared into the inky beverage. "I still find it hard to believe that some of the weaponized drones were stolen and made their way to Syria. Maybe that was the real deal she and POTUS had undertaken. Niger could've simply been a front."

The waitress returned with their meals and utensils. As soon as the woman left, Alisa dove into her meal, not realizing how famished she'd become.

"Damn, kiddo, you act like you're coming off a two-week survival course."

She was about to respond when she saw the guy in the hoodie near the sunglass display in the store. He had just averted his eyes from her and moved towards the T-shirt rack. Alisa removed the folding knife from her pocket that she'd bought at a roadside gas station in Montana. She clutched the weapon, fixing her gaze on the man, and began to slide out from the booth. A second later, he turned and exited the gas station, heading to a semitruck across the lot.

Alisa wasn't sure if the guy was just checking her out or was a tail. But then she'd felt like that at every stop she'd made today. She rubbed her eyes and leaned back. "God, I need sleep."

"You and me both. Been a long week with recent events in Washington, and now Idaho."

"You gonna fill me in on what you've been up to?"

"When we get to the rental house. It'll be a lot easier with my computer and the maps I tacked up on the wall. But I can tell you this is much bigger than just what happened to the senator's jet, tragic as that was. There's some major shit about to go down, so I'm glad you're here. I can use an extra set of eyes."

She studied his face for a minute. "Thought retirement was supposed to prevent the formation of more gray hairs. Guess I was wrong."

"Worrying about you and my daughter is what gave me all these gray hairs."

She noticed the order of his words, remembering how he lamented spending more time at the agency than with his own family. It eventually cost him his marriage and nearly estranged him from his only daughter. But for Alisa, he was like a second father, minus the drunken binges.

"How is Darla these days?" Alisa asked.

He stroked his beard. "Holding up, but Marple's no place to make it as a vet, and my harebrained plan to augment her business with an air-taxi service hasn't gone over well. Fortunately, the expenses are all mine."

She glanced out the window, watching a procession of semis drive into the lot. "How long a drive ahead of us?"

Kilkenny finished his coffee and threw down a fifty-dollar bill. "It's only an hour."

"And after we go over everything you need to tell me?"

"Oh, you're gonna love it. It's a clusterfuck of a mission that has harrowing odds and probably a decent body count. Just like old times."

She wiped her lips with the napkin and slid out of the booth, following beside him. "Sounds interesting… depending on whose side the body count is on."

CHAPTER 25

It was nine o'clock at night when Payne parked the car in the woods a quarter mile away from the airfield. The crescent moon hung in the clear sky like a wolf's fang, providing scant illumination of the forest. He and Walker pulled their Sig Sauer rifles from the hockey duffel bag and donned their daypacks.

He removed the Silva baseplate compass from his shirt pocket and aligned the red north needle to his surroundings. He pivoted to his right and pointed into the woods. "If we head due east for four hundred yards, we'll end up at the fence line near the back of the outbuilding and planes."

"Copy that."

Payne slid the small night-vision spotting scope from his pack's side pocket and put the device's lanyard over his head. Turning on the scope, he scanned the green-hued forest ahead. He took a few minutes to study his surroundings, causing Walker to move in closer beside him.

"Everything good?"

"Yeah, it's just been a while since I've used any sort of

night vision. Brings back memories of living in a green-tinted world for weeks at a time."

"Do that a lot?"

"Depended on the region of the world. There were times during missions in Afghanistan and Africa when my team and I would be sleeping in caves during the days and spending our nights sneaking around villages, pursuing insurgents. I remember once we did eighty-seven ops over seventy-one nights, searching a region for a chemical weapons maker and his network."

"God."

"And then two days after we got him, I was back at my apartment in Virginia and saw a ten-second clip on the news about how the guy had been *brought to justice*."

"What does that mean? You and your team didn't kill him?"

"We had a capture order for him, so he was turned over to my intel counterparts since he was a big fish. Though, there wasn't a capture order for the two dozen guys who were with him."

———

FIFTEEN MINUTES of slow movement through the forest and they arrived at the fence. Payne took off his daypack and removed the paintball gun. He leaned his left shoulder against a nearby pine tree and steadied the crude front sight on the nearest fence-mounted security camera twenty feet away. He didn't bother with accuracy, dumping a half-dozen paint rounds into the device until it was coated with red paint.

He moved a few yards to his right and peppered several more fence-line cameras with paint, then set the gun down.

Walker removed the rolled-up canvas tarp from the top of

her pack and handed it to Payne. Next, she slung her rifle and climbed the fence partway. Nearing the barbed-wire rim, she extended her hand and grabbed the six-by-eight-foot tarp, which Payne had rolled up. She waited for him to come up beside her; then they worked in unison to toss the tarp over the barbed wire so it rested squarely on top.

They took turns climbing over, with Walker arriving on the ground first and taking up a kneeling position with her suppressed rifle near the base of a hemlock tree.

A few seconds later, Payne descended and stood beside her with his rifle raised, both of them scanning the thirty-foot-long field leading up to the rear of the admin building.

He glanced through the night-vision spotting scope, sweeping the entire airfield. Other than a raccoon making its rounds near one of the dumpsters, the place was quiet.

Payne patted her on the shoulder. "Go."

She darted through the knee-high grass, plastering her back against the wall of the brick building.

He made a final pass around the immediate area near the buildings with the night-vision scope, then sprinted across the field.

Payne glanced down at the door, seeing the outline of the bronze handle in the faint moonlight. He leaned his rifle against the wall and removed the two-pound hammer and crowbar from his pack. He set the shorter, hooked end of the crowbar on top of the door handle, then slammed the hammer down so hard that sparks flew off the steel. The handle broke free and clanked to the ground.

He tossed down the tools and grabbed his rifle. Payne swung open the door and scanned the hallway ahead with the night-vision scope before stepping inside. The interior was modest with only two open offices on the right and a classroom on the left.

They moved through the rooms systematically, each of

them sharing common tactical skills that only required hand signals or shoulder taps to convey their thoughts.

At the front was a lobby with a counter and waiting area containing a couch and two lounge chairs that looked like they were garage-sale deals. After clearing the place, they lowered their rifles and activated their red LED headlamps.

Walker broke off into the rear office while Payne examined the counter drawers in the lobby. Other than a clipboard with some administrative documents and a maintenance log, the front of the place was devoid of anything useful.

"Payne, over here," Walker said in a hushed tone.

He retraced his steps to the back room. She had accessed a computer, the screen casting a blue glow across her face. He paused for a second, drinking in her beautiful features and high cheekbones.

"What is it?" she asked, glancing over at him.

"Nothing." He moved behind her, leaning over her shoulder and glancing at the data from the security logs. "How far back does this go?"

"Four weeks." She clicked through a time-stamped folder for the past seven days. There wasn't any activity until three days ago, the grainy camera footage showing still photos of a Gulfstream jet. It was identical to the K9 Air jet but lacking a logo. One figure emerged, and Payne immediately recognized Harrison. He headed down the steps and met an older man at the bottom. They walked to a black GMC Yukon parked near the east fence line, then got inside and drove off. Payne couldn't make out who the driver was. A few seconds later, the jet rolled slowly down the runway and turned, repositioning itself for takeoff.

"I knew he'd been here," said Payne.

She clicked on the flight log. "The jet's arrival was undocumented. Only they didn't cover all their tracks and erase the camera footage."

"Sloppy, but they probably had to leave the area in a hurry before the senator was spotted or someone looked into the landing." Payne rubbed the back of his neck. "The senator always traveled with a bodyguard when he was in the US. It was a Secret Service guy he'd used for years. Think his name was Reggie. That must've been who the remains belonged to at the crash site."

Walker leaned back, gazing up at him. "So he sent his bodyguard to meet with Whitmore in Seattle, but why would he stay here? What's in Marple?"

The soft crunching of a snapped twig outside drew his attention to the window.

Walker turned off the computer screen and slid back, moving to the doorway while Payne slid up beside the window and peered through the blinds.

"Four tangos with rifles and tac gear thirty yards away," he whispered. "And these guys don't move like they're weekend warriors."

CHAPTER 26

"How'd someone know we'd be out here?" asked Walker, focusing her rifle sights on the front door.

"Either we were followed, or Darla tipped them off about our interest in this location."

"Any suggestions on how to get out of here in one piece?"

The glass beside him shattered as a burst of gunfire tore through the window frame. Payne rolled to his left, taking cover behind the desk. The wood paneling beside his head splintered apart from incoming rounds.

"Best bet is to draw them into a kill chute where you are," he said to Walker, who was crouched in the hallway by the rear of the building.

"Got my hands full right now," she replied, firing off three controlled shots through the back door. A shriek on the other side confirmed at least one hit.

Payne quickly assessed the tactical situation. The administrative building's thin walls offered minimal protection against the assault, and he knew they couldn't endure a long standoff. Four enemies initially with at least one down from

Walker's shots, but he thought he heard the squeal of tires in the distance, suggesting that reinforcements had arrived.

He squat-walked to the office entrance, spotting a hulking silhouette in the glass doorway of the lobby. From the faint exterior lighting, he saw a man with a shaved head and a swastika tattoo on his right bicep. The man kicked in the door and began firing wildly with a shotgun, blasting holes through the reception-area furniture and paneled walls.

Payne waited for the shotgun to click empty, then rose and squeezed off two shots. The first struck the skinhead in the neck, while the second round hit above the nose. The man collapsed to the floor, partially blocking the entrance.

Walker moved up next to him, sweat trickling down her cheek. "Back entrance is temporarily clear. I took down one, but that means the other two must be circling around or waiting for us to exit."

A new barrage of automatic weapons fire ripped through the front of the building, forcing Payne to duck lower. This was a thunderous noise, and he immediately recognized it for a machine gun. Probably belt fed. Most likely a SAW, squad automatic weapon, that could punch finger-sized holes through flesh. The assault had just taken a major turn, one that they weren't likely to outmatch.

"Who the hell are these guys?" Walker shouted over the noise.

Payne pointed the muzzle of his rifle at the dead man's arm tattoo. "Just the local chapter of white supremacists. Must be out for their monthly meet-and-greet."

He returned to the back room, gazing out the corner of the window again. "I think this initial group was just here to test the waters. There's a truck that stopped by the gate, and the guy has an M249."

"Damn, he'll tear this place to pieces and us with it," said Walker from the hallway.

A second later a muzzle flash erupted from the truck bed, the next burst of gunfire peppering the building's east side.

He and Walker dove to the ground in the hallway, both of them keeping their eyes on the two entrances.

He slid closer to her, but found himself still needing to shout due to the cacophony of automatic weapons fire. "Back door on three. Then we run like hell into the woods."

She nodded, both of them elbow-crawling down the passage to the rear exit.

At the next pause in the gunfire, they moved into squatting positions. Payne reached the door first with Walker pressed into his back. They moved in synchronicity, as if they'd run operations together for years rather than days.

A crash from the classroom interrupted them. A wiry skinhead had kicked through a window and was halfway inside. Walker reacted first, but only heard the sickening sound of a dry click. She looked down in horror at her rifle, which had failed to discharge. She ran forward, slamming the butt of her rifle into the guy's face. The rail-thin figure tumbled backward, but managed to grab onto the edge of the window frame and then use it to push off towards her.

Payne was about to assist when the sound of boots on glass came from the lobby. Two more attackers had just rushed through the front opening. He pivoted, firing three rounds and dropping the first guy, but the other one darted off near the counter.

The hallway had just become a kill zone being used against them. They were caught between attackers from all angles, with the machine gun at the gate preventing any escape through the windows on the east side.

He could hear Walker struggling with the skinhead in the other room. He turned his head for a second, seeing her and the goon fighting for control of her rifle. The man let go of the weapon and shoved her back, using the momentary distraction to draw a Bowie knife from his belt.

"Carrie!" Payne said, but she had already seen the blade.

She had just regained her balance when the knife sailed through the air towards her face. She shuffled back, the tip of the blade nearly slicing her cheek. Walker dropped her rifle and transitioned to the pistol on her right hip, pulling it out and firing off three rounds into the man's chest. He staggered to the right and collapsed on a table.

Payne redirected his attention to the lobby again, seeing the faintest shadow of a muzzle tip beginning to slide out from the right side of the wall. From his squatting position, he angled his body to the left and fired off a burst of rounds through the drywall near the corner. A shriek was followed by the killer slumping forward on top of his rifle in the hallway as blood leaked out from below his jawline.

The deafening barrage from the machine gun filled the night air again, tearing through the building's brick walls and sending rivulets of drywall dust onto Payne. A few more passes from the SAW and the exterior wouldn't be providing much protection.

They could hear someone shouting to the far right as the remaining attackers coordinated their assault.

"This way," said Walker. "If we head out this window, we can angle off towards the utility building near the woods while this place provides some protection from the incoming rounds."

He rushed into the lounge, locking the door behind him. It wouldn't hold for long, but they only needed seconds. Payne used the bottom of his rifle to smash out the jagged glass shards along the bottom of the window while Walker overturned a table and shoved it against the door.

Without waiting for the next wave of attackers to breach the building, Payne helped Walker through the window, then followed on her heels. They darted twenty feet over to the utility building, crouching behind it and scanning the woods to the rear.

"We're gonna have a hell of a time getting over that barb-wire fence quickly," she said.

Payne glanced at the thick trees ahead, knowing that they first had to jog through the forest before they reached the barrier. He looked back in the direction of the main gate, thinking about their options.

"If they knew we were going to be here, they would've probably staked out our vehicle and posted a few guys in that direction, waiting for us."

"So what, then?"

"There's only one choice; we need to take the fight to them and get rid of that gunner in the truck. We duck into these woods and run a parallel route along the edge of the field so I can get within sniping range of the machine gunner."

"Is that all?"

He let out a faint chuckle. "One thing's for certain, whoever these skinheads are, they're willing to protect what-ever is going on here in Marple, which means we must be getting close to the truth."

Payne thrust his chin at the tree line, motioning she should go first. He remained behind and kept his rifle trained on the bullet-riddled building, which sounded like it was already being stormed.

———

SETH BECKHAM BRACED the butt of the tripod-mounted M249 SAW against his right shoulder as he stood in the truck bed. Sweat beaded down his shaved head despite the cool night air. The familiar weight of the SAW in his grip brought him back to his dishonorable discharge from the Marines eight years ago, before he found his true purpose in life with the White Nation Brotherhood.

He shouted to the other six men in the parking lot to take cover by a storage bay and dumpster as Beckham unleashed his fury upon the admin building. After draining the ammo belt, he yelled at his guys to head inside while he reloaded.

Sheriff Dwyer had been clear: eliminate the outsiders at any cost, then ditch their bodies in a canyon. It seemed like a simple job, but it was proving more difficult than expected. The fact he had already lost several men made him think that these two were experienced operators or undercover officers. He took some pleasure in being up against people who had seen real combat like himself, the realization bringing a tight smile to his face since it only made the hunt more satisfying.

As his men moved towards the building, Beckham loaded a fresh belt into the feed tray, slamming the cover closed with practiced efficiency.

In the red glow of the truck's taillights, the black SS tattoos on his forearms seemed to pulse with each beat of his heart. The pure, uncomplicated clarity that came with violence always made him feel alive in moments like this.

Let's end this and get the hell back to the compound. The other guys are gonna wanna hear about this.

A stocky man with an AK stopped outside the east window of the administrative building and shouted back, "Boss, I think they cleared out."

Beckham pivoted the SAW to the left, preparing to saturate the rear of the building and the forest beyond. *Whatever the outsiders found here, they ain't never gonna make it out in one piece to tell anyone.*

———

WALKER AND PAYNE slipped through the woods, disappearing into the shadows, the sounds of angry voices fading slightly behind them.

Fifty yards in, the sound of an approaching vehicle made them freeze in their tracks. Headlights cut through the trees from the access road, not where they parked, but coming from the direction of the main highway. The lights suddenly disappeared, but the sound of the vehicle continued.

"Shit, more of them," Walker whispered, her face seeming paler in the moonlight.

Payne muttered a curse under his breath. They were being further boxed in, caught between the machine gunner, the skinheads by the building, and now what appeared to be reinforcements approaching from the highway. The odds had just deteriorated further.

In his former line of work, he might've had the luxury of calling in for helicopter support, a quick reaction force, or even a drone strike. But now they were outgunned and outnumbered, and he was looking at their last stand in these woods.

He paused beside the trunk of an immense ponderosa pine tree, both of them taking up shooting positions on either side. He scanned the route ahead. "Plan is still the same: drop as many as possible, and get to the truck. If we can control the SAW, then maybe we can turn this to our advantage."

"It never boosts my confidence when someone uses *ifs* and *maybes* in their tactical plan."

"I hear that."

Payne could see a skinhead exiting the administrative building and moving along the edge of the forest in their direction. The machine gunner in the truck bed had adjusted his stance and was now swiveling the big gun towards the trees.

Payne braced for the coming battle. The unmistakable

sound of automatic weapons fire erupted along the airfield, but something was off. The gunfire wasn't directed at their position. Payne and Walker exchanged puzzled glances and cautiously moved out a few feet from the ponderosa.

From their vantage point, they could see the machine gunner in the truck frantically swinging his weapon toward the entrance road at a dark SUV that had just screeched to a stop. Its occupants hopped out and were firing from behind the doors and hood.

"What the hell?" Walker murmured.

The newcomers weren't targeting them at all; they were methodically cutting down the skinheads near the gate and in the parking lot. The main gunner fell backwards off the bed of the truck, riddled with bullets. Another goon by the driver's door ran for cover, collapsing in mid-stride as his torso began springing leaks.

Payne and Walker turned their attention to the three remaining skinheads near the forest to the left, dropping them with multiple shots to their torsos.

In less than thirty seconds, the firefight was over. Bodies lay scattered across the tarmac, blood glistening in the moonlight, the ground littered with brass shell casings. The quiet that followed seemed almost unnatural.

"Friends of yours?" Walker inquired, her weapon pointed at the shredded admin building.

"I was about to ask you the same thing," Payne replied, straining to see the figures who were moving along the road near the entrance gate.

A flashlight beam swept across the forest near their position, and Payne and Walker instinctively retreated into the shadows, lowering to the ground.

A lithe figure stood in front of the Yukon's headlights—one hand raised in the air, doing three rotations in one direction, followed by two vertical slashes with her spear hand.

Payne's breath caught in his throat. It was an old recognition signal he hadn't seen in years.

"What is it?" Walker asked, seeing his reaction.

His eyes strained to make out the face at this distance as he slowly rose to his feet despite Walker attempting to pull him back down.

But even at this range, there was no mistaking the silhouette—the confident stance and the way the woman held her weapon.

His white-knuckled grip on the rifle eased, and he motioned for Walker to come out. "Looks like we don't have to worry about the *ifs* and *maybes* after all."

CHAPTER 27

PAYNE AND WALKER HEADED ACROSS THE AIRFIELD, CRUNCHING along spent brass casings.

Alisa met them halfway, both she and Payne staring in disbelief at each other for a long moment. She finally shuffled forward, giving him a hug.

He pulled her in, averting his eyes from the splayed bodies to the left and wondering what stroke of fate had placed her in Marple.

She leaned back, brushing some flecks of drywall off his cheek. "You look a little worse for wear than when I last saw you, almost a year ago," said Alisa. "But then that's how I always remember you."

"And you look as angelic and youthful as ever," said Payne with a crooked grin.

"No one's ever accused me of being angelic. Not sure I like it." She shot a thumb towards the main gate. "We should go. We can talk more on the drive."

"Go where?" asked Walker, staring at the older man with a rifle beside the Yukon in the distance.

"We've got a rental house about thirty minutes away," she said.

They followed alongside her, constantly scanning the forest and buildings.

"I left a Subaru on the other side of the fence," said Payne.

Alisa chuckled. "Yeah, um, that's gonna need four new tires and new windows, by the looks of it." She lightly punched him on the arm. "Since when did you trade in your motorcycle for a car?"

He gave Walker a sideways glance. "That's quite an epic story, actually. Maybe another time."

They stopped at the pickup, Payne glancing at the SAW, which had a rivulet of smoke rising from the barrel. "Glad you got here when you did, Alisa."

"From what I've learned since being here, Marple has a dark underbelly of neo-Nazis, and these guys out here are just a small portion of them."

They continued to the SUV, Walker and Payne pausing to shake hands with Robert Kilkenny. They did hasty introductions, then hopped in the vehicle while Kilkenny sped off to the two-lane highway. Two miles later, the old man took the back roads south, avoiding driving through Marple.

Alisa turned in the passenger seat and glanced between Payne and Walker, who sat in the middle row of the Yukon. "So, how did you two meet, exactly?"

"You mean the first time when she and her fake FBI buddy tried to kill me or the time after that?" asked Payne.

He rattled off the condensed version of the events that had transpired during the past two days, including his meeting with Whitmore, Fiche's death at the rodeo grounds, and what led them to Marple. Walker sat in silence, occasionally nodding in agreement, but staring into the darkness after the mention of her partner's name.

"And how'd you drag your old boss out of retirement for this?" Payne said, shooting a glance up at Kilkenny, whom he'd met a few times over the years at Langley.

"Oh, it was the other way around, you could say," replied the old man. "A few weeks ago, my daughter, Darla, whom you already met today, was telling me about the livestock poisonings north of town. It was an interesting bit of sad news, but I knew my girl would eventually figure it out. Then last week, I got a call from Jim…Senator Harrison, about him needing my help with an illegal arms dealer who re-emerged in the Western US after being dead for two years, and how his activity might be connected with a militia group near Marple. Jim and I went way back, so we met at the airfield here where my canine-business jet is stored."

Payne recalled how the old man used to take ten minutes to answer a simple personal question. "So your specialized skills were in demand once again?"

The man pivoted slightly towards Payne. "And yours as well, it seems."

———

IT WAS a thirty-minute drive southeast of Marple to the two-story lodge in the woods. While Kilkenny often stayed with his daughter, he had rented the place to keep a degree of separation between him and Darla given recent events with the investigation he had undertaken with Harrison. It was close enough to visit Darla but far enough from Marple to be secluded.

The four-mile dirt road leading into the property crossed several one-lane bridges over small streams and ended at a lodge. A single porch light provided a faint outline of the front, the inky woods seeming to envelop the place.

Kilkenny parked the SUV, and everyone exited. A man

stepped out from the front door on the porch with a lever-action rifle. He looked to be in his fifties and had a wiry body with dark hair. Kilkenny gave him a friendly wave, causing the guy to lower his rifle.

"You sure we're gonna be off the radar here?" asked Walker. "We're not that far from Marple."

"Far enough," said Alisa. She motioned towards the tree line. "And we're pretty secure with trail cams and thermal devices set up around the place along with, shall we say, a small arsenal, courtesy of Kilkenny."

The figure on the porch stepped down and moved closer, and Payne felt a sense of relief wash over him as he glanced into the familiar face.

"Kyle, you have no idea how good it is to see you," said Senator James Harrison.

Payne took the offered hand, Harrison vigorously shaking, his grip akin to a rock-climber on a precarious hold.

"Likewise, sir." Payne felt like there was finally a head-lamp shining on the maze of trails it had taken to get to this point. "When I saw the crash-site photos of the victims and that your remains were lacking a hip replacement, I was immediately relieved but then even more worried about what was going on."

Harrison lowered his eyes. "My bodyguard, Reggie, and my aide, Jessica, insisted on going on that flight in my place so I could stay here and figure out the Marple connection. Next thing I know…" He bit his lip. Harrison rested a hand on Payne's shoulder. "Just glad you're alright. Let's go inside, and I can explain what the hell is going on."

———

THE INTERIOR WAS spacious with bedrooms on three levels, an immense kitchen and dining area, and a jacuzzi on the back deck. Kilkenny indicated that he had rented the house just a few days ago, but it looked like he had been staying here longer than that.

After Payne and Walker finished eating a reheated meal of leftover chicken wings and potato salad, they settled onto the bar stools around the large kitchen island as Kilkenny and Harrison laid out maps, photos and documents on the surface.

Payne heard an upstairs door open and saw Darla emerge from one of the bedrooms.

Maize darted past her, eagerly racing down the stairs and weaving between everyone.

Darla gave an uneasy glance at Walker and Payne as she moved up next to her father. "Sorry for being so curt earlier today. Things have gotten a little unnerving around Marple lately, and I'm pretty wary of outsiders rolling down my driveway."

"Don't worry about it. I understand," said Walker. She jabbed a finger towards Payne. "I'd be on edge, too, if he showed up on my doorstep."

Payne leaned over, rubbing Maize's neck as the dog pressed against him. "At least somebody here is a good judge of character."

Harrison stood at the far end of the counter with his hands on his hips like he was about to make a senate address. After looking at everyone, he settled his gaze on Payne. "Alisa mentioned you told her on the drive here from the airfield that you and Whitmore had previously met. What did he tell you?"

Payne recounted his discussion with the port official and the recent shipments that had passed through Indonesia from North Africa, along with mention of the mercs who spoke French Algerian.

"Why would Dresden load up his cargo on a ship heading

through Jakarta and not send it directly from Algeria to the East Coast, which would be a helluva lot quicker?" asked Alisa.

"I wondered that for some time," said Harrison. "Originally, I thought there were two logical reasons: one is that there must have been something specific he needed in Indonesia; the second was that any ship coming directly from Algeria is normally routed to the East Coast, which leads me to think he's planning an attack out west."

"You said 'originally'...has your train of thought changed?" asked Walker.

Harrison paced around the room. "Since lying low here these past few days, I've had plenty of time to think and do some research. I'm pretty sure this all goes back to Dresden and Secretary of State Colson's business relationship beyond her political role. Right from the early days of the drone-smuggling shipments to Algeria, she used Dresden for getting the weapons into the hands of the Niger rebels across the southern border. That's how this whole thing started. She seemed to have an easy-in already established."

He folded his arms. "But I've been thinking back to the way she always referred to her 'inside guy'...it wasn't impersonal. It struck me more as a trusted confidant, or at least someone she had relied on extensively in the past. That's kind of unusual, as something like that would normally be farmed out via State Department types, not agency case officers, especially since she *is* the Secretary of State."

Kilkenny had been leaning against the kitchen counter and now stood upright. "That's why the senator and I figured Colson's old man, Nigel, had to be involved. He had been a career diplomat, having served as the ambassador to Egypt for years, and later worked for several international consulting firms in Africa and the Middle East. The guy also had a major hard-on for artwork, from paintings to sculptures to ancient antiquities. He would have had extensive connections both politically and in the black-market world, which aren't necessarily mutually exclusive over there."

Kilkenny removed his prescription glasses and rubbed them on his shirt. "It wasn't unusual, back in the day, for collectors to ship their goods in insulated cargo containers back to ports in the US, then have them trucked out to their estates. But once the maritime laws changed, the only way to get such things shipped abroad was by routing it through different ports like Jakarta and Singapore while using cargo containers with specially engineered compartments to conceal the artwork from customs inspectors."

"And after the senator first approached me about all of this, I did some digging," said Alisa. "Every time Nigel Colson attended a major social event in Africa or the Middle East, there was a corresponding shipment of cargo containers departing Algiers for Jakarta and then on to Seattle within a week. Every time." She looked into each person's face. "And here's where it gets really interesting: Nigel Colson became the ambassador to Egypt the same week that a young Michael Dresden got bumped up to case officer in Cairo."

Payne let the information percolate through his weary brain. "So Dresden is using his knowledge of the Colsons' operations against them now. But what exactly was he shipping here? I'm guessing it sure as hell wasn't artwork."

Harrison replied, "All the investigating I did two years ago led me to believe that Dresden may have destroyed the drones in Syria, but he might have walked out of there with the microchips. Those were some unique, cutting-edge microchips for their time. They were designed for fast-moving weaponized drones that cope with high-altitude winds for sustained periods. The bodies of the drones them-selves required a specific type of carbon-fiber frame just to handle the g-forces. I think he sold some of them to fund his mission of retribution."

Harrison sighed, running his hand through his wavy black hair. "But the trip Kyle and I did to Algeria two years ago to search the warehouse where the weaponized drones were originally stored led me to believe that there were more microchips. If Dresden has those, then he would only need to create the carbon-fiber frames and then equip them with C-4 or something similar."

"C-4 won't be an easy item to obtain in quantity, at least in this country," said Alisa. "Hence, the cargo vessels arriving from Algeria."

Payne nodded. "With Dresden's former agency connections overseas, he may have smuggled what he needed into the port in Seattle."

There was a long moment of silence as everyone stared at the photos and maps on the counter.

"Like being back at the office," said Kilkenny, who glanced at his daughter.

"Your office was on a whole other level than the rest of us mere mortals." Darla called over Maize and sat on the floor against the couch in the living room, her head swiveling around as each person continued talking about the latest revelations.

Payne figured she was seeing a rare side of her father's former line of work, and wondered if it would create more distance between them or have the opposite effect.

Walker picked up an old photo of Dresden. "What's his endgame?"

Harrison rested his fists on the counter. "Algeria to Jakarta to Seattle, then Idaho. He has to be somewhere in this region."

"Why here, of all places?" asked Walker.

Alisa pulled up an image on her tablet, which had been

resting on the counter beside her. She flipped it around. "This is Paul Giletti. He was Dresden's right-hand man for years. They were recruited by the agency at the same time almost fifteen years ago. He grew up in Idaho; Boise to be exact. Last week when I was doing my initial research on everything the senator had brought to me, I created a search algorithm using old images of Giletti and Dresden. I got a hit on a Facebook photo from six years ago. It showed a bearded Giletti with a guy named Miles Dwyer. They were in the woods, standing over a dead deer with their rifles. I did a deep dive into the GPS tag on the image, and it was outside of Marple, on private land."

Darla stood up and moved to the counter. "That rat-bastard Dwyer is involved in this. Why am I not surprised?"

"Do you know where his property is located?" asked Walker.

She shook her head. "The problem is, he owns tons of land out here, mostly in the sticks. When I first moved here, I was told to avoid him and stay out of the forest in the north since there were rumors he was connected to some militia groups."

Payne gazed at Darla. "I've tracked down a few IED and drone makers overseas before. The improvised drone manufacturing process requires certain metal and synthetic compounds, things that can leach into the water table over time and have a detectable presence. I think that you're the key to finding Dresden."

"Seems like a call to Colson's Secret Service detail is in order," said Walker. "She should be notified of the potential threat and what we know."

"Pretty sure she's well aware of Dresden's intentions," said Harrison. "Especially since one of the Colsons' closest friends, Matthew Ellison, an art importer from Seattle, was recently murdered in his house. The word 'Paragon' was spelled out in blood in his kitchen."

Kilkenny moved closer, resting his meaty hands on the table. "From what I've been able to unearth from my colleagues at the agency, Dresden was a patriot. He may have been smuggling on the side for the Colsons, but he was a man with a personal code for most of his career. Then Syria happens, and he loses five of his eight-man team after destroying the missing drones that the Secretary of State tasked him with tracking down. His crew were largely French Algerians whom he'd worked with on countless missions, including a woman he was apparently involved with for years." He directed his gaze at Alisa and then Payne. "I don't have to tell you how devastating that must have been for him, watching his comrades-in-arms and the woman he loved getting vaporized before his own eyes."

"And my partner was gunned down because of this so-called patriot," snapped Walker. "Agent John Fiche. He was a husband and a father, and a friend."

"My apologies," said Kilkenny. "I'm not trying to excuse Dresden's actions but to explain his motivations. I don't think he's a terrorist planning to make a big splash in the headlines with a large-scale attack. This seems more personal and aimed at the Colsons."

"Its reach will be far beyond that," said Harrison. "POTUS would have signed off on anything Brittany Colson was doing in Algeria, providing those drones to rebel forces across the border. And you can be damn sure he's aware of the political fallout on his campaign for reelection if it gets out that Dresden and Colson were connected to all of it."

Payne and Alisa exchanged knowing glances. He knew she was wondering how soon before an agency strike team would be en route to the Western US to eliminate Dresden and anyone associated with his blood trail from Algeria to America.

Payne gazed at Harrison. "Dresden will want to strike at

the heart of the Colsons' empire, and he's using what he learned about their smuggling network to create their downfall. The guy has some balls." He put his hands on his hips. "So, why should we stop him, exactly?"

Walker punched him lightly on the shoulder. "You're shitting me, right?"

"Of course he is," said Alisa. "Payne's got smart-ass spliced into his DNA and can't help what pours out of his mouth most of the time."

Payne smirked, glancing at Harrison. "It seems like this is a good time to call in some reinforcements. You know people in DC you can reach out to. They're going to have far greater resources to locate Dresden rather than us poking around in the woods and getting into shootouts with angry skinheads."

Harrison balled a fist. "Believe me, I would have done so by now. I'm just not sure who I can trust beyond the people in this room."

Payne mulled over the latest revelations and recent events. "You're not entirely sure Dresden was behind your jet going down? If not him, then—wait, you don't think Colson would have orchestrated it?"

"She would have good reason if she thought the trail of clues about arming rebels was to go public," said Alisa.

Harrison let the comments hang in the air for a second before responding to Payne. "You were on the front lines plenty of times in your career; you probably recall the gut feelings that saved your ass, while your brain was telling you to do the logical thing." He put his hands on his hips, giving Payne a hard stare. "I need to stay dead for a while longer until we know all of the pieces in play and who can be trusted. In the meantime, I could sure use your help, and yours too, Agent Walker, to stop whatever Dresden is planning."

Aside from Harrison's impassioned plea, Payne wasn't

about to abandon Alisa, and he knew Walker wouldn't pull up stakes. Plus, he wouldn't be able to live with himself if he woke up in a few days to see news of a catastrophic attack on civilians.

He glanced at Walker and then Alisa, who both had expectant looks in their eyes. He looked beyond them towards the stove. "How much coffee's in the pot?"

CHAPTER 28

LANCE RAYBURN SLID ON HIS SHIRT AND GRABBED HIS DUFFEL bag from the locker at the Victory MMA gym in Alexandria, Virginia, when his phone rang. Seeing the number made him feel like he was back in the ring about to square off with another opponent.

He quickly walked to the rear exit, needing privacy for the coming call. Stepping into the alley, he answered, hearing Director Benjamin Stratton's gravelly voice.

"Sir, this is unexpected."

"You have no fucking idea. There's a situation I need handled with extreme discretion. How soon can you and a rapid-response team be wheels up for Spokane, Washington?"

Rayburn felt his pulse quicken even further. Usually when the head of the CIA rang him, it involved heading to a black site overseas or taking down a target in some less-than-hospitable region of the world. This was only the second time Stratton had requested his specialized skill set on US soil, and Rayburn was certain the memory of the first mission was the cause for his recurring ulcer.

He glanced at his watch. "Ninety minutes to depart Virginia for me and my crew."

There was a long pause before Stratton responded, "Good. I'm texting you the target package my analyst assembled. Name's Michael Dresden. He's a former case officer who was presumed dead in Syria two years ago but just resurfaced in Washington State. I have a source who indicated there is a high probability of him launching a terrorist attack on our shores, possibly using weaponized drones. Find him, find those drones, and then dispose of him and the tech."

"Copy that, sir. Rules of engagement?"

"Avoid collateral damage if possible, but I don't have to tell you that drastic measures are sometimes needed."

"Yes, sir."

"And there are a few other players you need to be aware of. I'll discuss how to handle them as more intel becomes available and from anything you might pick up in the field. For now, just assume this is a multi-varied operation."

The phone went silent. Rayburn slid it back into his sweatpants and stared up at the partial moon cresting the rooftops. *Multi-varied—that means a clusterfuck with a bunch of tentacles.*

———

TWO HOURS LATER, Rayburn unbuckled from his seat in the Gulfstream jet after it leveled off. He stood in the aisle, arching his back and stretching. The rest of his hastily scrambled team of three other operators were on their tablets, going over the mission briefing that Stratton had sent to Rayburn. Two men and one woman, each personally recruited from numerous countries he'd worked in over the years and with scars that rivaled his own.

He walked back and forth along the aisle, scanning the photos that Stratton provided. They were a mixture of black-

and-white profiles that looked like they were taken from CCTVs, security footage, and old personnel records.

Rayburn studied the accompanying files associated with Michael Dresden and Paul Giletti, committing the facial contours and eyes to memory, along with details on their builds and physical characteristics.

Both men were as experienced in wet work and clandestine ops as Rayburn. The difference being that Rayburn was what the agency referred to as a roving element. Where Dresden and Giletti had focused solely on one geopolitical region of the world, Rayburn was inserted into a country for a limited time to excise something or someone of concern to the agency. During his thirteen years in black ops, Rayburn had performed missions in fifty-nine countries. Most of them were a blur, but he was sure this one on home turf wouldn't fall into that category.

He pulled up another image and caption. This was a crisp photo of a man with a black beard and shaggy hair. Rayburn read the caption below several times.

Kyle Payne, former case officer with Ground Branch. Random variable. Was previously assigned to Senator James Harrison's protection detail in Algeria two years ago. Harrison's jet crashed outside of Seattle three days ago. Payne may be connected with a federal investigation into the senator's death.

The next photo showed a blonde-haired woman with blue eyes.

FBI Agent Carrie Walker. Currently aligned with Payne.

Rayburn gripped the luggage rack as a blast of turbulence rocked the jet. He scrolled back to the image of Payne.

Ground Branch. We probably know some of the same guys.

He glanced down the aisle, catching the eye of Tara Gibbons sitting three rows back. "What's up with this dude Payne playing watchdog for Harrison in North Africa a couple of years ago? Those champagne lovers out of DC usually have Statey's on their six."

The others looked up, their expressions matching hers.

Rayburn replied, "Good question, but if I had to guess, I'd say Harrison wanted people from outside his usual inner circle of State Department personnel for some reason."

Tara smirked. "Wonder if it has anything to do with Brittany Colson being in charge of the State Department? Everyone I've ever talked to in our community suspects she was the brains behind the drone debacle in Africa, which cost the lives of a recovery team sent into Syria."

The others nodded, a bearded man across from Tara swiveling in his seat. "And this guy Dresden was operational in Africa during that exact time. Can't be a coincidence since he's listed as KIA at the same time the Syrian team went boots up. Maybe we should be buying him a fucking beer instead of putting him in the ground. He was probably just following Colson's orders to clean up her mess."

Rayburn felt like nodding in agreement. He'd heard the same chatter within the spec-ops world, from respected case officers with field experience in North Africa. Specific details and names of those who were KIA might be redacted on paper, but people's reputations weren't something that could be blotted out with black ink. If anything, they were put under a great magnifying lens, and the image that repeatedly emerged about Colson was that she was a power-hungry, two-faced politician who would stab her own grandmother in the back if it meant advancing her career.

And when a covert ops team of eight operators mysteriously went missing after Colson's involvement in North

African affairs, no amount of media wrangling was going to squelch suspicions amongst experienced case officers.

But he also knew the job at hand was straightforward: put down a threat to the nation. He had to keep this operation on track and prevent any further sympathy for the target from entering the picture. Their role wasn't to interpret intel but to use it to eliminate Dresden. Period. And if Payne and the FBI woman interfered with that objective, then their bodies would end up beside Dresden's.

Rayburn looked into the eyes of each person. "Whatever went on two years ago is above our pay grade, and the job *is* to put Dresden in the ground before he can kill anyone else on our shores. End of story, so compartmentalize any shit that interferes with that and get your heads on straight."

He turned and headed to the cockpit, repeating his own advice a few times.

CHAPTER 29

It was nearing 1 a.m. when they finished talking and everyone retreated to their rooms. Payne and Walker were given two bedrooms downstairs. While she showered, Payne returned to the main level and sat on the back porch, taking in the silence. His ears were still ringing from the gunfight at the airfield, and his face and arms stung from the numerous cuts and scrapes from all the flying debris during their hasty escape.

He stared up at the crescent moon over the spruce treetops as a great gray owl hooted in the distance.

"Thought I might find you out here." The screen door opened, and Alisa stepped out, sitting in a wicker rocking chair a few feet away.

"Just need a few minutes to decompress."

"I imagine this is a far cry from sleeping in a hammock near the ocean while the breeze rocks you to sleep."

He grinned. "You and I have very different images of what being a provisional nomad is like."

"So you don't plan to drift around forever?"

He shrugged his shoulders. "I take it month by month, but

after the past few days, I'm considering disappearing into the wilderness and avoiding my fellow kind for good." He glanced at her. "Present company excluded."

"Does that also include Walker?" She had a coy smile. "I saw how you two looked at each other. Although your tells weren't as obvious as hers."

"Not sure what the hell you're talking about." He said it without much fervor.

"Yes, you do, Payne. You just don't want to admit it, or act on it, because it will mean adding a complication to your Jesuit lifestyle. Just like before."

"Says the woman who views a one-month relationship as a long-term commitment."

She leaned back. "I've actually been involved with someone for nearly a year, so kiss my ass, Payne."

"Damn, good for you. Can't say I've ever walked that road."

"That's because you're too busy running away from that road."

"Fair enough." He gave her a long stare. "So, is the lucky guy from within the community?"

"Not exactly. He's a former Navy intel guy and now works in the private sector like me. He's in London for a few months, so things are on hold for a bit, but not in a bad way."

He patted her on the hand. "I'm happy for you, Alisa. I really am."

"Thanks." She nodded towards the lodge. "I just need to get all this shit sorted out with Harrison so I can get my life back on the grid. While I didn't have a bunch of heavy hitters come after me like you did, I still had to disappear and get out of Dodge fast."

"I need to know: you trust Harrison?"

She angled her body towards him, lowering her voice. "You're asking me? You worked with him before."

"A couple of years ago. People change and, in his world, can change their stripes on a moment's notice."

"When he first approached me, he was transparent about his motives, laying things out like he did here earlier. I was moved by him being so forthright. It sounded like he just hitched his wagon to the wrong horse when he first took on his role with the Senate Armed Services Committee a couple of years ago. What he said about Colson doesn't surprise me a bit. She's always struck me as a true political animal who would do anything to stay on top."

"Yeah, her father was the same, I think. I remember hearing things when I worked in North Africa about how all roads of commerce led to him, in some way. Seems like a shady motherfucker."

"As long as we can put a stop to whatever Dresden is doing, then we should be able to get back to our lives."

He slid his chair closer. "Since hearing Harrison explain things earlier, I couldn't help but wonder what contingencies Colson has in place to prevent any blowback to her, especially now that she thinks Harrison is out of the picture."

"I've been wondering the same thing from the get-go. When I dodged whoever was shadowing me in Virginia, I figured it was some of Dresden's crew, but now I'm not so sure. What if Colson has her own assets in place?"

"We need to assume she does. And she probably has the blessing of POTUS since neither of them can afford their past fuck-ups to be painted across the news—again." He rubbed his aching shoulder. "My guess is she has a crisis-reaction team on standby, former agency guys or independent contractors who will clean up her mess along with the necessary media puppets to run cover."

"All the more reason to make sure Harrison comes out of this unscathed. He's going to be the only one who can run cover for us and get our names off her shit list if we're implicated in some way."

Payne sighed; the lure of riding off on his motorcycle never seemed more appealing. "Did I mention I might move to Alaska and live in a tiny cabin, days from the nearest town?"

She smirked. "*After* this is over, Payne. Then you can fulfill your Jeremiah Johnson dreams all you want, while I get back to my boyfriend and paved roads."

———

AFTER ALISA LEFT, Payne lingered on the porch for a few minutes before heading inside. He grabbed a bottled water from the fridge and headed downstairs. His bedroom was at the opposite end from Walker's, with a couch, a TV, and a pool table spaced around the central living area with a bathroom off to the side.

He took a hot shower and then sat on the couch in his shirt and boxers, applying a few bandages to the various nicks and cuts on his arms.

Walker's door opened, and she stepped out, wearing a white bathrobe.

"Sorry to wake you," he said.

"Not at all. I was just staring at the ceiling. Not gonna be getting a lot of sleep after tonight's events." She sat down beside him, grabbing a bandage off the coffee table and applying it over a small cut on his neck. "You missed one."

She sat with her silky legs crossed, and he noticed her red-painted toenails. The look of alluring femininity pushed back the veil of the fierce exterior she'd projected since they met. And her eyes held a softness that he could lose himself in for a while.

She almost rested a hand on his arm but pulled back. "So, are you and Alisa a thing...or were you?"

He pursed his lips. "No. She's more like an annoying sister, or at least how I'd imagine a sister being. She was my eyes and ears during missions, and there's no one I trust more in this world."

Walker let her hand slide forward until it settled on his shoulder. She was close enough now that he could smell the sweet scent of her shampoo. As she slid in towards him, her robe parted slightly. "What are your instincts telling you right now about trusting me?"

She asked in a soft voice that he could listen to all day. He leaned in, brushing his lips along her neck. She pressed into him, kissing him and pulling him closer.

A few seconds later, Walker slid back and smiled. "I don't want to be alone tonight." She stood, clasping her hand around his and leading the way to her bedroom.

CHAPTER 30

THE PLUM-ORANGE FINGERS OF DAWN SLICED THROUGH THE TREES outside the second-story bedroom window. Sheriff Dwyer sat up on the side of the bed, grabbing his phone and checking for messages. Nothing from Beckham or his crew who had gone to the airfield last night.

Not good. I shoulda heard something by now. Unless those idiots are all passed out back at the compound.

He pulled the blanket up over his wife's bare shoulder. He brushed a long strand of her red hair off her cheek, then kissed her softly.

After using the bathroom, he got dressed and headed downstairs to the kitchen. The coffeemaker had already completed its daily sunrise brew, and he poured the contents of the pot into a Stanley thermos.

Grabbing his lunchbox from the fridge and a bagel from the counter, he headed out the back door to his 4x4 vehicle adorned with the Marple County Sheriff's logo. Again, he checked his phone, silently cursing Beckham.

He'd have to head up to the compound thirty miles north of town, which would add an extra hour to his day.

Eight miles later, he decided to pull off onto the county road that led to the airfield to make sure Beckham hadn't left any signs of his handiwork.

Dwyer nearly choked on his bagel when he pulled up to the main gate. Beckham was lying facedown on the driveway, his torso peppered with bullet holes. Beside him were thousands of rounds of spent shell casings. Dwyer parked and got out, staring at the other dead men splayed out along the tarmac.

Assholes. I said make the outsiders disappear, not obliterate the property.

He spit out the remains of his bagel and leaned a shaking hand against the side of Beckham's truck. A third of his family from the Brotherhood had been gunned down like animals. He slammed his fist against the truck, staring at the belt-fed machine gun in the back.

Dwyer moved closer to Beckham, kneeling and resting a hand on the man's shoulder while muttering a prayer.

Shit, who'd Beckham go up against? Those two outsiders had to be undercover cops, if they dropped a bunch of well-armed shooters.

Dwyer returned to his vehicle and drove slowly to the admin building, pausing on occasion to glance at the dead men, envisioning their mothers' faces after they'd learned of the tragedy.

Fuck! His rage balled up inside him, and he hoped he would find one of the outsiders still alive.

He parked around the back of the building, which looked like it had been hammered by mortar rounds. He grabbed his duty rifle and headed in through the rear door, stepping over a dead body. Three more of his brothers' lifeless figures were scattered around inside.

He thought of their laughter, jokes, and the deer-hunting trips he'd been on with all these fellas. They were more family than any he'd grown up with, and now he'd be muttering prayers at their funerals.

Dwyer dragged a sleeve across his misty eyes, then removed his cellphone, dreading the forthcoming call.

Dresden picked up on the first ring. "Is it done?"

Dwyer kicked a broken lamp down the hall. "They must have gotten away and had help, since eight of my guys are dead. It was a fucking slaughter."

"The slaughter part was supposed to be dealt by your crew."

The sheriff's voice cracked. "Look, these were friends of mine. Brothers to the bone. Shit, I officiated at most of their weddings. Whatever you got them into was way over their heads."

A long pause followed; then Dresden replied, "You're right. I'm sorry for your loss. I'll be sure to compensate their families. Get over here, and we'll talk about what happens next."

He couldn't tell if the man was being sincere or just trying to placate him, since he needed the use of his land for a few more days.

Dwyer ran a hand along his smooth chin. "I gotta get more of my men out here to clean this place first. It's a fucking graveyard."

"I assure you, there will be two graves in the backwoods soon, once I zero in on their location."

There was no mistaking the conviction in Dresden's voice this time. Dwyer hung up, feeling the adrenaline surging through his veins and thinking of the medieval pain he'd be inflicting once he found the man and woman behind this bloodbath.

CHAPTER 31

PAYNE AWOKE TO AN EMPTY BED. HE GOT DRESSED AND WAS heading upstairs just as Walker was descending with two bagels in either hand. She met him at the bottom, remaining on the last step and moving closer. He slid his hands around the gap in her robe and pulled her in. "How did you know I would wake up hungry?"

"Haha." She kissed him, wrapping her forearms around his neck. "Everyone is already up and gathered around for breakfast, so we should go." She leaned back, shoving a bagel towards his lips. "This will have to do for now."

He frowned. "I guess."

Payne only wanted to take her into the bedroom and spend the morning beside her. Maybe the afternoon, too. But that would have to wait.

He gathered his pack and headed up while she got dressed. When he entered the kitchen, everyone stared at him, then quickly averted their eyes and returned to their conversations.

Alisa sidled up next to him as he grabbed the pot of coffee

from the maker and poured it into a cup. "Carrie seemed in really good spirits this morning," said Alisa.

"A solid night of sleep will do that."

Alisa leaned into his ear. "She does know that your only possessions are that bike and your hammock, right?"

"Maybe that's the appeal."

She smirked. "You still wanna disappear into the woods and live in a cabin miles from people?"

He gently pushed her back, grinning. "Just one person in particular right now."

Walker arrived in the kitchen and sat on one of the stools around the island. Harrison, Kilkenny, and Darla sat on the other side, all of them partaking of toasted bagels.

Harrison motioned to Alisa. "It's your show. Fill us in on what you found."

She tapped on her dormant tablet. "Since we know the common denominator in the events of this week involves whatever was delivered to the Port of Seattle and what was bound for Marple, I hacked into several of the local security feeds around town here to see if any convoys or air couriers arrived."

Payne leaned over Walker, resting one hand on her shoulder. She gave him a surprised but pleasant look at the gesture.

"Outside of the usual delivery trucks emanating out of Boise, there were two semis that passed through Marple two days ago, heading north." Alisa enhanced the license plate of the rear truck.

"Washington State," Payne muttered.

Walker tapped her finger on the four-digit number on the bumper to the right of the plate. "That's for vehicles originating out of Seattle. Washington Department of Transportation requires that for semis."

"Doesn't mean it's connected with the port," said Harrison. "Could be anything from clothing to electronics bound for retail shops."

Alisa pulled up a map of western Idaho. "Except they didn't stop in Marple; and the next closest town, and I use that word lightly, is two hours to the north. Then, later that morning, they passed back through Marple."

Payne analyzed the map, noting the winding roads that he and Walker had driven the day before. "We only went a short ways up that way, but from the looks of it, there were millions of acres of wilderness." He glanced over at Darla, who was finishing an apple. "You must know every back road around here?"

"And then some," interjected Kilkenny.

Darla walked closer, briefly gazing at the map and rolling her eyes. "No-man's land. Most of us avoid venturing into the areas up north. Too many militia types, pot growers, and whacko hermits."

"And dead livestock, from what you said," replied Walker. "What's the story on that?"

Darla leaned forward, resting her forearms on the kitchen counter. "Started about a month ago. Originally, I thought it was connected with a bacterial outbreak but quickly ruled that out after sampling the water. Further testing didn't reveal anything viral or fungal, so I sent off a batch to a soil scientist with the USDA in Boise. He indicated the water was laced with a distinctive ratio of copper, zinc and magnesium."

She nodded towards the forest beyond the rear window. "Those things are normally found in nature, and even in the water table in many regions, but in minuscule amounts as to be barely detectable. My samples from north of town were found in high enough concentrations to be toxic to mammals. And many of the ranches up in those parts have been there for generations and never had issues like this, so it's clearly a recent development."

"When did the first reports of the poisonings occur?" asked Walker.

Darla's eyes darted around the ceiling for a second. "Four weeks ago, and the first rancher I spoke to took me out to where his cattle had been drinking from the stream, which had a pink residue along the shoreline. Same coloration was found at other sites I surveyed."

"Sounds familiar," said Harrison. "Just like in that warehouse in Algeria two years ago."

Payne nodded. "Whitmore said he noticed that in the containers at the port too." He turned to Darla. "Any luck on tracking down the source of the pollution in the stream?"

The veterinarian shook her head. "It's plural. There are hundreds of rivers and streams along the mountain ranges north of here. And the reports are too few at present to pinpoint ground zero. There is one river basin where the majority of poisonings have occurred, but I have no plans to venture up in those parts unless I have an armed unit of Fish & Wildlife officers with me."

Alisa had been working on her tablet and spun it around. "I mentioned reviewing the security cams around Marple and just found this, from the site of your welcoming committee last night."

The group huddled around, watching black-and-white video footage from the main gate at the airfield as Sheriff Dwyer squatted beside the body of the dead machine gunner.

Darla's eyes filled her face. "Jesus, when you said that there was a gunfight at the airport, I wasn't figuring it was an all-out war."

"The sheriff looks like he was pals with those animals," said Walker.

Darla balled a fist. "I wondered if that bastard was tied up with those guys. Those goons were always getting slaps on their wrists by Dwyer for harassing the hell out of women in town."

Alisa pointed to the time-stamp on the video. "That was from three hours ago. And when I just examined the security cameras in downtown Marple, I didn't see any indication that the place was swarming with LEOs from outside the region."

"How many deputies does Dwyer have?" asked Walker.

"It's just him," said Darla. "He's got a couple of part-timers he uses during weekend festivals, but he's a one-man show. At least during the four years I've been livin' here."

Payne slid towards Alisa. "Can you get me the sheriff's address...his home address?"

"Coming up," she replied, turning her device around and getting busy.

Payne looked around at the others in the room. "This is the part where the rest of you should probably take a coffee break on the back porch. The less you know about what happens next, the better." He directed his gaze at Walker. "That goes for you too."

She smirked. "Not likely. Whatever happens next is going to include me."

He rested a hand on her shoulder again. "I envision you having a long career in law enforcement, and this is something that won't further that goal."

"I'm coming, Payne. Someone has to keep the violence from going off the rails."

Alisa grinned. "I like her. And I also like that she thinks she can control you."

CHAPTER 32

It was 6:30 p.m., and the sun was just dipping below the horizon when Payne drove Alisa's rental vehicle down the dirt road. A few minutes later, the route split off in two directions. From the plat map Alisa had pulled up earlier, the road on the right headed to Dwyer's place while the other route led to a vacant lot slated for a new house.

Payne drove for three hundred yards up a slope towards the cleared lot, stopping beside a bulldozer and Porta Potti. He exited the vehicle and walked ten feet into the tree line, then returned a minute later. "Dwyer's place is directly below, about sixty yards away. There aren't any other vehicles in front. Darla said his wife works overnight shifts during the week as a paramedic in the town south of here, so the house should be clear."

Alisa opened the vehicle door and swung her feet out. "My device has an amplified antenna that can feed off of both Wi-Fi and satellite, allowing me to intercept or infiltrate signals across multiple frequencies, but it won't work smoothly if I'm in here with the windows up."

She accessed Dwyer's network by exploiting an outdated

software vulnerability in his exterior security system, using a modified Kali Linux distro that had been developed for cyber-penetration testing. After establishing a foothold, she implemented a man-in-the-middle attack to intercept the CCTV feeds and freeze the cameras.

After that, she disabled the motion sensors along the outside of the house and replaced the active signals with looped data to prevent triggering any failsafe alerts on Dwyer's monitoring dashboard, which she figured was located inside the house or on his iPhone.

"Give me a minute to breach the Wi-Fi in the house, as his exterior system was on a separate setup from what's inside," said Alisa, typing on her laptop.

"Only 'a minute,'" quipped Payne. "You're rusty."

"Screw you, Kyle. Your joints make the same sound as the coffee maker at the lodge, so I wouldn't talk."

Walker flared an eyebrow. "Sheesh, and you two used to work together."

"She used to work for me, as the targeter for my team," said Payne with a grin.

Alisa didn't bother looking up. "Actually, he worked off of *my* hard-won intel, so it was the other way around."

"Seems like a frictionless environment," said Walker. "I'm sure you two were very productive."

"I'm just giving Alisa a hard time. She was the best in the business. I don't care what the others said about her."

"How 'bout I push in your face after this," replied Alisa, her fingers suddenly stabbing away at the keypad.

"He's a charmer, alright," said Walker as she scanned the forest ahead. "I can see how he must have been great at recruiting assets."

"I recruited Alisa," said Payne.

The cyber expert shook her head. "Hell you did. You

merely nudged me in the direction of doing intel after I was medically relieved from field ops."

"Was it due to the psychological trauma of working with Payne?" inquired Walker. "I can see how that would wear you down."

The two women laughed; then Alisa said, "Blew out my knee, actually. And while there is some validity to his statement, Kyle was actually the best case officer I'd ever been around, despite what everyone said about him suffering from delusions of godhood, or something to that effect."

Payne waved his hand. "If we're done with our mutual admiration fest, I'd like to get inside Dwyer's place."

Alisa leaned closer to her device, her typing increasing. "Almost there. Just bypassing the pathetic Wi-Fi on his smart fridge, which will give me a pathway into the house's main Wi-Fi router. From there, I'll be able to hack into the security system, which appears to be an older model."

"You can gain access from the fridge?" asked Walker.

"Smart appliances, smart utility meters, and even Wi-Fi thermostats. Those are always the weakest links into a person's house. From there, I can penetrate computer firewalls and gather information on their world, their families, or, if I were so inclined, hack into their bank account."

"Something to be said for living off-grid," Payne quipped.

"You mean living off the back of your motorcycle and sleeping in budget motels without streaming TV?" asked Walker.

"You almost sound jealous of the nomad life," he said.

She chuckled. "You mean vagabond. Nomad is too respectable a term."

"All set. Security systems are neutralized," said Alisa. She set her tablet aside on the back seat and unzipped a side pocket on her go-bag. She removed a black pouch, pulling out a set of earbuds and a two-way radio. She handed one earbud each to Walker and Payne. "This will allow me to communicate with you from my position, but you won't be able to relay anything to me. Fortunately, this guy has a long driveway, so I'll be able to give you plenty of notice if he shows up."

Payne removed the FN pistol from his beltline along with a Surefire flashlight that Kilkenny had provided.

"Hang on," said Alisa as she handed him a small nylon pouch. "Here's that lock-pick set you gave me a few years ago."

"Thanks."

Walker leaned back. "Like I said, he sure knows how to woo the ladies."

Alisa chuckled. "Not sure 'woo' and Payne are two words I'd ever put in the same sentence."

The three of them exited the vehicle and headed through the woods. Alisa remained along the tree line with her eyes trained on the driveway, while Payne and Walker moved towards the house.

The sun had disappeared beneath the horizon, casting the forest in shadows. A dusk-to-dawn light above the garage door flickered on, illuminating the front.

"Ever done this kind of thing before?" whispered Walker. "Breaking into the house of a law-enforcement officer."

"Not in this country, not that I can recall anyway."

"Forget I asked."

"Besides, it doesn't sound like there's much actual 'law enforcement' that Dwyer does in this town."

THE LOCK-PICKING WAS STRAIGHTFORWARD. It was clear that Dwyer relied on his security system since the antiquated deadbolt and door handle looked like they were originals from when the place was built, probably sometime after World War II.

The house smelled like an Italian restaurant. Payne proceeded past the kitchen and into the living room while Walker cleared the upstairs. The residence was well organized and resembled an arts-and-crafts store with its countless handmade baskets that adorned the walls and shelves in nearly every room. He figured Dwyer's wife had a part-time business either selling her wares or teaching workshops.

Basketmaking 101; only neo-Nazis need apply.

He wondered if Dwyer's wife even knew about her husband's militant predilections. *She has to if she grew up here.*

He recalled a twelve-year-old child soldier he'd encountered in Sierra Leone during his early days in the field. The boy had been the only survivor of a massacre, following the attack by a rival warlord who decimated his village. After being attended to by the medic on Payne's team, the boy asked if he could have his AK-47 and ammunition back. The look in his eyes haunted Payne—not hatred or anger, just absolute conviction. The kid spoke of destroying the other faction, using phrases that his former commander had ingrained in him, the boy's trauma being weaponized to suit the cause at hand.

Payne realized then that the most dangerous weapon wasn't the rifle in the child's hands but the unshakeable belief that violence was not only necessary, but a virtue.

He heard Walker's footsteps as she came downstairs. "So far, there's no evidence anyone other than a woman lives here. All the bedrooms could be featured in *Good Housekeeping*."

She nodded towards a closed door beside the fridge. Walker opened it and turned on the light. The odor arising from the basement smelled like an old dishrag. "Guess we found where Dwyer spends most of his time."

They moved down the steps with their pistols drawn. At the bottom, Walker went left while Payne headed right. The place had a larger footprint than the main level. It was completely paneled with faux wood and a floor covered in off-white carpeting except for a small portion near the wet bar, which was tiled.

Bookshelves adorned the right wall, while a showcase with bowling trophies lined the back. A pool table was in the middle near a faded couch that faced an immense widescreen TV mounted on the wall. Several open beer cans were on the table by the couch along with an empty paper plate with dried ketchup.

"Talk about a man cave," said Walker.

Payne paced around the room, stopping by the wet bar and examining the walls and flooring. "I think the real man cave might be over here." He motioned for Walker to help him, pointing at the scuff marks on the tiles. She grabbed one end of the six-foot-high liquor cabinet and rotated it out away from the wall. The recessed wheels underneath made their job easier than expected.

They stared past the narrow entrance, the main lights of the basement illuminating the room enough to see that it was roughly bedroom-sized.

Payne pulled out his flashlight and stepped inside with his pistol aimed ahead. He examined the string hanging from the rafters and saw that it connected to a fluorescent light overhead. Payne yanked on it and turned off his flashlight.

He and Walker stared at the large vintage paintings of a half-dozen Nazi officers adorning the left wall. Goring, Himmler, Goebbels, and others had their names listed on shiny bronze plates attached to the frames. On a shelf below were numerous antique belt buckles, hats, and WWII paraphernalia. Payne glanced at a bronze sheath that held a pearl-handled officer's dagger with the insignia of the German navy.

"Damn, this stuff looks legit," he said as he surveyed the collectibles.

"Not sure if this is a man cave or Dwyer's place of worship. What a psycho." Her mouth hung open, and she pulled on Payne's sleeve.

He turned to the right, seeing the wall covered with several dozen rifles, pistols, knives and a tarnished samurai sword. "Those firearms are one-offs—Dwyer probably acquired those from various criminal cases he worked, or covered up."

"The latter for sure since those should've all ended up with ATF."

"No wonder that ape at the airfield was sporting a submachine gun."

Walker opened a metal cabinet near the corner, staring at stacks of cash, a few bricks of cocaine and clear plastic bags filled with blue pills. "This guy has amassed a fortune down here."

Payne rifled through the table drawer and a small desk near the entrance, giving up after a few minutes and returning to the weapons wall. "Nothing here is going to point us to their little hideout in the woods, but these will sure come in handy." He removed several rifles and their corresponding magazines and boxes of ammo from a shelf below, setting them on the table.

"I think I saw a golf-club bag near the basement steps," said Walker as she exited. A second later, she leaned in, her eyes like saucers. "Shit...someone's upstairs."

CHAPTER 33

PAYNE TURNED OFF THE LIGHT AND BOLTED OUT THE ENTRANCE. The person lumbering around upstairs didn't sound like the dainty person Darla had described when discussing the wife. This was a big man, and Payne knew he would be sweeping through each room of his house with a weapon after discovering the alarm system had been disabled.

He heard Alisa's voice in his ear, realizing the primitive comms had been hampered by their presence in the Nazi vault. "Payne, do you copy? The sheriff has returned and just gone inside."

No kidding. He motioned for Walker to move to the far corner and conceal herself beside the bookcase. "We need him alive," he mouthed to her.

Payne retreated behind the wet bar, squatting beneath the counter. He suddenly realized they'd left the lights on, and he ran back to the base of the stairs, flicking off the switch. He carefully retraced his steps to the bar, relying on the slivers of dusk stabbing through the narrow privacy windows. He intentionally left the vault door open, wanting Dwyer's attention drawn away from Walker's location.

A minute later, the basement door opened. The stairs creaked, and heavy breathing emanated from the shadows. Payne heard the familiar sound of a shotgun being racked. A tactical flashlight turned on and flooded the first half of the basement.

"You'd best be spread-eagle on my fuckin' floor when I get down there," said Dwyer. "Or me and my deputies are gonna plug you full a holes."

Payne clutched his pistol, replaying Alisa's words. There had been no indication of anyone other than the sheriff being on-site. However, that could change if he'd called in a bunch of skinhead reinforcements.

The creaking stopped, then resumed as the man made his way to the bottom. Payne saw the tactical beam float over the bar, the light reflecting off the mirror on the wall. Payne canted his head, seeing the opposite corner where Walker was suddenly exposed.

So much for her being concealed.

Payne leaned out from the edge of the bar as Dwyer turned towards Walker's position. Payne squeezed off a single round, striking Dwyer in the left hip. The man groaned and swiveled towards Payne, firing wildly and shattering the mirror and liquor cabinet. Payne dropped lower, squeezing off another round that hit the sheriff in the other hip. This time, the man toppled onto the stairs, collapsing on his back. He squealed like a wounded bull and curled in a fetal position.

Payne trotted up and kicked away the shotgun, then turned on the lights. He removed Dwyer's duty pistol from his belt along with his Taser, then grabbed the guy by his shirt collar and flung him forward onto the carpet.

"What happened to taking him alive?" asked Walker as she moved up next to Payne.

"He had the drop on you." Payne moved closer, standing

in front of the guy. "Besides, he'll live long enough to answer a few questions."

"Fuck off," muttered the sheriff in between pained groans.

Payne pressed his boot on the man's leg. "Who sent your little band of broken toys out to the airfield last night?"

Dwyer's face was growing pale; the blood loss from the two shattered hips was significant and was soaking through the thick carpeting.

"Clock's ticking. The human body can only part with about the equivalent of three spaghetti jars of blood before you're done for, and you're almost halfway there."

Walker pulled Payne's arm, shaking her head as she cast an apologetic look at the sheriff. Payne removed his boot and stepped back.

Dwyer chuckled in between winces. "You let your whore run the show. You're pathetic." The man arched up. "I'm not gonna beg for my life. Dresden will find...find you. Then he and my guys are gonna take their time cuttin' you both to pieces."

"Tell me where he and his crew are. I know they smuggled weapons of some kind into the US. I'm guessing drones based upon his prior MO." He nodded at the open vault. "You really believe that helping Dresden murder a bunch of innocent people in your own country is going to right some warped notion of injustice you think you've suffered? That bullshit thinking was already attempted by the monsters in those paintings, and it set humanity back generations."

"Screw humanity and screw your hero complex. Whatever Dresden is planning is big, man. It's going to be...to be epic and will make the sheeple in this country come to their senses for once. That's when the real uprising will...will happen, and my brothers will be there."

"And don't forget about the promise of a hefty paycheck

from Dresden." Payne raised his pistol and fired a single round into the man's head.

Walker's face turned red. "What the hell—you can't just execute people."

"He was going to be a goner in five minutes, and I'm not about to stick around in case his buddies show. Plus, Alisa probably has what she needs by now from his vehicle's GPS transponder, which will help us locate Dresden." He stepped towards the stairs and grabbed the golf-club bag. "I'm gonna load up the weapons and ammo; then we need to high-tail it out of here."

She followed him into the vault, helping to stow the rifles. "So you and Alisa already figured you could track down Dresden using the sheriff's vehicle? Yet we came here anyway, and now Dwyer is dead."

Payne grabbed the stuffed bag and exited the vault while she followed with a handful of remaining rifles. "It's never linear like that, Carrie. You gather as much information as you can from tech, from your surroundings, and from the players on the field. Sometimes, that means the latter ends up in the crosshairs. And like I said before, I'm not going to lose any sleep over someone like Dwyer going down the drain."

They walked up the steps and exited the house, heading back towards Alisa and the vehicle. Whatever tenderness he had felt from Walker last night had just evaporated. And he didn't know if her feelings for him had just been permanently severed.

It would have to be added to his growing list of concerns, the latest one being what they were going to do once they finally caught up with Dresden.

CHAPTER 34

THE DRIVE BACK TO THE LODGE ALONG THE BACK ROADS OUTSIDE of Marple took longer than expected due to a light rain, which made the dirt roads slick. Payne kept his gaze ahead as much from the driving conditions as from the feeling Walker was shooting daggers from her eyes when she glanced his way.

"I wish we could have gotten some information from Dwyer on how many guys are out at his compound with Dresden," said Walker.

"That would be great, but once I locate the property, I might be able to hack into their security cams and get some numbers for you," said Alisa from the back seat. "It's probably the same setup as his home system...Costco special... buy one, get one half off deal. Perfect for safeguarding your Nazi collectibles."

Walker glanced from Alisa to Payne. "This really doesn't bother either of you at all—killing a man in cold blood?"

"You can't possibly feel remorse for that monster," said Payne.

"It's not about remorse. It's about following the law.

Otherwise, we're not much different than him, bending things to suit the agenda at hand."

"So you wanted to cuff him, read him his rights and call the EMTs, some of whom might be members of the Brotherhood; only this time they show up with a shitload of their buddies armed with more than just machine guns."

Walker shook her head. "You've got it all figured out. No need for a judge or jury because no one can be trusted to do the right thing in your world. But you know what's best. Payne's rule of law."

"You know I'm right, but you can't see beyond the protocols you've adhered to during your career. My former career required more flexible protocols. Ones that involved making sure scumbags like that don't continue spreading his horror show upon the folks in Marple or elsewhere."

———

THE REMAINDER of the drive was punctuated by uncomfortable silence, and Walker felt like they were seated in a cavernous bus.

Pulling in beside the back door of the rental house, Payne exited and headed inside, leaving the two women in the vehicle.

Walker swiveled around to face Alisa, who was packing up her radio and binoculars. "It's like there was no other outcome in Payne's mind for the sheriff despite him saying we needed the guy alive. Dwyer was guilty and was going to die. End of story."

Alisa flared an eyebrow. "Sounds right."

"And you don't have a problem with that?"

Alisa glanced out towards the forest for a second. "Look, you have to remember that there was no immediate oversight in the field for Payne when questioning a target. People like him had to make split-second decisions based upon what their environment and the individuals in it were indicating. Logic and actual intel aside, relying on gut instinct is a prerogative associated with that line of work. There is no time to radio back to a Langley lawyer and weigh who gets a round in the head and who walks away. The case officer in the wilds decides that based upon the need in that moment, and the potential blowback in the future, if that guy turns out to be a much bigger player in the terrorist network."

Walker blew a strand of blonde hair off her nose. "Your world seems built around moral flexibility."

"I imagine that doesn't sit well with your FBI code of conduct."

"People like Dresden and Payne and others in that line of work see targets instead of suspects. That's just not how I'm wired."

"First off, don't compare a lunatic like Dresden to Kyle. They're polar opposites. One is bent on retribution regardless of the collateral damage, while the other is driven by a duty to country and protecting it at any cost, even if that means sacrificing his own life. And Kyle's come close to doing the latter more than anyone I've ever met in the clandestine world. As someone who was his eyes overseas, I can tell you that his body count eliminating the bad-guy population wasn't in the double digits. He knows how to get that done efficiently and with minimal fallout."

"This isn't Afghanistan or Africa."

"No, but wolves cross geographic boundaries, and sometimes it takes another wolf to hunt them down." Alisa leaned in closer. "You need to stop viewing Dresden and his crew as suspects with Miranda rights. They need to be put down and fast, before the civilian loss of life becomes something for the history books.

"I don't know what Dresden's endgame is, but he's probably not planning on a small splash, more like a crater…and he's had two years to plan out every operational detail and contingency. Even if I had a team of analysts, we are way, way behind the curve in catching up to him. We need to avoid doing anything that will slow us down, hence Dwyer being boots up." Alisa grabbed her pack and exited the vehicle, heading into the house.

Walker opened the car door, feeling the rush of cool air upon her face. She lingered with one boot planted on the ground, wondering if she was stepping into quicksand.

Last night, her feelings for Payne had been so clear, and she had seen a gentleness in him. Now, it seemed like he was someone else. But as she mulled over recent events, she knew the inconsistency wasn't with him. All of her training with the FBI hadn't prepared her for breaking the law to suit the mission at hand. For outright killing of the guilty. For residing in the shadows and running solo apart from her own colleagues.

She glanced up at a passing cumulus cloud, unsure what was worse: that Payne and Alisa had their own fluid rules of engagement, or the uncomfortable realization that a small part of her was being drawn to their way of thinking.

CHAPTER 35
JACKSON HOLE, WYOMING

Vintage wines, German ale, imported cigars, and rare caviars were stacked on the lengthy kitchen floor and marble counter in the two-story estate as the waitstaff wheeled in the last shipment on dollies.

Nigel Colson did a cursory inspection of the items, seeing it matched the twelve dozen of each that he'd told his head chef to order. All of it amounted to a quarter of a million dollars in products, but Colson's accountant would barely register the expenditure. Besides, in Colson's world, it was par for the course. And the event in two days was going to be historic, so every facet of the weekend had been meticulously planned.

Entertaining diplomats and politicians had once been a weekly affair when he was the ambassador to Egypt. Afterwards, when he'd worked as an economic consultant throughout North Africa and the Middle East, he maintained his habit of hosting lavish banquets. Naturally gregarious, he cherished, and perhaps pathologically required, being in the spotlight. But the main reason for his sumptuous feasts was to strengthen his ties in the art world and expand his black-market network for acquiring antiquities.

Until recently, his business undertakings as an art collector had been going smoothly. But the brutal murder of his importer, Matthew Ellison, had created an undertow of anxiety that had put a halt to his overseas ventures. Temporarily. No one fucked with Nigel Colson or his daughter Brittany.

Nigel cracked open a crate containing Cuban cigars and removed a box, tucking it under his arm and heading down the hallway to the curved mahogany staircase. He walked briskly up to the second floor. At seventy-eight, he still had a punch to his gait, and his daily walks around the groomed paths on his one-hundred-eighty-acre property had kept him spry during the past two years of retirement.

He walked past the six other bedrooms and movie lounge, then entered his private den. The smell of dinner wafted over him, and he saw his head chef setting down a silver tray with a plate of Wagyu ribeye, roasted duck-fat potatoes, and truffled mushrooms, along with a dry martini.

"Leave it on the tray. I'll be pecking away at it while I'm working." He shot the man a plastic smile, his indication the servant should leave.

The portly chef retreated and disappeared down the hallway, leaving Colson in solitude in his immense office.

He set down the cigar box and grabbed the martini from the tray before opening the French doors onto the balcony and heading outside. The cool mountain air stung his face, but he found it energizing. He walked the length of the porch, occasionally leaning on the varnished teak railing and drinking in the vista of the Grand Tetons to the south. Every view from his various balconies on the thirteen-thousand-square-foot estate partook of the wilderness splendor that bordered the property on all four sides.

Colson's father, Edgar, had built the mansion after World War II, buying up parcels of land fourteen miles northwest of Jackson Hole. The structure was made from locally harvested ponderosa pines and river rocks, a visual tribute to the Western frontier. Over the years, it had been expanded upon, and it was one of the oldest and most renowned properties in a coveted region that had filled with Hollywood celebrities, doctors, lawyers and media moguls, many of whom had danced with Edgar Colson in the dark corners of black-market art deals.

He looked beyond the horse barn and planetarium and followed the movement of two black SUVs in the distance as they made their way along the three-mile serpentine road that wound through his property.

He sipped on his martini, watching the vehicles come to a halt below him near the side entrance. Brittany stepped out of the second vehicle while her six-man Secret Service detail trailed behind her into the estate.

Out of his three children, she was the only one who made him feel like there was hope for the Colson legacy. His other daughter was a pediatrician, more interested in her volunteer work abroad than in his empire; and his wispy son resided in Berkeley with his wife, both of them wasting their lives as professional dancers.

He finished his drink and set the glass down on the railing, hearing the clacking of his daughter's heels on the flooring. A second later, she stepped into his den and came up alongside him on the balcony. He waited for her to initiate a hug, then turned and embraced her. It was another of his micro-loyalty tests with those in his inner circle. He never offered a handshake or hugged first. They needed to make the effort, and then they had to wait, however briefly, for his response—for acceptance into his domain. And even when he reciprocated, he pulled the individual in towards him, as if they had been enveloped by his presence, a gift from a god to a mortal.

Except in his case, with this rare individual in his life, he actually relished his daughter's hug. It was the only time he ever truly let anyone beyond the prickly barriers erected around his soul.

"Good trip?"

She sighed, unzipping her leather coat. "Turbulent as hell, but then so is my life these days." She watched the waitstaff unload another truck of supplies near the far right corner of the estate. "What are the numbers attending the summit so far?"

"Forty-three guests along with their significant others. And everyone responded, which shouldn't be a big surprise since this is a landmark gathering of dignitaries that hasn't gone on in Jackson Hole since 1989."

"Except when my predecessor, James Baker, did it at his ranch back then, it was with the Russians. I think it was the only time I saw President Bush with a smile that filled his face. I wish I could have pulled off getting the Russians this week instead."

"This will be quite a feather in your cap, and your boss'. Having the crux of Middle Eastern leadership in the heart of the American West will be auspicious and will help further your efforts with the international arms agreement POTUS has worked so hard to solidify."

"You mean that I've worked so hard at. He just signed off on it." She clutched the railing with her pale hands.

He studied her face. "But this event isn't why you're tense, is it?"

She glanced back in the den, then moved closer to her father. "The Dresden situation has not been resolved yet. He's still out there. Still planning something. I know it. Especially after the message he sent with Ellison's murder and the senator's plane crash."

He rested his hand on hers. "Well, if he is, it won't impact us here. This property is outfitted with so many security measures and personnel that it could withstand a parachute brigade of commandos. Not to mention that Jackson Hole is about to be the epicenter for hundreds of federal agents and foreign security services. We're safe here, Brit."

"I'm not just concerned about an actual attack. The optics on this summit are critical. This has to go off without a hitch. It's about an arms agreement, for God's sake, and the irony of Dresden, my former arms dealer, being behind a potential attack would be the end of both our legacies and the president's."

He squeezed her hand. "I know it's who you are, but you can't control all the variables, no matter how much you try. This event will be smooth, and you will not only be on center stage during it, but in the annals of history afterwards. The things within your grasp right now are your composure and the image of strength you project to our guests. Focus on that, and let me and your security detail worry about the rest."

He tapped his knuckles on the railing. "I should have cut Dresden loose a long time ago, after he got things underway with my art-smuggling enterprise. I knew he was a wild card, but he knew how to get things done and had the black-market connections. My one regret is introducing you to him."

She frowned. "He was a necessary cog in what POTUS needed done in that region. I couldn't have pulled off arming the Niger rebels without him. And if that shipment of drones hadn't gone missing and turned up in Syria, then we wouldn't even be having this conversation, and I wouldn't be worried about having another ulcer."

"You said you spoke with Stratton about having a CIA

team handle Dresden—he seems like a capable lad from what I've heard, and he certainly has the resources."

"Stratton's a Boy Scout. I had to remind him that political appointments can be fleeting. But he knows POTUS will have his head on a platter if he doesn't eliminate Dresden."

"There you go. You can ease your mind, then. You are not only protected on many fronts but have the most powerful spy agency in the world hunting down the man. And soon, your bright, beautiful face will be on the cover of *TIME* and *Newsweek* as woman of the century."

She leaned in, entwining her hands around his arm. "Thank you for getting me this far. I couldn't have pulled this off without you."

"Getting *us* this far, my dear." He gazed towards the open doors. "I have something for you. Something to commemorate your achievement." He motioned for her to follow, both of them walking through the den and down the hallway. They proceeded down the steps, and she gestured for her head Secret Service agent to remain at his post near the bottom of the staircase as both Colsons moved past the spacious foyer and into the west wing of the estate.

Nigel stopped before the door to his personal library, pausing to remove a bronze key from his pants pocket before unlocking it. They headed inside and closed the door, Nigel twisting the deadbolt in place. Sunlight passing through the ornate stained-glass windows illuminated the thirty-by-thirty-foot room, which was filled with floor-to-ceiling bookcases made of bird's-eye maple and lined mainly with first editions from around the world.

Behind the central bookcase on the right lay the true heart of the Colson legacy—a vault that few beyond the family had ever seen. He slid back a leather-bound edition of *Crime and Punishment*, revealing a biometric and retinal scanner known only to Nigel and his daughter.

After his identity was authenticated, the bookcase swiveled inward, attached to a reinforced steel door. A short passage lined with motion, humidity, and heat sensors opened into a room whose walls were constructed with eighteen-inch reinforced concrete sandwiched between layers of hardened steel.

The wall to the right showcased what Nigel proudly called his "liberation collection"—artwork and artifacts that had disappeared from museums and private collections during periods of political unrest across North Africa and the Middle East.

On the left wall stood perhaps the most significant piece—a limestone bust of Nefertiti that Egyptian authorities had been searching for since it went missing during a transport between museums seven years ago, thanks to Dresden.

But the wall directly ahead contained what both father and daughter considered their personal life insurance policies —a series of fireproof filing cabinets and digital storage systems containing documents detailing American intelligence operations in eleven countries, with names of assets and operatives that would devastate US foreign policy if revealed. Nearby sat Brittany's contribution: a series of external hard drives containing intercepted communications with foreign governments that had never been shared with oversight committees, alongside records of weapons shipments diverted from their congressional-approved destinations.

Despite the small size of the room, it was the heart of the Colson empire—each stolen artifact and document representing a story of power wielded without constraint, protecting them from the accountability they had spent their lifetimes evading.

Nigel reached behind a leather recliner in the corner and removed a wrapped blue box.

She tore off the paper and flung it on the ground, then removed the lid. She pulled out a delicate Iznik pottery vessel, holding it up to the overhead lights and staring at the intricate tulip and carnation motifs, the vibrant glaze still intact after four centuries. Her mouth curved up in such an unfamiliar manner that it threatened to strain her facial muscles.

While Nigel revealed that he had acquired the item on a business trip last summer, he left out the part about how it had vanished during the cataloging of a Turkish private collection.

"Oh, I love it, Father." She squealed out the words, leaning her shoulder into his.

"I thought you might. It's for your office upstairs."

She stared at it for a few moments, rotating it and stroking the surface with her thumb, then returned it to the box. "Unfortunately, duty still calls. I need to take a shower, and then I have some online meetings to attend to for the evening. If you could have the chef bring me some dinner in my room, that would be amazing."

"Join me for breakfast tomorrow, then?" Nigel inquired.

"Yes, of course. After that, I need to go into town and pick up an order of two dozen custom-made cowboy hats from the dealer on Main Street. They're presents for the visiting heads of state."

"Have an aide handle that, my dear."

"I may have leaked it to a few journalists that I'll be in town. It will be a good prologue of media coverage for the summit." She gave him a hug.

He responded with a kiss on her forehead, another gift he rarely bestowed.

CHAPTER 36

ALISA WAS SEATED ON THE COUCH IN FRONT OF THE FIREPLACE, poring over the GPS data from Dwyer's vehicle while Darla was on the phone with her vet tech, going over tomorrow's schedule. Maize slept curled up next to her hip, occasionally glancing up at the commotion in the kitchen.

Payne and Kilkenny stood by the counter, inspecting the newly acquired rifles from the sheriff's arsenal as Payne recounted the Nazi museum in Dwyer's vault.

Harrison and Walker were engaged in a heated conversation on the back porch, and from what Payne could tell, it was connected with her wanting to notify her boss back in Seattle about recent findings. Harrison's body language was defiant, and Payne could only assume the senator was still determined to keep a low profile, but even Payne was beginning to think that someone outside of this circle should be notified about Dresden's potential plans. Of course, actual proof would be helpful, and right now they didn't have much to go on. Hopefully, that was about to change once Alisa narrowed down Dwyer's travel patterns.

Kilkenny relayed the information from the weapons on

his side of the kitchen island. "We've got a Ruger Mini-14 rifle, with four thirty-round mags of 5.56, an Uzi 9mm with six thirty-round mags, a 12-gauge Benelli shotgun with a bandolier of forty-two assorted slugs or buckshot, and a Saiga AK with three forty-round mags of 7.62."

"You've got me beat for sheer firepower," said Payne, running through his acquisitions. "A pair of next-gen night-vision goggles, a Remington 700 rifle in .308 with a pricey scope, a Marlin .22 rifle with a bull barrel, three tactical vests, two Glock 17s with a dozen mags, and a Kimber 1911 with ivory grips that probably cost more than the damn pistol."

Kilkenny grinned. "I'd leave that Kimber with me. It weighs too much."

Payne slid it towards him. "It's a safe queen and not something I'll use anyway." He pulled out his FN 5.7 pistol and removed the mag, then cleared the chamber before passing it to Kilkenny. "A Glock with more happy sticks will be a better bet than just a pistol with a lone mag."

"I'll treat her well," said Kilkenny.

Walker and Harrison came inside, both of them gathering around the counter. "Carrie agreed that she will hold off on contacting her boss in Seattle until we can scout the compound where Dresden is supposed to be. Last thing we need right now is to spook him by having a legion of feds showing up in Marple, in a town where he probably has lookouts."

"Sounds reasonable," said Payne, noting that Walker hadn't made eye contact with him since returning from Dwyer's.

Alisa came over, setting her tablet down and rubbing her temples. "The sheriff's GPS data shows him repeatedly going to a site thirty-one miles northeast of Marple. All the rest of his travel patterns are local within a mile or two of town, so that remote property must be the place."

"What's the nearest road?" asked Darla, getting up from the couch and joining the group.

Alisa enhanced the image, handing her the tablet.

The vet scanned the tangled array of county and forest service roads. She pointed to a blue line on the map. "This property is eleven miles upriver from where the majority of livestock poisonings have occurred. It's right on the Black River, which is the headwaters for numerous streams in the area."

Payne leaned in next to Darla. "Can you point out two routes we should consider using?"

She went over the details, mentioning road conditions and pullouts. "Keep in mind, I haven't been out that way in a long time. That's one of those areas most locals avoid due to all the checkerboard private and state holdings and the shitty roads, not to mention the 'subculture' of folks out in those parts."

"You can take my truck," said Kilkenny.

"I'll go get my boots," said Harrison.

Payne shook his head. "Not gonna happen, sir. It'll be me, Carrie and Alisa. Besides, like you said, this is just a scouting trip. We gather info on the layout of the compound and the numbers on-site, then we're back here, and Carrie gets on the horn with her agency."

The senator started to talk, but Payne raised a hand. "Too many good people have already been lost, and as your former bodyguard, I can't allow it. Sir."

Harrison ruffled out an exhale, folding his arms. "I'm ready to be done playing hermit in this cabin. After tonight, I need to get back to work. In the meantime, what can I do to be of use?"

Payne nodded towards the forest. "You can take these weapons out back with Kilkenny and fire off a few rounds from each to make sure they're runnin' smooth. After that, pack 'em all in the truck along with some water, chow and the first aid kit from the bathroom." He looked at Alisa and Walker. "I need to get my gear and a sandwich. Let's plan to leave in twenty minutes."

"We're driving out there in the dark?" asked Walker.

He slid the night-vision goggles towards her and pulled the Benelli closer. "You are. I'll be riding shotgun. Pun intended."

———

WHILE PAYNE and Kilkenny loaded up the Yukon, Walker exited the lodge and headed around back. She palmed the burner phone, debating whether to make the call. It had been long enough, and she was already overdue on checking in with her boss in Seattle.

She took in a deep breath of cold air and punched in the numbers.

Derek Mentzer picked up, speaking in a groggy tone.

"It's good to hear your voice, sir. Sorry for calling so late."

"Carrie…is that…is that you? What the hell? Are you alright? Where are you?"

"I'm holding up despite everything that's going on. And we've made some major inroads into what Senator Harrison was investigating. It's on a whole other level than what any of us out here could have imagined."

"Wait, slow down. Who's 'we'? You make it sound like it's more than just you and Payne."

She rubbed her aching neck. "You could say that. Some of Payne's old crew from the CIA are involved in tracking down a weapons shipment that left the Port of Seattle and is somehow connected with a potential terrorist attack in the US."

A pregnant pause followed, and then Mentzer replied in a voice devoid of weariness. "You've gotta give me more than that. Who are the players, and what's the intended target, for God's sake?"

"The player is a rogue CIA agent named Michael Dresden. He and a crew of mostly French Algerians are in league with a bunch of white supremacists in western Idaho. Payne, myself and one of his colleagues are actually heading out right now to recon their location, so I should be able to provide actual numbers of personnel and the property's layout shortly."

"Idaho...where exactly? I'll contact our office in Boise. They'll handle this, Carrie."

She shook her head, wishing she were face-to-face with the man. "No, this is happening on the outskirts of a small town that probably has a decent amount of locals in bed with the extremists. Plus, there's just no time. You have to trust me on this once more, sir."

She couldn't believe the way she sounded, asking him to buck the protocols and just let her wing it. Maybe Payne was rubbing off a little too much on her, but she also knew this was the only way, for now.

The man seethed out a breath. "This has been the biggest clusterfuck of a week since I began with the bureau. First, Fiche is killed; then Zhang melts down our entire network here. Now, you want to keep running a rogue undercover op...and it involves taking down some terrorists. You're really pushing my buttons."

"Wait, what do you mean about Zhang?"

"He was behind surveilling you and Fiche in the days leading up to those impostors showing up at the expo looking for Payne. And he tampered with the video footage from the rodeo grounds to make it look like Fiche wasn't taken out by a long-range sniper round." Another sigh followed. "Before Zhang disappeared, he left some malware on his computer, which infected everything in our building. We've been royally crippled here since you left, and I'm working around the clock with a digital forensics team out of Washington to unravel the damage he did, along with debriefing, via polygraph, I might add, everyone who works in our building. It's been a helluva week, and that was before I answered your fucking call."

Walker felt like she was trying to stay afloat in the same whirlpool that was conspiring to suck Mentzer down.

She watched Kilkenny slam the rear hatch of the Yukon and move back towards the lodge. "I gotta run, boss. And there's one more thing you should know: Senator James Harrison is alive. It was his bodyguard who was on that downed jet. Harrison's here with us, helping get to the bottom of an investigation into Dresden he started two years ago."

"Shit, Carrie, you could have led with that."

"Sorry, it's been a chaotic couple of days. I'll be in touch soon. I promise." She hung up before he could respond. She knew that was a horrible idea, just like she knew saying "sorry" multiple times to her superior wasn't a confidence builder for either party involved.

As she mentally prepared for what lay ahead, she knew a reckoning with Mentzer would be coming after the conclusion of this mission. She just wondered if her friendship with him, along with her career with the bureau, would survive the fallout of her actions.

CHAPTER 37

THE QUONSET HUT AT THE BACK OF THE BROTHERHOOD'S property was busy with activity as Dresden's six remaining French-Algerian mercs loaded up the utility vans for the road trip east. Giletti was busy doing a weapons check and gathering their personal gear, while Dresden and Keen were putting the finishing touches on the new fleet of weaponized drones on tables at the back of the building.

The gleaming carbon-fiber surfaces of the jet-shaped devices caught the harsh overhead lights, causing them to resemble dormant predators as Dresden gazed at the additions to his team.

The eighteen-inch-long drones had a wingspan of only twelve inches with a central cavity containing the palm-sized lithium battery Dresden had obtained from the Spokane facility. The sleek shape was driven by a single propeller mounted at the rear, while the nose section housed a tiny camera gimbal and the receiver that was linked to the handheld controls that the pilot would be using to fly them.

The undercarriage of the drone contained precision-engineered claws, resembling miniature mechanical talons, that carried the deadly payload of C-4.

Dresden stood patiently beside Keen, watching him insert the last brick of explosives into the remaining drone. It was something he'd seen the man do dozens of times in the past, but tonight it brought a sense of excitement laced with something else he couldn't quite pinpoint. It almost felt like relief, but he knew it was more than that.

For two years he'd waited for the time to arrive when he could strike back at the woman who had signed off on his death and the murder of his friends—and of Danielle and the future they could have had together. And when this whole thing was over, he was uncertain what would be left of his life. He had pushed away that thought for so long in favor of this singular objective, that the aftermath, assuming he was alive and not in shackles, was a big blank spot in his psyche.

While Dresden and the rest of his crew had evasion plans in place for separately fleeing the US after tomorrow's attack, he knew there would be no high-fives or celebration. Just new lives in foreign lands, while spending the rest of their days avoiding the public eye. After tomorrow, they would be hunted men. No one pulls off a devastating attack like they had planned and then spends quiet lives on a distant beach, enjoying the sunset.

For Dresden, the thought of going down in a hail of bullets was much preferred to hiding away for decades in some obscure village. He'd already endured hardship and agonizing loss, and he had no interest in continuing down that path. He recalled the saying one of his mentors used to mutter. *A man who has lost everything is the most dangerous person in the world.*

Dresden watched Keen's meticulous calibration of the drone, cognizant that the coming sunset tomorrow would not merely mark the conclusion of another of his tortured days on this earth, but the ending of the sociopolitical order he had once worked so hard to protect.

———

AN HOUR LATER, after the drones had been secured in padded containers in the three vans, along with several Yamasaki dirt bikes, Dresden joined his crew around a campfire behind the workshop.

Giletti handed him a cup with bourbon in it. Dresden glanced at the firelit faces of his team. In addition to Keen, there were six French-Algerian mercs who had been with him for years. Most of them had lost brothers or close friends in the missile strike in Syria, and their allegiance to Dresden went far beyond the money he'd been paying them.

He noticed Zhang sitting in the open door of one of the vans in the distance, doing something on his laptop. His absence from this gathering didn't bother Dresden. He was a paid instrument and didn't share their sense of duty and commitment to the cause.

Dresden spoke in French, recounting their struggles since that tragic day, their lost comrades, and the painstaking efforts to make it this far. When he finished, he held up his cup, gazing into each man's eyes and making a toast.

"Few pick up the sword. Even fewer care to wield it, and fewer still are those willing to strike down their enemies on the battlefield when the odds have turned against them and death is certain. But, you, my brothers, have done that countless times and never wavered. Here's to you and to those who were with us in Syria. You are what is best in a warrior."

———

From a distant ridgeline, Payne swept the night-vision scope around the property below while Walker and Alisa squatted beside him in the shrubs. The sound of heavy-metal music emanated from a building near the driveway.

He settled his eyes a hundred yards below. "I count eight skinheads hanging out on the front porch of the lodge by the trucks. They seem pretty hammered by the way they're staggering around."

Alisa leaned in. "There's some activity by the rear of that Quonset hut. Looks like a bonfire and shadows moving around, but I can't tell how many people." She pulled out her ruggedized tablet and examined the layout of the property based upon the last county assessment records she'd located online.

"The drones have to be in that hut," said Walker, peering through her night-vision goggles. "There's a pretty steep cliff along the right side that drops down to the river below, so we'll have to approach from the other direction."

He set the Remington 700 sniper rifle beside Alisa and swapped it out with her Saiga AK and mags, which he slid into his vest. "Walker and I will recon the Quonset hut. My first choice would be to disable the drones, but if that isn't possible, then we'll have to find a way to torch the place and everything in it."

Payne nodded towards the lodge, then looked at Alisa. "Wait for my hand signal. And we may need a distraction. A .308 round through that propane tank should do the trick."

"What are you talking about?" asked Walker. "You said we were only here to scout the place."

"That was the plan, but the vans are on the other side of the hut, so that must mean they're loading up. There's only four hours until sunrise, so they're probably going to use the cover of darkness to get out of the region."

"We're going to be picked apart if we go up against an armed group down there," Walker said.

"I have no desire to engage them. I just want to blow the shit out of that Quonset hut and the vans along with it."

CHAPTER 38

WALKER KEPT PACE BEHIND PAYNE AS THEY MADE THEIR WAY down the steep incline towards the Quonset hut. They moved from tree to tree, pausing briefly to scan for sentries before continuing their descent. The patchy wet snow muffled their footsteps but made for slow going as they tried to avoid slipping.

Arriving at a small storage shed, they stopped and studied the property again. All the activity still appeared to be by the cabin on the far left by the driveway entrance and the distant side of the Quonset hut.

"One guard by the side entrance of the building," Payne whispered, pointing towards the shadowy figure near a door of the metal structure.

Walker nodded, raising her Mini-14 and peering through the scope. "I count another guy patrolling on the far side."

They moved ahead, pausing again a minute later and crouching behind a fallen log fifty feet from the building. Payne studied the layout, noting the large rolling door on the south side that probably served as the main entrance. The muted voices of Dresden's French Algerians carried through the night air, punctuated by occasional laughter from the direction of the bonfire.

"I need to get inside that hut," Payne said. "If those drones are prepped for deployment, we've got to sabotage them before they can be launched."

"And if they're not there?"

"Then we'll make sure this place isn't useful for anything after tonight." He pointed to a bunch of red plastic gas cans near the side door beside a large generator. "After I see what's inside, we can use those to torch the place."

Payne focused on the sentry and removed his knife, a seven-inch fixed blade Kilkenny had lent him, though, after tonight, the old man might not want it back. He glanced at Walker. "Stay here and cover me until I give you a signal to head over. If something goes wrong, then hoof it back to Alisa, and both of you follow the route back to the truck."

She gripped his forearm. "We're all going back to the truck after this."

With a nod, he disappeared into the darkness, moving towards the east side by the cliff overlooking the river, where the shadows were deepest.

Payne reached the wall of the Quonset hut, pressing his back against the corrugated metal. He edged toward the corner, stopping by a stack of discarded boxes and listening to the guard laughing about something on his phone while taking occasional puffs on a cigarette.

Peering through gaps between the boxes, he noticed the guy standing beneath a dim exterior light just on the other side of a silent generator. The man was facing the driveway, his nose buried in his phone screen. Payne took a deep breath, clutched his knife tighter and slipped out from the shadows. He closed the eight-foot gap and rushed forward.

The guard barely had time to look up before Payne clamped his hand over his mouth, driving the blade into the base of his skull. The man went limp, his nervous system still causing his limbs to twitch slightly. Payne lowered him to the ground and dragged him into the darkness.

Payne entered the side door and slipped inside. The interior was surprisingly well lit, with rows of workbenches on the left side. Along the wall beside him was another bench, a trailer with welding equipment, and empty storage crates tipped over alongside a large pile of broken rocks next to what looked like an industrial-sized 3D printer.

He skirted past the long workbench, pausing to gaze down into a twelve-inch-diameter hole in the middle. It had a coarse screen glued over the top. Payne could hear the gurgle of water below and figured it was where they dumped their waste by-products from the 3D printer into the river.

Darla's ground zero.

Payne worked his way down to the printer, examining the laser-cut remnants of carbon-fiber panels piled in a heap on the workstation. He held up several pieces, studying the outline of the components that had been manufactured. It reminded him of the plastic cutouts for airplane models he'd built as a kid but on a scale ten times the size.

He set down the junk, noticing an angular white object protruding from under the refuse. He pulled it out, marveling at the foam prototype of a drone. It was roughly eighteen inches long with a wingspan of twelve inches. The design was unlike anything he'd seen before, and was clearly engineered like a falcon for speed and maneuverability.

He set it down and scanned the other items. Jeweler's glasses, an array of tiny screwdrivers, and stacks of fine-grit sandpaper that he figured were all used to shape and polish the completed carbon-fiber hulls of the drones for less drag.

Whoever built them really wants them faster than an ordinary drone and able to cope with excessive wind shear.

The real find came when he plucked a small leather journal off the top shelf. Flipping through it, he saw notes in French coupled with trigonometry equations and sketches of dozens of trajectories between drawings of mountains.

Payne tucked the journal into his vest and headed deeper into the building, making his way to the opposite bay door. He peered through the corner of the window, seeing eight men standing around the bonfire. Twenty feet to the left were three white vans whose rear doors were ajar, and Payne could make out dozens of elongated plastic crates inside, along with several dirt bikes.

He glanced back at the workbenches, not seeing any other drones besides the prototype by the printer. *They're ready to roll, like I thought. This needs to end here.*

Payne retraced his steps back to the side door and stepped out. The heavy-metal music by the front cabin hadn't let up, and he could still see the skinheads on the front porch, most of them glued to a movie on the large TV screen they'd set on top of two coolers.

He glanced in the direction of Walker and waved her over. He returned his blade to the sheath and now began grabbing gas cans. Only three were full, and he carried them inside the hut, heading to the far corner that was closest to the vans outside.

Just before he was about to pour out the first gas can on some empty pallets, he saw it. The pink hue on the ground beside the rock piles. He stepped closer, picking up one of the halved specimens. He was shocked at the weight, expecting it to be heavier. It was made of some kind of synthetic material resembling a realistic specimen. Inside were white flecks of a claylike substance. One whiff told him it was C-4. He glanced around at the hundreds of discarded shells, his pulse quickening.

They must have a few hundred pounds of explosives at this compound.

He grabbed a gas can and doused the rock pile instead.

The side door opened, and Walker entered, trotting up beside him.

"Just watch the entrances while I finish what I started," he said.

Walker took up a position near the north bay door, peering out towards the campfire. "What about the skinheads at the lodge? They're going to see us on our way back along the ridge if this place is lit up."

"I'm going to set a fuse of sorts, so we'll have a little bit of time to get back to Alisa." He finished dumping the last can and ran to the other side of the hut. He hopped up on the flatbed trailer with the welding equipment, turning the dial on the argon gas tank. He grabbed the sparking tool and ignited the end of the arc welder, averting his eyes from the intense flame. Payne set it on the ground in the direction of the stream of gas that was trickling across the pavement.

He removed the AK slung on his back and motioned for Walker to follow, both of them trotting back to the side entrance. After peering through the window, he stepped outside and moved back past the generator and up the slope.

A sudden burst of gunfire shattered the quiet. Both of them froze behind some trees, exchanging alarmed glances as the bark around them splintered apart. Payne squatted, peering out long enough to see one of Dresden's men standing by his dead compatriot.

"I'll cover you," he said. "We need to get the hell away from this hut, and now." He leaned out, firing off a burst of rounds that strafed the side of the building, sparks flying off the exterior wall as Walker bolted along the ridge.

The guard responded, moving behind some empty barrels and peppering the trees above Payne's head.

Payne heard men shouting by the campfire and the sound of the vans starting. *Shit, I need this building to blow.*

He waited a few more seconds for Walker to gain some distance; then he lowered further to the ground. More shooters had emerged from the main lodge, and a group of skinheads were firing blindly from the front of the Quonset hut, following the lead of the guard by the barrels.

Payne elbow-crawled ten feet to his right, concealing himself behind a chair-sized rock and pressing his body into the wet earth. He was on the downward slope of the cliff that led to the river. He just hoped the angle and the rock cover would provide enough protection for what came next. The trees around him were splintering apart now, bark and wood slivers raining down on his back. He slid the AK barrel forward, focusing his front sight on the gas generator near the side door, sixty feet below.

The AK barked out two rounds. The explosion took out the guard near the barrels, tearing through the bottom portion of the hut. Payne slid back, balling up and covering his ears as he pressed his back into the rock.

The second blast from the gas inside the building shattered the night air, sending a shock wave that Payne felt through his ribs. It tore through the roof of the hut, sending metal shrapnel in every direction. The flames that shot out either side of the bay doors resembled orange pythons racing towards the victims in their paths. Six skinheads and two of Dresden's men were incinerated in seconds.

Payne saw a steel sliver the size of a two-by-four land near where he was previously standing, the pine tree's green needles now blackened. He propped himself up, glancing towards the north side of the hut's bay door. Or where it had been. One van had been toppled on its side, and a charred corpse was lying near the mangled door of the driver's side. The other two vans were gone.

He moved up into a squat and crouch-walked to where Walker had gone, darting from shadow to shadow as the flames flickered against the forest. Then he stopped and glanced back at the smoldering van, remembering it had been filled with crates. Crates that probably had drones loaded with C-4.

Payne skipped concealing himself, sprinting along the ridge and making a beeline back to Alisa. Seeing Walker ahead, he waved and shouted, "Run! It's not over."

"What'd you do now?" she shouted as they bounded through the forest.

"Get ready for round three."

The van explosion dwarfed the previous blasts. Payne and Walker dove behind a fridge-sized boulder. He threw himself over her as another shock wave rippled through the trees.

This time, he was sure there wouldn't be a building left standing.

———

DRESDEN DROVE for another mile and stopped the van. He left it idling and got out, heading to the vehicle behind him. The paint on the side of the van was glazed over and slightly charred near the rear bumper, and he was shocked at how close they'd come to losing everything, including their lives.

He leaned in the driver's open window of the second vehicle, glancing at his three men inside and then over at Zhang, whose face had grown a shade paler. "You guys good?"

"Yeah, but we lost Anton, Theo and Luis," replied Keen, who had a white-knuckle grip on the steering wheel.

Dresden glanced back at the orange glow to the southeast.

"Fuck!" He stomped his heel down on a stone, driving it into the ground. "We've still got enough drones to complete this. Let's split up, like we intended. Both of our routes will take five hours. Plan on stopping twice to swap out business signs and skins." He glanced into Keen's bloodshot eyes. "See you at the rendezvous site by 9 a.m."

CHAPTER 39

AFTER THE TIRING WALK BACK TO KILKENNY'S YUKON, IT TOOK ninety minutes for Payne and the others to reach the rental house, sticking to the back roads again. And once more, they assembled in the kitchen, going over the night's events and their findings at the Brotherhood's property.

"Well, this town just got a whole lot safer," said Darla.

"Everyone just loves the Wild West justice that appears in Payne's wake, it seems," quipped Walker.

"Dresden is still bent on his own justice—any ideas on where he might be heading?" asked Payne as he glanced at the other faces.

"Got any favors you can call in at the NSA?" asked Alisa as she looked at the senator.

"I wish. Even if I did, I'm sure it would trickle back to POTUS, and he would shut it down. He's not going to want anything related to Dresden coming to light."

"It's going to get aired all over the internet if we don't stop him," said Walker.

"They took off in vans, so that means they were either planning on a nearby target, or they were going to load the drones onto a plane and fly to it," said Alisa, who was pacing around the living room as Maize followed her.

"Is there anything of significance happening in DC, outside of the norm, that Dresden could be targeting?" asked Walker while gazing over at the senator.

Harrison shrugged his shoulders. "Great question. If there is, I'm not privy to it. Although Colson was supposed to be involved with an international summit this month. Most likely in DC, of course. She's probably been instructed to keep that on a need-to-know basis, especially given all the foreign dignitaries flying in. Events of that nature usually aren't even broadcast to the public until the night before, when the journalists arrive and are allowed to set up."

"Maybe it's time to come out of the shadows, Senator," said Walker.

Payne grabbed the leather journal from his dirty vest and tossed it on the counter. "This might help."

IT WAS another three hours before Alisa and Payne had translated the French notes, but it was what she discovered from the flight trajectory calculations and wind-shear data that allowed her to pinpoint the target's location.

By now, everyone else was asleep on the couches or recliners. Payne poured himself another cup of coffee, knowing that rest was nowhere in his immediate future. He roused the others and set down the fresh coffee pot on the living room table by the fireplace, along with five mugs.

"Good news?" asked Walker, rubbing her eyes. Even with her groggy expression and tousled hair, Payne could still stare at her all day.

He sat down beside her, nodding to the dozens of pieces of Alisa's notes spread around the table. "Using the vector formulas found in the journal, along with altitude and weather data from the weather service database online, Alisa determined that the attack must be slated for a region around the Grand Tetons. Since the only thing of significance there, population-wise, is Jackson Hole, that must be the target."

He glanced at the senator, noticing the man's flat expression. "The summit is taking place there. It's been on the news," said Payne.

"That's right—the Colsons have an estate there, as I recall." He said it in a terse manner, then grabbed a mug and poured his coffee.

Payne glanced at his watch. "Dresden's already gotten a head start. He could even be staging in the area right now. And with the drone design I saw, he could be set up thirty miles away, outside of the Secret Service security perimeter. We need to get to Jackson Hole before he unleashes those weapons."

Alisa swiveled towards Kilkenny. "You any good at flying that bird of yours at the airfield?"

The older man glanced at his daughter, then down at the golden retriever curled up next to her. "Maize seems to think so."

CHAPTER 40

PAYNE STARED OUT THE WINDOW OF THE CHARTER CITATION CJ2 jet, wondering how Kilkenny had managed to hit every air pocket since they'd left Marple. The six-seater would have normally been a luxury ride compared to the cargo and military planes he'd been on during his many government-sponsored trips around the world, but the dog hair floating around the cabin coupled with the pilot's flying was aggravating his headache.

"There's one thing that's been bothering me since I arrived in Idaho," said Alisa, who was sitting across from him, while Harrison and Walker were on the opposite side of the tiny aisle. "Those two semitrucks that passed through Marple a few days ago to deliver the shipment from Seattle... remember I said that they passed back through again later that morning after what we know now was from dropping off their payload at the skinheads' compound."

She swiveled her seat towards Harrison. "You told me when I first started helping you that Whitmore had noticed a discrepancy with two other shipping containers arriving along the same route through Jakarta, which is what first tipped you off that there might be a potential connection with your Algerian investigation from two years ago."

"I'm not following," said the senator. "What does this have to do with a potential drone attack?"

Alisa fixed her gaze on Payne. "Did the supplies and remnants of materials in that Quonset hut reflect four or more semitrucks' worth of items?"

Payne and Walker exchanged nervous glances. "Far from it," he said. "I'd say maybe one eighteen-wheeler's worth of goods, and that would include the drones that were in the vans."

The air in the cabin suddenly grew heavy, and Payne was certain it wasn't from a climb in altitude. "So somewhere out there are two semitrucks loaded with—what—more C-4?"

Alisa turned her tablet around, showing the time-stamped image of the trucks from three days ago as they passed south through Marple. "They could be anywhere by now."

Harrison leaned in towards her. "Let me have your burner phone. I need to get a hold of Homeland Security. This has gotten much bigger than just a personal attack on Colson."

———

ANDRE BOUCHER'S alarm jolted him awake. He shoved the sleeping bag off him and quickly sat up in the sleeper cab of the semitruck, putting on his boots and a ball cap as beads of condensation dripped down on his neck. He opened the mini-fridge under his bed and pulled out a can of double-shot espresso and a ham sandwich. These he placed on the front seat of the rig.

He closed the black privacy curtains and pulled out an empty Gatorade bottle to relieve himself in. Two days of living inside the semi had made him and his surroundings smell like a locker room. But he had experienced far worse in urban observation hides in North African cities during his many years working under Dresden, in the days before his sister Danielle perished in the blast in Syria and his world had unraveled. Now the Americans would feel something similar, but on a scale that not even their pricey high-def TVs could ever capture.

Boucher finished and screwed the lid back on the bottle, placing it in the Styrofoam cooler on the floor. He zipped up, then dabbed hand sanitizer on his palms before climbing into the driver's seat. Most of the other rigs had left the overnight lot next to the truck stop, but there were still plenty of stragglers around him, so he didn't stick out.

It didn't matter if he lingered a while this morning, since his upcoming destination was only thirty-eight miles to the southeast. His older brother, Gabriel, was behind the wheel of a similar truck some nineteen miles to the northwest and would soon be moving into position at another location.

Thankfully, it would be the last time either of them would be chained to their rigs. And the first and last time they'd ever be in this country.

Andre started the engine, letting it idle while he ate his breakfast, feeling like the two thousand pounds of plastic explosives in the cargo hold were pressing against his back.

CHAPTER 41

FROM HIS VANTAGE POINT ON THE NINE-THOUSAND-FOOT mountain, Dresden could take in a three-hundred-and-sixty-degree view that felt like it reached all the way to Canada. An ocean of conifer trees extended in three directions, while a vast prairie dotted with patches of snow occupied the area to the south that led to Jackson Hole.

The town was nine miles distant, but it was the old log mansion four miles to the east that his eyes fixated upon. It stood alone, carved from the forest nearly seventy-five years ago and expanded to its present, spacious form, which made it appear like an abnormal blight that had sprung from the earth.

Dresden had only seen it on satellite photos and studied the layout from blueprints, but he felt like he was staring at a place he knew better than any other in his life.

The particular location below had been revealed to him years ago after he'd GPS-tagged some of the crates of stolen artwork bound for the US and tracked them to Colson's property. Initially, it had been done out of curiosity, seeing what he had been risking his life for, but later he looked upon it as insurance for blackmailing the former ambassador if he ever tried to threaten Dresden or his crew. Little did he know the information would culminate in the coming attack.

A cold breeze swept up from the valley, bringing with it the scent of elk mingled with the aroma of spruce trees. In another reality, he would have found this to be a paradise for hunting wild game, but his quarry was of the two-legged variety, and he'd waited so long for this hunt to begin.

He returned to the vans, helping Giletti offload the three Yamasaki dirt bikes. Each would carry two individuals and were the escape vehicles for the mission's end. His three other men were carefully removing the drones from their padded cargo crates. These would be arranged alongside one another, with eight of the ten planned for other estates to the south while the remainder were pointed on precise trajectories to the east.

Zhang sat with his laptop on a foldout camp chair near the weather service building. When Dresden had finished with the dirt bikes, he walked over to the cyber guru, standing behind his left shoulder and peering at the satellite images around Jackson Hole.

"How many personnel at the Colsons' ranch?" Dresden asked.

Zhang pulled up a minimized screen that showed numerous red blips on the property. "Thermal imagery indicates fourteen individuals. Two of those appear to be some of the Secret Service detail doing sweeps on the outside of the mansion, while the others inside are mainly situated around the kitchen and dining room, so I assume those are the staff."

He enhanced the master bedroom on the second floor, pointing to a single red dot. "This guy has alternated between his room and the adjacent porch since we arrived."

"Has to be Brittany's old man, Nigel. Probably waiting for

the sun to go down so his flesh doesn't burn. Speaking of that coffin witch, where is she?"

Zhang returned to his original screen, showing the layout of the roads south of Jackson Hole. He enhanced the map, zooming in on real-time footage of two black Suburbans parked along Main Street. "From the inventory list I hacked into at that Old West store, she's picking up two dozen cowboy hats worth nine grand."

"Sounds like a cry for help," said Dresden. He waved his hand out to the valley below. "Looks like you'll have quite a seat. Just make sure to put a blanket over the comms in this region ten minutes before the allotted time."

"Copy that." Zhang glanced at the Colsons' mansion in the distance. "With all the logs in that place, it should go up like a bonfire in June."

"That's the plan. The first phase, anyway."

He whistled in the direction of Giletti; the lanky operator responded with a nod as he grabbed two suppressed MK12s from the van and leaned them by the bikes.

"You've done an excellent job tracking Colson's whereabouts these past few days. We're all grateful for your services, Marcus." Dresden patted Zhang on the shoulder. "Once this day is over, the rest of your funds will be wired over; then you're free to go your own way."

"I appreciate that, sir. Anytime you need another job in the future, I'll be a call away."

He nodded. "After today, my list of objectives will be nearly nonexistent. But then again, the future is very malleable at this point."

Dresden moved to the open passenger door in the lead van. Keen was seated inside like he was prepping for a space launch. Around his neck was an FPV headset that was connected to the leads extending to the handheld controls in his lap. The headset would allow him to maneuver the kamikaze drone and view what it saw through the forward-facing camera right up until the moment of impact.

"Everything's ready, my friend," said Keen, the sun on his mottled skin already causing the old burn marks to swell.

"After it's done, don't wait around here for us."

Keen nodded and extended a hand.

Dresden pulled him closer for a hug. "See you in the next world, brother."

CHAPTER 42

Brittany Colson was never so grateful to leave Jackson Hole. The short shopping trip to a local Western outfitter had been essential and provided her with some brief media exposure, but she was ready to get back to the estate and enjoy her last day of quiet before the summit tomorrow.

Her bodyguards loaded the boxes with the custom-made Stetson cowboy hats into the rear of the black Suburban while she settled into her seat in the middle row.

She twisted around, ensuring that her Secret Service cyborgs were careful with the hats, which were made from premium beaver fur and were going to be presented as gifts to several prominent heads of state from the Middle East.

The two bodyguards returned to the vehicle, with one sitting near her and the other riding shotgun. The driver radioed to the companion Suburban parked at the front that they were ready to return to the ranch.

Since her father had been an ambassador, she had been surrounded by armed Neanderthals in suits and shades. It went with the territory, and most of the time she was oblivious to the extra appendages shadowing her every move. But these next few days were different, and her normal four-person detail had been doubled, with several staked out at the estate. A historic meeting with visiting dignitaries from the Middle East, Africa and Europe would forever cement her status as the most accomplished Secretary of State the nation had ever known, so she would tolerate the extra muscle for now.

As the convoy drove north of town, she rubbed her sweaty palms along her navy slacks. Her diazepam was wearing off and a trickle of anxiety returning. She tried to convince herself the summit was the sole reason for the excitement and adrenaline, though she was sure the latter was coursing through her veins for the one loose end that hadn't been tied up yet.

Once the outskirts of the city were left behind, the procession moved along the winding road through the forest. Seeing the sea of evergreens on the mountaintops eased the tension in her neck. She glanced out the window at a fast-moving stream parallel to the narrow two-lane road, recalling an afternoon of horseback riding with her father last summer.

A bump in the road jarred her back to reality. She drummed a finger on the leather seat, then slid out her iPhone, calling Stratton's personal number at Langley.

The man took three rings to answer. "If you're calling for an update, my analyst is currently working on something promising," the director said in a bored voice.

"Unacceptable. You should have already wrapped this thing up by now. For God's sake, you and your people target and eliminate threats for a living. Am I missing something?"

"Dresden has proved more elusive than expected. Right now, I assume he's—"

"The word 'assume' doesn't mesh with your job title. But shit-canned and blacklisted do if you don't get this done. I'm twenty-four hours away from the meeting at my estate. The other diplomats are arriving soon. You know what's at stake, yet you sit on your fucking hands."

"It's not like I can get a Predator drone in the air or shut down the interstate. This isn't Kabul or Tikrit."

"Maybe I didn't make myself clear before, but you can skip the posse comitatus bullshit. If a Predator is needed, then make it happen. You have a garrison of lawyers at your disposal, so figure out the low guy on the fucking totem pole you're going to hang this on and get it done."

She ended the call, her head pounding as much from the elevation change from the East Coast as from the lack of sleep this past week. She wasn't sure if Stratton was really that in the dark about Dresden's location or if he was holding back from revealing his whereabouts. She removed the bottle of diazepam from her pocket and dry-swallowed half a tablet.

From the sight of the approaching tunnel under the two-lane bridge ahead, she knew they'd be pulling up to the family estate in fifteen minutes. Then she could relax. At least until tomorrow when she'd be putting on her game face.

And hopefully Dresden will be nothing but ashes by then. That bastard. This is my moment. He can rot in hell.

As the two Suburbans slowed and entered the twenty-foot-long tunnel under the road, she felt the vehicle vibrate, then shudder as the lead SUV exploded in a ball of red flame.

CHAPTER 43

HER DRIVER SLAMMED ON THE BRAKES AND PUT IT IN REVERSE, the other agents barking orders into their ear mics.

Her Suburban only retreated five feet before the ground exploded, sending rocks and a cloud of dirt into the air. Colson felt like her organs had just turned to jelly, her ribs rattling from the intense blast. She wanted to vomit, the meds being overridden by sheer terror.

"Hold on," yelled her driver, who drove forward a few feet toward the flaming wreck, then quickly backed up, but immediately stopped as they all stared back at the jagged hole in the ground blocking their retreat.

She glanced at the normally stoic faces of the remaining three agents inside with her as they clutched their MP7 rifles, which had been concealed under their jackets. "Comms are down," said the senior agent in the passenger's seat. "We're trapped."

Colson was about to scream at the man to do something. Anything. Then she saw it. A figure emerging from the side of the flaming shell of the lead vehicle alongside the tunnel walls. He was wearing body armor from head to toe and a ballistic helmet with a tinted visor that resembled a welder's headdress.

The man paused a few feet from the hood, leveling a black shotgun with an extended magazine.

CHAPTER 44

DRESDEN DUMPED HIS THIRD 12-GAUGE SLUG INTO THE Suburban's front hood near the release. Giletti and two of his men were standing on either side of the vehicle with their MK12s pointed at the side doors. There was little point in firing at the ballistic glass, but it prevented the agents inside from thinking about stepping out with flash-bangs, foolish as that would seem.

He lowered his weapon, letting it hang off its shoulder sling, then grabbed the hood and pushed it up. He retrieved his weapon again and dumped six QB-8 buckshot rounds into a thumb-sized gap in the ballistic insulation where a conduit of wiring extended into the interior just above the brake pedal. The specialized steel buckshot punched a baseball-sized hole in the barrier.

He set his Mossberg 590M shotgun down on the side of the engine and removed a narrow smoke grenade, pulling the pin, then leaning over the side of the engine block, shoving it into the jagged hole. He grabbed his shotgun and stepped back, watching the interior fill with reddish-gray haze as the pepper-spray solution dispersed.

A few seconds later, the doors opened. The security detail inside never had a chance and were quickly dispatched by Giletti and the other mercs.

Dresden moved to the rear door, grabbing Colson's arm and yanking her out. He shoved the gagging woman to the ground and sent his boot into her ribs.

"Brittany, I hope you got my RSVP for the summit."

CHAPTER 45

KILKENNY BROUGHT THE CITATION CJ2 JET TO A STOP AT THE FAR
end of the runway, then turned to the east and drove it into
an open hangar.

Harrison descended the steps first, stopping at the bottom
and shaking hands with a thirty-something man in a black
suit. "Jenkins, right?" he asked the Secret Service agent. "You
served on my protective detail a few months back when
Reggie was out sick."

"That's right, sir." He looked over the senator's shoulder
at the four other people disembarking the jet. "You wouldn't
believe my surprise, and my relief, when my boss called and
told me you were coming here...that you were alive. Glad to
see you, sir."

"Thanks, buddy. I appreciate that. Your boss probably also
told you about what I relayed to him and the items we need?"
Harrison asked as Payne and the others gathered around him.

"Yes, sir. He said you would require some wheels and an
escort. I can get you an SUV, but all of our units and the local
SWAT and DHS guys have been pulled away to the south.
There was a massive explosion at a fertilizer plant about

twenty miles outside of Jackson Hole. Surprised you didn't see it upon arrival."

"We were in the clouds until just before touchdown, son, but that sounds like a helluva problem," said Kilkenny.

"Dresden's trying to drain off the first responders from the north end," said Payne. He moved closer to the man. "Got those keys? We need to get going."

The agent thrust his chin towards a black SUV in the right corner of the hangar. "On the front seat." He walked with them to the vehicle. "You won't get very far on a lot of the main roads except on the interstate to the east and west. Everything else around Secretary of State Colson's place was supposed to be sealed off by now, but there've been some comms issues, so I'm not sure on the status."

Harrison replied, "When you get through to your boss, tell him we're coming onto the property, but we'll be staying out of their way at the estate. And trust me, he's going to want us nearby."

Once the agent departed, Payne and Walker trotted back up to the Citation jet and removed the duffel bags full of weapons. Payne just hoped it would be enough.

CHAPTER 46

AFTER BEING DRAGGED THROUGH THE WOODS, BRITTANY COLSON was shoved to the ground again, landing beside a fallen aspen tree. She felt like her head was the size of a bowling ball as she struggled to open her burning eyes. The lingering effects of the pepper spray were causing a continual blur despite her flowing tears.

The hazy image of a large, black bird overhead slowly came into view, and she wondered, prayed even, if she was lying on a recliner on the upstairs porch at her estate, enduring a nightmare.

The image came into focus, and the supposed raven turned out to be a man in black body armor, removing his dark helmet. The scarred cheek was something new, but recognition of the familiar face caused her heart to punch against her ribs. She thought she'd pass out again. Or vomit. Then a hand passed in front of her nose, and smelling salts assailed her senses, causing her to arch up.

"Brittany, or I mean Madam Secretary, you haven't aged a day since I last saw you." The gravelly voice of the man penetrated her weary brain.

She slid back, pressing into the log. Her eyes darted wildly around, the road and her Suburban nowhere in sight. "You son of a bitch. I'll see you live a long life at a black site in Yemen or some other shithole for this."

Dresden smiled. He glanced at the three men in black to his right, who were standing in defensive positions with their rifles aimed at the forest, all of them chuckling momentarily.

"Hear that, boys, we're gonna be shipped off to Yemen. I hope it's along the coast and comes with a view of the Red Sea."

He sent a boot into her ribs again. She was sure something cracked. She leaned over and began vomiting, a coppery taste mixing in with the bile.

Dresden squatted down, grabbing her brunette hair, which had come free from its bun. He yanked her into an upright position, then removed a tattered photo from his vest and placed it in her right hand.

She held it up, staring at the image of a thirty-something woman with blue eyes and freckles, her blonde hair tousled about her tan shoulders. She reminded Colson of the minority of Anglo explorers she'd seen around North Africa. People of French or German descent who ran some of the hotels and cafés in Tunis and Casablanca. Only she had a weathered look like someone who had spent her days living under open skies.

She handed it back to him. "A colleague of yours. Let me guess, she was part of your ill-fated cadre who ventured into Syria. And you blame me, is that it?"

He smacked her across the cheek. "You've got some nerve playing the 'not me' card. But then you and your old man were always good at dodging responsibility for your actions, regardless of the devastation in your wake."

"I'd offer to pay you, just like old times, but you won't live long enough to spend it. This county is one of the most heavily armed places outside of DC right now, given tomorrow's event. You'll be in cuffs by nightfall."

"You're assuming escape is in my plan."

His words sent an icy chill down her spine. She glanced around the forest, then up at the skies, but there was no rapid-response team on the way. Then she realized they had been attacked just outside the carefully constructed security perimeter her father had created. And as far as he knew, she was still shopping in town.

She needed to stall. She had to get him talking about his grievances, even if that meant enduring a beating. *He must want something, or I'd be dead by now.*

Dresden grabbed her by the arm and hoisted her to her feet. "Let's take a hike. There's something you need to see."

"You're insane. I'm not going anywhere. Within the hour, you and your pathetic group will be surrounded or dead."

He put a pair of zip ties on her wrists and cinched them down until they cut into the skin. "I promise, this isn't a show you'll want to miss."

THE HIKE only took ten minutes of uphill trekking through a sparse forest of pines and spruce. Cresting the top, Dresden paused and sucked in a lungful of cool mountain air. "They say that people born at higher elevations live longer and have a higher red-blood cell count than those at sea level."

"Fascinating," Colson replied, her chest heaving from the exertion. "You always were as sharp as a marble."

He rested his hand on the back of her neck and squeezed until she winced. "You grew up here, as I recall...or was it at one of your daddy's other posh estates in Belize or Spain?"

He pointed to the log mansion below a few miles to the northeast. "Nah, I know it was here. I know because this is where your old man always kept his collection of stolen art and antiquities. You remember, the ones I helped smuggle out of Algeria for years."

"And you were paid for your services, beyond anything you could have possibly made at the agency."

He let go of her neck, stepping around to face her. "You know, I put aside those funds, planning to buy a small beach house in Thailand with the woman in that photo. Danielle, that was her name." He slid forward, grabbing Colson's chin. "I want you to say her name."

Colson looked like a caged animal, the color draining from her face. "Danielle."

Dresden released her. "Simple things in life: a place to call home, good food and wine, friends who have your back, and someone to share your life with. Most of those things are probably foreign to a creature like you, but it's what me and my friends wanted; what Danielle and I wanted for ourselves. You took that away from all of us. From me."

He grinned. "I had my tech guy do a deep dive on the building schematics of your daddy's place here. It seems old Nigel did a lot of retrofitting on the main level in his library. He built quite a vault there to protect his holdings. I was impressed. It's quite an engineering feat but nothing a weaponized drone with a shitload of C-4 can't handle."

Dresden removed a small tablet from his BDU pocket and tapped on the screen, turning it around and showing her a red blip on the blueprints. "And it looks like Nigel is in his library as we speak, probably checking out the vault since I had my hacker trip the humidity alarm inside."

She gasped, reaching for his arm with her bound hands, but Giletti pulled her back. "No, please. You don't have to do this," she said. "There must be something…some amount of money, or immunity for you and your men…something you all want."

Dresden tapped on his earpiece, calling Keen. "Send it."

He held up the photo of Danielle and another with his old teammates. "Your fate was sealed long ago, Brittany. Now you'll know what it's like to truly have your world shattered."

Everyone looked up at the sight of four drones racing toward their target, the birdsong in the trees disappearing.

A few seconds later, he watched the first drone strike, the west end of the estate splintering into a thousand pieces as debris and glass formed a gray-orange blaze that billowed skyward.

He turned, watching the flicker of flames dance in Colson's teary eyes as the next drones hit their targets.

CHAPTER 47

PAYNE BROUGHT THE SUV TO A SCREECHING HALT ON THE DIRT road, staring at the smoking wreckage of a mangled Suburban and an intact one at the rear whose doors were wide open.

"God, we're too late," said Walker.

Payne backed up forty feet towards a cluster of thick pine trees. All of them quickly exited, grabbing the assorted rifles from the back cargo hatch and taking up defensive positions around the vehicle.

"There should be a shitload of Secret Service agents swarming this area," said Harrison.

"Jenkins said comms were down, so Dresden must have put a net over the region," said Alisa.

Payne glanced over at Kilkenny, who was struggling to be on his knees. "You got a bird's-eye view as we flew in...was there anything that stood out as far as nearby peaks that could be used as a staging area, besides the Grand Tetons?"

"Yeah, like about forty of 'em. All of them were covered in snow except a couple."

"Which ones?"

The old man got his bearings using the sun, then thrust his fingers to the left. "There's a National Weather Service tower not far from here. Has lots of repeater towers, probably some of which are also used by the airport. Those towers are often on lower-elevation mountains or hilltops so the snow isn't an issue right now."

Alisa nodded, keeping the Uzi focused on the trees across the road. "Their hacker is going to be able to use the signal from those towers to bounce off of, for setting up a comms blackout in the area."

"Walker and I will inspect the Suburbans and see if we can pick up Dresden's trail while the rest of you stay in this area and try to locate that weather service tower."

Payne grabbed the rest of the mags for the Saiga AK and slid them into his vest while Walker did the same for her Mini-14. He tossed Alisa the keys to the SUV; then he and Walker skirted through the woods, trotting parallel to the dirt road turned war zone.

Approaching the vehicles, Payne raised a fist, he and Walker pausing and staring up at the four drones soaring across the sky. A rumble of explosions filled the air to their right, as if a crack in the earth had just formed. He knew the sound and the resulting aftermath too well.

A second later his thoughts were confirmed as a blood-orange ball of flame erupted east of their location.

"Shit, did the Colson place just take a direct hit, or do you think the vehicles or grounds were targeted?" asked Walker.

"Cars and bare ground have a different ring to them. That was a pretty significant charge of explosives taking out a building or buildings." He surveyed the smoking tunnel and the interior of the derelict vehicle at the rear.

Heading inside the tunnel, he pulled his shirt collar over his nose as the sickening odor of charred flesh and burnt metal wafted over them. They stared at the blackened corpses in the mangled Suburban from a distance, then glanced inside the rear SUV.

"These guys never had a chance." He looked at the red residue on the leather seats. "Must have suffered a blast from an OC grenade before being taken down."

Walker pointed her rifle muzzle at a woman's handbag on the floor and a cracked iPhone, along with fingernail marks on the back of the leather seats. "The Secretary of State must have been taken alive. But why? You think Dresden is going to make demands with her as hostage?"

Payne shook his head. "He'll want to gloat. Hold his victory over her as he dismantles her little kingdom out here. I just don't see his endgame being about kidnapping and ransom. He's probably going to kill her."

"You'd think he would have staged this tomorrow or the next day when the summit is in full swing with the other leaders at her estate."

"Five times the eyes and ears on this place with security details from each head of state along with a beefed-up Secret Service presence. Today was strategic, especially since Dresden lost some of his shooters during our skirmish in Idaho."

She flared an eyebrow. "I'd hate to see what you call a major firefight."

He stepped away from the vehicle and gestured at the drag marks along the ground and the game trail to the west. "Pretty sure we're both about to experience that."

———

"Damnit, I can't get any reception out here," snapped Alisa as she redirected her mini satellite dish on top of the SUV's hood. "There's something blocking even that signal."

From their new location a half mile west of where they'd

left Walker and Payne, the two men were standing in a cluster of juvenile pines, scanning the ridgelines to the north with binoculars.

A few minutes later, Kilkenny froze, zooming in on the top of the closest peak. "Got a utility van parked up by that weather service station I mentioned, almost a quarter mile out. I'd say one, no...two guys, and..." He leaned in, his mouth hanging open. "It looks like that's the launchpad for the drones. There's eight of 'em lined up side by side." He glanced back at her. "Shit, that explosion to the east was just the beginning."

"Tell me about the two guys—what are they doing, exactly?" she asked.

Harrison replied, "One of them is in the passenger's seat, and I can only see his leg hanging out the open door; the other fella is sitting on a...get this...a goddamned camp chair like he's about to roast s'mores."

"He's about to roast a lot more than that if those other drones get off the ground," Kilkenny muttered.

"Any chance you can shoot the explosive payload on one of those drones with the Remington?" asked Harrison. "That would end this whole thing pretty quick."

Kilkenny sighed. "Not from this angle. I can only make out the tops of the damned things from here."

Alisa glanced in the direction of the mountaintop, then readjusted the satellite dish towards the weather station to amplify her laptop's reach. "If I can bounce a signal off the repeater towers on top of that mountain, I might be able to disrupt the satellite connection used by their cyber guy."

"You say so, kid," said Kilkenny. "You're using Greek as usual, or maybe you forgot I retired when Gmail was all the rage."

"Pretty soon, you're gonna be of real interest to archeology students." She began typing furiously, navigating through the antiquated security network of the tower.

Kilkenny walked back to the vehicle, grabbing a large olive-drab duffel bag from the back seat. He unzipped it and slid out the Remington 700 and a telescopic monopod. He inserted a single .308 round into the bolt-action rifle and tucked the box of ammo under his arm, then returned to his scouting perch. "I'll be able to get off one clean shot, maybe two, so do you want that cyber guy liquified or just his laptop?"

"They might have other laptops in the vehicle, so drop both guys if possible with the nerd as primary."

Kilkenny extended the monopod to its fullest length, then set the rifle barrel onto the Y-shape. "Nerd-sniping followed by sidekick removal, got it."

Harrison was alternating between glassing the weather-tower region and scanning the surrounding forest. He kept his Uzi at a low ready and leaned against the tree while Kilkenny got into position.

"Accessing the repeater tower now and sending a feed-back loop that should momentarily interfere with our pal's laptop connection to the satellite, or at least hamper the inter-face. How much longer 'til you can put down those vermin?"

"Another minute at least. This is a low-angle shot and, of course, it's gotta be a gusty day, like there's any other kind out West." Kilkenny cursed as he adjusted his scope's dials for elevation and windage. Finally, he settled the green reticle on the computer operator's chest. "Asian guy. Thought Dresden worked with an all-Algerian team?"

She glanced up from her laptop. "Payne didn't mention anything about that guy at the Idaho compound. Maybe he just arrived."

"We have a slight problem. Actually, a major fucking problem," said Kilkenny. "The other dude in the van just stepped out and walked around the far side of the van. He had a headset around his neck."

Alisa's lips flattened. "Shit, we can't wait. Drop them now, or cripple the hell out of him if you have to."

Kilkenny steadied his breathing, his finger sliding onto the trigger. He focused on the Asian man's chest and squeezed the trigger. Despite a suppressor, the rifle still cracked the still air. He saw the round punch a gaping hole through the guy. He collapsed, falling off his chair.

He refocused his rifle on the last known location of the other merc, sending a round downrange. It tore through the right quarter panel of the van. Kilkenny was sure he saw a brief puff of pink mist beyond the side of the vehicle. He blinked hard, then moved his rifle slowly, searching for movement through the scope. "One confirmed kill, and one possible kill."

"I've got satellite access and will see if I can hack into those drones and disable 'em, but I need to check on Walker and Payne first." Alisa pulled up the satellite imagery for the immediate area, studying the map and enhancing the region where Payne was last headed.

She zoomed in on the live feed, seeing a man and woman trotting northeast a half mile away from the smoking tunnel. "Gotcha."

Her eye caught movement along the right side of her screen, where four other figures were moving across a ridge-line. They flowed like a single-celled organism, reminding her of agency kill teams like Payne's she'd observed over the years. "There's a group of heavy hitters moving in on Payne's position. I need to warn him."

Harrison retrieved the extra mags for the Uzi from the

back of the SUV and did a second chamber check on his weapon. "You and Kilkenny need to get up to that weather station and eliminate the rest of the drones and that operator. I'll go warn Payne."

Alisa shook her head. "No, sir. Not a chance. You're not going—"

He raised a hand. "I've sat on the bench long enough. Besides, this all unfolded because of actions I took two years ago when I signed off on those funds for Operation Paragon. It's time to rectify that."

Harrison slid on a tactical vest and inserted three twenty-round magazines into the front slots. "Once you eliminate the comms interference, contact the Secret Service detail in Jackson Hole. There has to be a secondary command post there, providing overwatch for the foreign dignitaries. The detail will be working in conjunction with the local PD. Start there and tell them to ground their helos and air traffic to the region until those drones are taken off the board."

———

PAYNE'S LEGS were burning as he and Walker paused beside a fire-killed tree, scanning the game trail ahead. He caught a flutter of movement on a small knoll forty yards up. "Got 'em. Dresden and three other guys—and the Secretary."

They took turns bounding between trees until they reduced the distance to only twenty yards. He waited for Walker to get into sniping position.

Payne rested his left shoulder against a tree for stability, then squeezed off two rounds from the AK, which struck the nearest henchman in the jaw and left ear, dropping him instantly, while Walker's rifle barked out several shots, taking down the man on Dresden's left.

Dresden grabbed the Secretary's arm and yanked her back

behind a large tree. The other mercenary stepped off into the scrub, dropping to a squat and firing off a burst of rounds that peppered the pines beside Payne.

Payne made his way around the other side, arcing up the hill and darting from stump to fallen log until he was thirty feet away. He could see the amorphous shape of two people semi-concealed behind the largest pine on the hill.

"Payne, that you again?" shouted Dresden. He shoved Colson out slightly as he continued speaking. "You put a lot of my people in the ground lately."

"You're gonna meet up with 'em soon," Payne said. He heard a faint sound behind him and swiveled around, seeing Walker coming up.

Payne spoke in a hushed voice. "I'm going to take Dresden. He'll drag Colson along as a hostage for now. He must have an escape vehicle nearby, so she might not live long past that point. Once I move on him, make a wide circle around to the right and take out that other shooter. That should give you a slight advantage since he'll be focused on me."

"Copy that."

He peered out from the fallen log, seeing Colson's bruised face and bloody lip, wondering how much more trauma she could take.

"Hey, Payne, you can have the Secretary. She's all yours. I've got a little life insurance plan besides the drones."

"Yeah, what's that?"

Dresden held up a small detonator with a red switch beside Colson's head. "Somewhere just outside of town is another truck with the rest of the C-4. It's parked on a gas pipeline that serves the entire region. It'll make that explosion out at the fertilizer plant seem pathetic. I give you Colson and you let us head off, and there'll be no mushroom cloud over Wyoming."

Payne was sure his petrified expression matched Walker's

as he glanced at her. "He isn't just here to take down Colson, he wants to destroy the entire region," he said.

"Jackson Hole is also the headwaters for the Snake River —he blows that gas pipeline and it'll pollute the rivers and streams in every state from here to the Pacific Ocean."

"Jesus." Payne clenched his jaw, staring up the hill. "You've done enough. I know what happened to your team in Syria. Isn't this payback sufficient? You've proved you're formidable." He tried to appeal to the man's ego but wasn't sure that would work with someone so twisted by revenge.

"That depends on you. I'm going to leave Colson right here and be on my way. What happens after that is on you."

He saw Colson get yanked back and then heard a shriek. The woman staggered forward, clutching her left arm as bright red blood streaked down her sleeve.

"A cut in the brachial artery means she's dead in ninety seconds unless you intervene, Payne. You save her and I get away. You come after me and she'll die along with eleven thousand people in town being incinerated."

He caught a glimpse of Dresden trotting off, but Payne couldn't get off a shot. A second later, he saw the other man spring from the shrubs and split off apart from Dresden, veering to the right.

Payne rose and sprinted up the hill. Colson collapsed onto him as he approached, and he lowered her to the ground. He slid off her silk scarf and removed her jacket, then quickly wrapped the scarf around the gash on her inner arm.

Walker squatted beside him, her rifle trained on the trees ahead.

"Madam Secretary, hang on," said Payne, propping her feet up on a broken branch he slid over.

Her eyelids fluttered. She grabbed Payne's jacket. "That missile strike. It had to be done. He knew too much. He would've brought this...this country down."

Walker and Payne pivoted around at the rush of footsteps behind them.

"At your six," said a labored Senator Harrison, who was running up the hill, keeping his Uzi pointed beyond the grisly scene.

"Where's Alisa?" asked Payne, still pressing his hand on the bound silk scarf on Colson's arm.

"Trying to put a stop to the drones up by the weather station, northwest of here."

"Dresden's got a truck planted somewhere along the gas pipeline and is going to blow it. Can you take care of the Secretary?" Payne asked.

The senator nodded, slinging his rifle and kneeling beside the trembling woman, whose face had grown further pale.

Payne picked up his own rifle, patting Walker on the shoulder. "Remember what I said, once you see your target, take a wide arc out and hook in from his two o'clock."

She nodded, a faint smile emerging. "Just be careful, Kyle."

He trotted after Dresden while she veered off to the left. He just hoped he would be in time to stop Jackson Hole from living up to the latter part of its name.

CHAPTER 48

Rayburn paused beside a concrete pillar supporting an old water tower and scanned a forested hilltop on the northern outskirts of Jackson Hole.

It had been a long stretch of travel as he and his team, with the assistance of Stratton's analyst, pieced together the bloody trail that led from the murders at the aviation repair facility in Spokane to the skinhead compound outside of Marple. Satellite and signals intelligence had now pointed to this location, and he hoped it would put Dresden in his crosshairs. Instead, he found himself peering through his MK12's rifle scope at a surprisingly familiar face. He blinked hard, confirming whom he was looking at.

His earpiece crackled, and the voice of Stratton's intel analyst flooded through. "Dresden and Giletti split off and are heading in almost parallel routes north," she said. He didn't know her name or need to.

Rayburn took in the information, as did the rest of his team, who were lined out on either side. Using hand signals, he motioned for them to pursue the two men.

He lingered, speaking in a hushed tone to the analyst,

"Relay this to the director...Senator James Harrison is alive and kneeling beside the Secretary of State, who is wounded. Ask him if he wants them handled, as well."

"Copy that," she replied. "I'll be in touch. And it appears there's a shooter and possibly his spotter nearly a quarter mile to your southwest. Facial recog indicates they're former agency personnel as well, but I'm assuming they're not associated with Dresden since they engaged two individuals near a weather station atop a small peak to the north. One is dead, and the other is crawling on the ground beside a van."

"Affirmative. Dresden was veering off in that direction, so we'll handle him and the drones."

Rayburn watched an armed man in khaki pants who had been talking to Harrison sprint off in the direction that Dresden was reported heading.

Pretty sure that was Payne. Maybe he's on the right side of this thing after all. Not that any of that matters if he comes between me and Dresden.

CHAPTER 49

PAYNE SPRINTED OFF TO THE LEFT, RUNNING THROUGH THE woods on a parallel route to the game trail he'd seen Dresden on. Thirty yards ahead, he caught a glimpse of movement in the trees. Payne made a wide arc out to the right, cutting across the trail and then sweeping back in towards where he'd seen Dresden, near a dense area of car-sized boulders.

A second later, he took up a shooting position beside an immense pine tree. He peered around the side, but there was no one in sight. He shot a nervous glance over his right shoulder, hoping the man hadn't anticipated this move and come up behind him.

Where the hell is he?

Payne bolted to a cluster of fallen logs twenty feet ahead. Again, there was no sign of Dresden. He wondered if the man had taken off in a dead run or was waiting in ambush.

The smart move, the move Payne would've made, would be to get some distance. *Surely Dresden has an exit strategy that doesn't involve foot travel. Has to be one of those dirt bikes I saw loaded in the vans.*

Payne caught the faintest rustle of leaves to his left,

causing him to drop to a squat. He pressed his back against the nearest log, leveling his rifle at the scrub oak ahead between some boulders.

A second later Dresden appeared. Payne swung his rifle towards the man, but the trees above his own head suddenly splintered apart from gunfire. He dropped flat, rolling away from the log and sprinting towards the boulders to the left of Dresden's location.

He had a sinking feeling in his stomach—that Walker had failed to take out the other shooter. *Damnit, Carrie, you'd better still be breathing.*

Another blast of gunfire strafed the woods, this time in Dresden's direction.

Payne slid lower, taking cover against a desk-sized rock barely tall enough to hide behind. He leaned out to the left, the muzzle of his rifle fixed on the trees in the direction he'd just come from. He figured there was a shooter set up on the distant hill, while several others were probably crossing the narrow valley and making their way up this one. Payne glanced at the topography in the opposite direction of the threat. It looked like a sixty-degree slope dotted with more rocks and boulders. Escape was possible, but it would be slow going.

"Looks like they got us pinned down, eh?" said a disembodied voice somewhere to his right. "It's Payne, isn't it... Kyle Payne?"

"And Michael Dresden, the man with nine lives, it seems." Payne glanced in the direction of the valley below. "So if these guys aren't with your crew, then who the hell are they?"

"You probably have an idea. I imagine POTUS has a mop-up crew that's been waiting to pinpoint my location for some time."

Another round of gunfire struck the rocks in the direction of Dresden.

"I sure as hell hope you were bluffing about taking out that gas pipeline. A lot of people are gonna die who weren't even connected with what happened to you and your team overseas."

"I've reached a point where I really don't give a shit anymore, and since a lot of people in this town benefited from the Colsons, I have no problem incinerating all of his pals."

"And your old crew, like your friend Danielle—would she want that too?"

"Nice try, but any shred of remorse I had for what I'm doing here today disappeared a long time ago. You of all people know about the shady shit and backhanded deals that go on with the Colsons, and even the higher-ups at Langley, using us as pawns along the way."

"Of course I've seen it, but that doesn't mean I'm gonna go waste civilians because I'm pissed about a bunch of two-faced politicians. Sounds like buyer's remorse—you're telling me you didn't know what you were signing on for when you joined the agency, and now the world needs to burn."

"Maybe I should've become a drifter and put my troubles behind me like you did. How's that working out so far?"

He heard the man whisper something. It sounded like he was talking to someone on a radio. Payne couldn't make out the details.

His attention shot back to the woods to his right where he heard movement in the brush. He figured the other members of the strike team were making their way up from either side.

"Well, I'd love to talk more, but I have a city to torch. And if you survive this little encounter, I suggest you head in any direction but south."

Payne saw something being flung through the air from Dresden's location. Payne's heart slapped against his ribs as he saw the grenade, grateful it was headed in the direction of the shooters. He braced for the explosion, but when it didn't come, he glanced around the side of the rock, seeing a thick haze of red smoke spiraling up towards the treetops.

A second later, he heard snapping twigs near Dresden's location and the sound of someone crashing down the steep slope below them.

Shit, he must have called in a drone strike!

———

LANDON KEEN'S breathing was ragged, his left arm useless after having his shoulder joint destroyed by a rifle round. He lay on his back near the front of the van, staring at the clouds for a second while gathering his last vestige of energy. Given his blood loss, he knew fulfilling Dresden's latest command would be his final act.

He pulled out the ruggedized tablet from his vest and pulled up the controls for the remaining drones. Keen leaned over on one elbow, wincing as he stared out beyond the front bumper at the rivulet of red smoke in the distance. He returned to the tablet screen, tapping in the coordinates Dresden had provided, and activated a single drone.

The edge of his vision was blurring as he fought to choke down another breath while his fingers grew numb. *See you, my old friend.* He pressed Enter and heard the hum of the drone's rotor before it took off.

He tried to launch the remaining fleet, which were programmed to strike the outlying estates surrounding the Colsons', but the tablet slid from his grip. He slumped back, clawing for the device as he gasped out his last breath.

———

PAYNE WAS ABOUT to bolt from cover but caught a sliver of movement to his left. He dove onto his stomach, rolling on his right side and shooting at a dark-haired woman who had just crept out from a berm. Two of his three rounds struck, hitting her in the neck and head and sending her back down the hillside.

He sat up, quickly examining the rocky route below. That was when he saw a murder of crows take flight a half mile away across another valley. His gut told him to run. Now.

He zigzagged down the steep incline, then ran from tree to tree, heading downhill, just as the woods behind him exploded.

The blast rocked him forward. It felt like he'd just been struck in the back with a baseball bat. Payne lost his footing and tumbled forward, dropping his rifle and rolling down the hill for thirty feet. He felt like his body hit every branch and rock in Wyoming, and he hoped all the cracking sounds were just branches succumbing to his weight.

When he came to a stop, he felt a heat wave from the orange cloud on the other side of the hill.

He slid over to the other side of a tall spruce tree, taking cover behind the trunk.

A bolt of agonizing pain shot through his right arm. He pulled up his jacket and shirtsleeve, wincing as the fabric passed over a slight lump halfway between his wrist and elbow. From the grinding sensation when he articulated his arm, he could tell the bone was broken. At least it hadn't perforated the skin.

He leaned his head back, feeling like he was gonna pass out...or vomit. He sucked in some deep breaths, scanning the forest floor around him for his weapon.

Without any luck, he used his left hand to remove the Glock 17 from its holster on his right side.

He shifted his weight, scanning the area to his right, where Dresden had descended. The man was still out there somewhere and about to obliterate half of Jackson Hole and poison the water supply for a huge chunk of the Western US.

Payne looked around at the litter on the forest floor beside him, not seeing a single straight branch that he could slide into his sleeve to stabilize his forearm.

Damn, things get any worse and I might have a bad day.

He pressed his back into the tree trunk and pushed himself to his feet, tucking his right hand into his belt line and moving at a quick enough pace so the agony was manageable.

Payne trotted along the base of the slope, pausing frequently from the jarring agony in his arm. He came across an area of disturbed leaves and crushed stands of dead grass along with a large boot print in the exposed dirt. Scanning the forest ahead, he could pick out a crude trail that snaked through the brush.

He followed it for sixty feet, coming across more boot tracks in the patches of snow. He continued on, noticing that the tread patterns on the left side were clearly visible while the right were being partially dragged. He wondered if Dresden had sustained an injury similar to his during his sprint down the hill.

Coming to another slope, he surveyed the route below. This one was more gradual and much shorter. At the bottom was a shallow but wide river that snaked through the forest. He glanced across at the other side, but didn't see any mud or water on the rocks.

Payne descended, walking on a parallel path next to the river. Again, the same boot and drag marks were evident along patches of bare ground. A hundred yards beyond, the river curved and dropped precipitously to the right.

He paused, hearing something faint above the gurgle of the rapids. It was the familiar sound of a dirt bike engine.

Payne increased his pace, following the tracks and running towards a grove of mature spruce trees ahead.

The throbbing in his arm was threatening to overtake his willpower. He bit down on his lip, forcing himself to sprint the last forty yards. As he broke into the stand of spruce trees, he saw Dresden in the distance, speeding away.

———

WALKER'S LUNGS burned as she tore through the dense forest, snow and pine needles crunching beneath her boots. The roar of a motorcycle echoed between the trees as she wove through the undergrowth. She vaulted over a fallen log, her tactical vest catching momentarily on a jagged branch before she wrenched herself free.

The motorcycle's engine screamed as the man opened the throttle and slammed back the kickstand.

Walker cut diagonally through a thicket, emerging onto a narrow animal trail and gaining precious ground.

The driver glanced over his shoulder, his face contorting with surprise as he spotted her closing the gap.

The trail opened into a small clearing, and the rider gunned the engine, pulling away.

Walker skidded to a halt. In one fluid motion, she raised her rifle, steadied her breathing, and tracked the fleeing motorcycle. Time seemed to slow as she exhaled, her finger applying precise pressure to the trigger. The first shot missed, splintering bark from a nearby trunk. The next three shots found their mark, blowing out the rear tire. The motorcycle fishtailed wildly before careening into a shallow ditch.

The man tumbled across the ground, scrambling to his feet with surprising agility.

Walker squeezed off another round, striking him in the

left shoulder. He collapsed to one knee, clutching his wound and trying to reach for the pistol on his hip.

"Don't. The next shot will take out the back of your head."

The man chuckled, pressing his wrists together in front of his waist. "Go ahead, Agent Walker. Arrest me. You're not the murdering type, not like Payne." He said it with a smile as he stared into her eyes.

"You think you know me?"

"I knew your partner, Fiche, through the other end of my rifle scope."

She shuffled forward, thrusting the rifle barrel towards his face. She desperately wanted to pull the trigger. There was no one around. No witnesses. She could get away with it, and the world would probably be a better place.

But she thought of Fiche. He wouldn't have wanted this. It wasn't who he was. Not who she was. Payne saw the world through another prism, and it had kept him alive all these years, but his path was not hers.

She closed the distance, sending a vicious kick into the man's jaw and driving him back onto the ground.

She realized she didn't have her handcuffs and had no way of restraining the man. She'd have to wait until help arrived or walk him down towards a main road. Either of those meant he'd try to find an advantage. She opted for staying put, which allowed her to control more of the variables.

"Enjoy the sight of blue skies because the supermax only allows twenty-minute walks outside once a week," she said. Walker lowered the rifle towards his groin. "And mention my partner's name again and see how that turns out for you."

———

Payne emerged on the other side of the trees, seeing Dresden fading in the distance and well out of pistol range. He glanced to his right, noticing the terrain sloping further towards another valley. Directly below him was a series of trail switchbacks, which looked like they had been made by the forest service to prevent erosion and keep hikers on the path.

He slid the Glock into his belt line and searched along the ground for spent limbs until he found a relatively straight branch that was close to his height.

Leaning on his new walking stick, he took a zigzag route down to the next switchback. He had just emerged from the brush when Dresden sped past. Payne didn't waste any time heading down to the next level below. He picked up his pace, leaning his good arm onto the walking stick to stabilize himself while he moved as quickly as possible.

Hearing the rumble of the dirt bike in the distance to his right, he broke into a slow trot, arriving at the switchback just as Dresden came into view. The man flicked his head towards Payne at the last second, but it was too late. Payne thrust the walking stick into the man's ribs like a spear as Dresden drove past.

The violent force caused the rider to pivot his upper body to the left, twisting the handlebars abruptly and sending the front tire into a stump. Dresden flew over the handlebars, landing on his back. Payne thought he heard something crack, and by the way Dresden staggered to his feet, he was sure the man had broken something. The look of predatory rage in his eyes told a different story.

As Payne went to pull out his Glock, Dresden charged forward, slamming his shoulder into Payne's waist in a wrestler's clinch. Both men tumbled down the remaining slope leading to the next switchback. Only this time there was no dirt pathway below.

The river from earlier had cut a swath through the hills, making its way west in its rapid descent to the lower valleys. The two men fell into the icy water, the cold shock causing Payne's chest to rapidly constrict. He fought to grab onto the roots dangling off the riverbank.

Payne pulled himself up the muddy bank, his right hand barely able to assist. Three feet away, Dresden was doing the same, except he swung his legs up and kicked Payne in the ribs. Payne felt his handhold slip away, and he was swept up by the current. He rushed by Dresden but managed to grab onto his belt loop. The man clawed at the embankment but fell back, both of them swirling into the rapids.

Payne felt his tailbone dragging along the rocky substrate as he fought to stay above the water. He spewed out a mouthful of sludgy fluid, seeing Dresden bob behind him as they spun in the turbulent waves.

For a microsecond, Payne caught a glimpse of a slow eddy on the left. He tried to upright himself enough to kick off the bottom and then speared his body towards the sluggish water, but it was just out of reach. The effort wasn't wasted. He sailed towards a partially submerged tree branch jutting out of the savage water like a bony finger.

He turned just in time to see Dresden pulling himself up on the opposite side of the main log that extended halfway out into the river. The man swung his legs up and straddled the center column, inching towards him.

Payne glimpsed the lanyard for the detonator that was dangling out of Dresden's vest pocket; he was close enough to make out the numbers, which were either five or fifteen minutes. He hoped it was the latter, but all he could do right now was hang onto the weaving branch as the river yanked at his body.

Dresden was only three feet away, an animalistic stare in his eyes. He reached for the pistol on his right side but only made contact with an empty Kydex holster. The enraged figure slid closer, pulling out the fixed blade from his vest and slashing at Payne's neck.

Payne ducked, the tip nicking his cheek. It was nothing compared to the torturous stinging in his broken arm. Another surge of waves hammered Payne's body, his grip slipping on the branch. Dresden moved closer, preparing to stab down onto his hand, but the man kept pausing to stabilize himself on the slippery log.

Payne leaned back, hooking the crook of his injured arm around the branch. He'd only have one chance at this, and he wasn't even sure it would work. But there were no alternatives.

As Dresden shimmied forward and steadied himself for a strike, Payne let go with his good arm and kicked off the rocks beneath his boots. The momentum was enough to send him towards his attacker. He thrust his left arm up and grabbed the nape of Dresden's vest, yanking him forward with the man's momentum working against him.

Payne pulled down with violent force, slamming Dresden's head onto a jagged branch. The stick pierced his right eye and came out the back of his skull.

He let go of his other handhold, clutching Dresden's vest and trying to grab the detonator, but the man's limp body slumped to the side, taking Payne with him back into the current.

Payne's body was hypothermic and his limbs barely functioning. The only relief coming from the cold numbing his damaged arm. A brutal wave slammed them together, and Payne fought to stay afloat in the frothy water while trying to yank out the detonator.

Finally, he grabbed it and slid the lanyard around his neck, then shoved Dresden away, but the man's pistol holster had gotten caught up on Payne's pants pocket. He tugged on it, but his fingers were too frozen to pull it free.

Payne heard a deafening roar and shot his gaze ahead. A half mile up, the river suddenly disappeared.

Waterfall!

He yanked on the holster, using his injured hand as well. Finally, he tore free and shoved away the dead man. Payne made a mad dash for the riverbank, swimming as hard as he could until he felt his limbs burning and the pain returning to his broken arm.

His peripheral vision sent a terrifying image that the river was about to open into a giant maw. He fought for every inch of distance to reach the nearest rootlets hanging out of the bank. Payne flutter kicked like there were crocs in the water, his left arm stabbing forward and grabbing the last cluster of tree roots.

He held on, pulling himself up only to slide down again, his body's fuel exhausted. The bank was steep, and he had only three feet to climb, but it felt more like fifty. His fingers were locking up, the last vestiges of energy withdrawing from his limbs as his body fought to conserve what was left of its life force.

Payne felt something on his wrist. A hand reached down and tugged on him. Above, a man with a stubbly face was straining to yank him free of the river's grip. Payne felt his boots gain purchase on the rocky shoreline, and he forced his body up as the stranger pulled.

The guy slid him over the lip of the muddy bank and released him, standing back and panting.

Payne latched onto the detonator dangling around his neck and set it down. He leaned on his side, trying to flip the disarm switch before the twenty seconds were up, but his hand was shaking uncontrollably.

The man moved closer, pointing his rifle barrel at Payne's chest. "I assume this is a countdown we don't want to complete?"

Payne shook his head, his purple lips trying to mutter the word "no," but even that was a challenge. He finally flipped down the red switch, the counter stopping at three seconds. Payne let the device fall from his grip and slumped back. It was only now that he could see he had been just twenty feet from the plunge into the rocky chasm below.

The guy stood back, waving towards the ridgeline above them. "This whole area's going to be swarming with Secret Service agents anytime now, so I need to be on my way. Just one question: did you take out the female shooter back on the hilltop before the drone struck?"

Payne felt powerless to move and saw no point in lying to the guy, who was probably her team leader. He was going to do what he had to do, and there wasn't any way Payne could alter his situation right now.

"Yeah, it was me."

The man glanced back at the waterfall. "I appreciate the honesty. Frankly, I thought about putting a round in you once I caught up with you and Dresden, but now I doubt you'll last long enough for any rescuers to even make it here. Plus I've still got some drones to take care of."

He moved closer, pointing his rifle at Payne's head. "But the choice is yours: you want me to end this, or you want to ride it out, enjoying the scenery for a few minutes more?"

Payne thrust his chin at the river and forced out a thin smile.

"You got it." The man stood and headed back up the slope.

Payne felt a warm sensation flooding over his body, his remaining life draining from his limbs into his chest. He'd had hypothermia before, but nothing on this scale, and he knew the end was near.

He thought about his father. Alisa. His friends spread around the world. And he thought about Walker. He would have liked to see her smile one more time and hold her close.

CHAPTER 50

THE NEXT MORNING, STRATTON WAS ALREADY IN HIS OFFICE WELL before his secretary and the rest of his staff. He'd had plenty to mull over and satellite images from Jackson Hole to review…again.

His encrypted cellphone rang, and he picked up without looking at the number. "Other than the Colson estate being obliterated, was there any other fallout from Dresden in that region?" he asked Rayburn.

The man responded in a monotone voice like he was reading off stock-market figures. "Colson's security detail was wiped out along with the remaining guards at her estate, but I haven't heard the final numbers. A large blast at a fertilizer plant south of the city created a massive crater, but no one was inside the facility at the time. Dresden and his crew were eliminated, and the remaining drones from his hilltop staging area were disabled and removed before the feds arrived. They're in my possession and will be passed on to Langley R & D unless you say otherwise." He cleared his throat. "Regrettably, my entire team was KIA."

"Damn, I'm sorry to hear that." Stratton rubbed the back of his neck. "Take whatever time you need."

"I'll be fine, sir."

He glanced again at his laptop. "You indicated Harrison was in the region, tending to Colson, is that right?"

"I only saw him for a minute. She was on the ground and had sustained a significant injury to her left arm, but that's all I know. Why?"

Stratton zoomed in on the recorded satellite feed from yesterday, seeing Harrison standing over Colson's dead body with an Uzi pointed at the forest, his hands bloodless. Moments later, a quick reaction force of Secret Service agents showed up, followed by a helicopter.

"Seems like history is sometimes shaped by those willing to let events take their natural course."

"Sir?"

Stratton cleared his throat, walking to his window. "Good work."

"I can't take the credit, not for all of it, anyway. That former agency guy, Payne, killed Dresden and was able to prevent a catastrophic explosion along the gas pipeline that ran through Jackson Hole. If Dresden had succeeded, you'd be looking at a lot of the Western states' water sources being toxic and a moon-sized depression where the city's at."

"God, that's incredible." He let out an audible sigh. "And where's Payne now?"

"Apparently, he survived and is at Jackson Memorial Hospital after being airlifted out."

Stratton mulled over the recent revelations. This was the largest terrorist attack on US soil since 9/11, and federal investigators and reporters were going to be swarming Jackson Hole for months. Recognition of Payne's involvement and background was going to invite questions. And questions could lead back to Langley.

"Anything you need me to do before I leave Wyoming, sir?"

"No, Payne understands the rules of engagement and what follows in the aftermath better than most. He shouldn't be a problem. I'll have to scrub the hospital records so no one can access his name and whereabouts."

He walked to the windows overlooking the courtyard. "Now, tell me more about these drones and how Dresden managed to get as far as he did."

CHAPTER 51

THE CLOUDS HAD CRACKS IN THEM. SPIDERWEB CRACKS THAT spread along the entire surface. Or were they fissures that opened up into another layer beyond this world? Payne blinked hard, his hazy vision growing clear as he stared up at the white ceiling.

A beeping sound coursed through his ears, and the air had a faint bleach odor to it. He felt something heavy on his chest and glanced down, seeing a thick layer of blankets over him. A blood-pressure cuff on his left arm released, and the beeping noise stopped.

"Hey there," said a woman off to his right. Alisa's face came into view, and she stood, resting her hand on his shoulder. "We thought you might stay on the other side for good. You were nearly dead when the helicopter crew spotted you, but once you were wrapped in heated blankets and they got an IV going, you stabilized."

He went to reach for her hand with his right hand, but the pain from before returned with a vengeance.

"Yeah, the doc was waiting to get that in a cast once you were, um, alive."

He gazed around the room. Bare bones with only the city logo for Jackson Hole adorning the wall. He looked at the blue skies beyond the window, grateful, for once, to be indoors.

Alisa smiled, wiping a tear off her cheek and looking away. "Thought my days of watching out for you were over."

He chuckled, pushing himself up with his good hand. "Just glad *you* are alright." He gazed past the open door. "Walker and the others?"

Alisa gave a hearty nod. "All good. Walker went to see Kilkenny off. He's grabbing a taxi back to the airport and returning to Marple. Then she's gotta check in with her boss in Seattle. Harrison returned to DC and is the subject of every news outlet in the world. The image of him standing guard over Colson's dead body has gone viral. When I watched the live TV interview this morning, he was nearly in tears as he described her life slipping away."

Payne's eyes widened. "Colson had a fighting chance when I left her in Harrison's care."

Alisa had the faintest of smirks on her face as she relayed the senator's self-described valiant efforts in the forest. "It's like Kilkenny always said: the only truthful part of the news is the weather report." She leaned in closer. "Before Harrison left here, he asked if I would consider being a part of his presidential campaign in the near future, but I politely declined. I can tell you there's also talk about the connection between Dresden and Colson...and now POTUS, so Harrison probably won't wait too long to announce his candidacy."

"I expect not. I just hope that's the last I hear from him, or anyone from his world."

"Well, actually, he insisted on springing for a vacation rental either here or in Seattle so you can recover for a few weeks...or months. I'll arrange it for you after you decide."

"Seattle," he said, watching Walker head inside.

Alisa laughed. "Good choice." She leaned in, giving Payne a hug, then grabbed her shoulder bag from the chair. "I've got some calls to make, so I'll be in the hallway."

Walker sat on the edge of the bed. She smiled, brushing her fingers along his cheek. "Almost thought I was flying back home alone."

"To sell off my motorcycle and live off the spoils."

"Something like that."

"How severely were you chewed out by Mentzer?"

She looked down for a moment, sighing. "I think my ear is partially burned from holding the phone too close while he reprimanded me, but, apparently, Harrison made a call, explaining how my involvement was essential to the operation." She drew out air quotes at the latter words. "I'm not sure I'm going to be heading back into a frictionless work environment, but Mentzer did tell me to report for duty next week, so that's something."

He reached up with his left hand, resting it on her arm. "What about us...we good?"

She slid in closer and kissed him. "It's going to take me a long time to process everything that just happened, but one thing I'm sure about is that we're still good."

He hugged Walker with his left arm, feeling true warmth. The muscle memory of constantly being on the move had become so ingrained that staying put felt like a rebellious act. He didn't know what came next, besides a cast and physical therapy, but he figured he could get used to having a roof over his head for a while, especially with her in the picture.

ABOUT THE AUTHOR

Did you enjoy *Kill Shot*? Please consider leaving a review on Amazon to help other readers discover the book.

———

JT Sawyer is the pen name for author Tony Nester who writes survival and vigilante-justice thrillers. Before becoming a full-time writer, JT spent 30 years teaching survival courses in the American Southwest for the military special operations community, at the university level, and for a variety of federal agencies. He also served as a consultant for the film industry and provided training in mantracking and fieldcraft for actors Josh Brolin and Emile Hirsch. Nowadays, JT prefers having a roof over his head and placing his fictional characters in dire straits. He lives with his family and several rescue dogs in Colorado.

———

Want to connect with JT? Visit him at his website:

www.jtsawyer.com

ALSO BY JT SAWYER

Printed in Dunstable, United Kingdom